The Boy at Booth Memorial

The Boy at Booth Memorial

Raymond DeTournay

North Star Press

www.northstarpress.com

ISBN: 978-1-68201-095-2

Author's Note

This is a work of creative non-fiction based on a true experience. I have modified some details to better tell my story, and to protect the privacy of some of the people involved. Names and identifying details have been changed, and the timeline of events adjusted for that purpose. Conversations in this book do not represent word-for-word transcripts but were written to capture the meaning and feeling of the moment. All in all, I have tried to honor the truth of my experience as accurately as my memory allows.

First edition: September 2018

Printed in the United States of America

Published by:
North Star Press of St. Cloud, Inc.
St. Cloud, Minnesota
www.northstarpress.com

This book is dedicated to my mother, and to the women of the Salvation Army, who had the social courage to provide care, concern, and guidance to young women experiencing a life crisis.

~1~

THE SHRILL CRY OF A NEWSBOY was our introduction to the Twin Cities. "Read all about it. Girl leaps to her death."

Mom and I stepped from the Greyhound bus into a confusing swirl of noise and traffic. Even though I was fourteen, I'd never been in a town this big, and the hustle of the city was scary. The newsboy's piercing voice cut through the din.

"Getcher latest copy here. Only five cents," he shouted and waved an afternoon edition of the *St. Paul Dispatch.*

It first sounded like an old 1930s movie, but this was 1949, and he was real, not some play-pretending actor. Mom tugged at my arm.

"Here's a nickel," she said. "Get a copy, and we'll read it on the way. Might as well learn something about our new town." The headline fairly screamed, "SNELLING AVENUE BRIDGE SUICIDE. GIRL LEAPS TO DEATH ON RAILROAD TRACKS." Scanning over the crowd, we searched for the last connection to our destination. Mom pulled an edge-worn piece of paper from her purse, offered it to a porter and put her finger on the address.

"Como Park, Snelling Avenue, and Fairgrounds streetcar, over there," he said, and pointed to a traffic island. "Should be here any time now. Careful gettin' on with all them suitcases."

Did he say Snelling Avenue? I pointed to the headline and he nodded.

"Careful of them bridges, too," he said and shook his head.

Modern streetcars zipped by us as we waited, and I pictured myself getting in and riding right up front. As I stood on my toes to look down the tracks a COMO PARK, SNELLING AVENUE AND FAIRGROUNDS sign came into view, but instead of being one of the sleek new post-war streetcars, this was one that could have been around since World War I. It looked like something out of the comic strips—a Toonerville Trolley—even down to the chimney pipe for the on-board stove. Inside the car had the worn look of an old timer. Paint on the handrails was worn through to the metal, and the varnish on the wooden seats had a soft glow from the buffing of thousands of bottoms. Little did I realize this noisy, faded-yellow relic of transit history would soon become part of my daily existence.

We rumbled past the state capitol with its impressive dome, skirted the edge of Lake Como and wound our way through neighborhoods nicer than anywhere I'd ever lived. On that warm September afternoon, we passed broad, neatly landscaped lawns and large houses sheltered by trees that shadowed their sizeable screened porches. The sound of metal wheels screeching on steel rails seemed out of place in this beautiful setting.

When Mom opened the paper, I asked for the comics. This was a new town, and I was curious to see if they had my favorite funnies. The suicide story must've gotten to her. Anytime she read something sad, Mom made little *tsk tsk* noises with her tongue. I counted seven.

"The police found a blue winter coat and suitcase on the bridge," she said to no one in particular. "It happened sometime this morning. Poor thing. *Tsk.*"

The conductor called, "Pascal Street and transfer to Fort Snelling." Then he turned to Mom. "It's your stop, ma'am. Next one's Snelling Avenue."

We stepped off, luggage in hand, and dodged traffic as we made our way to the curb. Directly in front of us began a long sidewalk and, at its end, stood our destination, a dark, brick, three-story structure that resembled a castle. Passers-by might think it was a private health-care center or sanitarium, but the neighbors knew better. At curbside a discreet sign read, "BOOTH MEMORIAL HOME AND HOSPITAL," the last stop for Mom and me.

As we neared the building, a group of girls played touch football at the far end of the lawn. *Just girls*, I thought. *What do they know about football?* One of them caught a wobbly pass, and the others charged after her, all moving in a sort of slow motion. Some even waddled. As they closed in, it was clear this was no ordinary football game. In this one, all the players were pregnant.

While Mom rang the doorbell, I tried not to stare. The girls milled around pretending not to notice us, but they were no longer interested in football.

A young woman in a military uniform led us into a large, somber anteroom where we sat on sturdy, old-fashioned furniture upholstered with dark-green naugahyde. Hardwood floors and dark-stained wood paneled walls gave the place the unwelcome feel of an institution. Just off the reception desk stood a telephone booth, one of those wooden ones with glass in the folding door. It looked so old it might have come with the building. Totally out of place was a small display case with embroidered baby clothes, booties, and scarves. They all looked hand-made.

"I'm Lieutenant Olson, and I'll be right back," she said. "Just wait here."

A framed portrait of an old man wearing a uniform hung in a prominent spot. A small placard identified General William Booth. From behind a closed door I heard a piano and a girl's voice singing a familiar hymn. The heavy odor of fresh paint and varnish drifted in from the hallway.

On the other side of the room I saw an imposing limestone stairway whose steps showed the wear and tear of heavy foot traffic. From upstairs I heard girls' voices and laughter while familiar kitchen smells drifted up from below—familiar because they smelled a lot like school cafeteria food.

I didn't need the large hallway clock to tell me it was almost time for dinner, or supper as it's called in the Midwest, because my stomach was already making noises.

Lieutenant Olson asked Mom if she had an appointment.

"It's rather late for any sort of placement today," she said. With a puzzled look, she glanced at our luggage and then over my shoulder.

"Is your daughter in the car?"

"I don't have a daughter," Mom said. "Just Rene is with me."

"Well, where is she?"

"Who?"

"Renée."

I winced at this mispronunciation of my name because it almost always ended up being pronounced like a girl's.

"This is Rene," Mom said, pointing. "He's my son."

The lieutenant looked at me and then slowly back at my mother.

"Well, then, why are you here?"

The confusion stopped when an older woman stuck her head in the room, someone I recognized. It was Major Ellen Swensen.

"Mrs. Dardenne, thank God you've arrived," she said. "We could use you on the floor right now. Two in labor, one dilating. How was your trip?"

She never waited for Mom's answer.

"Please excuse the mess," she said pointing down the hallway. "We're almost done with New Year's Eve and expecting Prom Night any day, so we use this time to paint and clean up the dorms."

The clock chimed the hour, five on the dot. A shrill bell triggered the sound of shuffling footsteps. Down the stairs came a line of girls that snaked its way toward the basement. They all wore similar smocks—small flower prints or faded pastels, with not much attention paid to style or fit. On some they were baggy, and on others the smocks were so tight the hem rode up above their knees.

As they passed, I tried not to stare at their bulging waistlines.

Most looked back at me with a vacant gaze, not smiling, not friendly. Several turned their heads away, probably afraid of being discovered in this place where they came to hide. Suddenly my face felt warm from embarrassment, but was it for them or for me? All these girls were about my age and pregnant and, according to what I'd been taught, every single one had sinned. As I looked over the strange parade, I had no idea that our destination, Booth Memorial Hospital, had played a role in the death of the girl who jumped from the bridge that day.

~2~

B ARELY A MONTH EARLIER, Mom and I were in Chicago. After three days and two nights on a train from Arizona, we stood on the platform of Dearborn Station and waited for the connection to our Illinois hometown. Air travel was getting popular, but going cross-country by train was still a big event. A shiny new diesel, painted in the red, yellow and silver colors of the Atchison, Topeka, and Santa Fe Railroad, was the locomotive for our Super Chief. It was sleek and modern with a big Santa Fe plastered on the nose. Still, the low hum of the diesel engine idling at the platform was no match for the excitement of real steam locomotives nearby. They skulked at their platforms and hissed and chuffed, their pop-off valves shot off bursts of steam. Dearborn Station was noisy and hectic—it was big time. For a fourteen-year-old who'd boarded at a single-platform station in the desert, this was heady stuff.

Focused on exploration of the station, I barely noticed Mom speaking with a woman who wore a Salvation Army uniform, just like ones who stood by a tripod ringing a little bell at Christmas. When money dropped in the pot they'd say, "Thank you and God bless you." Having been raised Catholic, I thought the only people who could bless you were priests and nuns. Since they also could smack the hell out of you, I was a little wary of anyone who said, "God bless you."

Major Ellen Swenson was waiting for her train to St. Paul. She started the conversation when she noticed a pin my mother wore. Mom was the first of her family to graduate high school and acceptance into nurses' training strengthened her immigrant parents' belief in the American dream. They had three other daughters to educate and little money to do it but promised to help Mom as long as possible. After all, in 1928 jobs were plentiful, wages were good, and everything was booming.

Mom loved learning to care for others and finished her first year with honors. Then two things happened; my father's insistent proposals of marriage and the Depression. Money from home dried up. Reluctantly, she put nurses' training on hold.

After a seven-year try, the marriage failed, so, with promised financial support from my father, Mom refocused her attention on nurses' training. It was 1937, the depth of the Depression, but Dad found a job with a promising future in a distant city. Mom was required to live at the nurses' home, so, at age two, I began the trek from grandparent to grandparent, uncle to aunt, one ghetto to another in our small Illinois town.

Three long years ended when Sisters of Mercy Hospital presented Mom with her pin and certification as a registered nurse. In 1940 things improved financially, but physical problems appeared. My low resistance to diseases progressed from winter-long colds to a mastoid infection to the first signs of tuberculosis. In 1945 the doctor advised a move to a dry climate until my body healed. Tucson, Arizona, was the destination, and off we went, dragging a used travel trailer behind the car of a friend who had "B" coupons for wartime gasoline.

After four years, nature's desert cure worked. Mom sold the trailer and spent the money for coach seats on the Super Chief. We arrived back in Illinois much the same as we left, almost flat broke. Her certification had supported us, so it was no surprise, in or out of uniform, that she proudly wore the pin of a registered nurse.

At Dearborn Station, Major Ellen spotted that pin, said a quick prayer and started a conversation. She had been in Chicago to recruit a nurse with experience in obstetrics, but was heading home empty handed.

"OB's my specialty," Mom said. "Tell me about your hospital."

As we boarded our train, Major Ellen's last words were, "Just think about it, and God bless you."

There it was again, that "God bless you" thing. Something was going to happen, probably not good. On the short ride to our hometown, my mother seemed distant, and I asked what happened.

"It's nothing," she said, looking at the business card in her hand. "Major Ellen is the administrator of a Salvation Army hospital in St. Paul. It's called Booth Memorial, and she desperately needs a head obstetrics nurse. She seemed depressed, and I tried to cheer her up, but really Rene it's a home for unwed mothers!"

~3~

WHEN THE BELL SOUNDED for the evening meal, the piano stopped and the door opened. Two girls, in tightly fitted street clothes, came out to join the file downstairs.

"They're new," Major Ellen said. "The new ones always stick to-gether." Nodding toward the line, she added, "All residents take their meals in the dining room downstairs. The first bell is to call them to the door. When the second bell rings, an officer takes them to the tables. We live by bells around here. You'll find that out soon enough."

Major Ellen Swenson was a tall, stately woman of Swedish stock and appeared to be in her fifties. Her slightly wrinkled face showed no trace of cosmetics, and her trimmed fingernails were naturally pink. She had a pleasant smile and spoke with a voice of gentle authority. Her dark brown hair, with light streaks of grey, was wound tightly in a bun.

"You call them residents?" Mom said. "They're just girls."

"We try not to call them girls even though they are," Major Ellen said. "In a small way we're preparing them for adulthood and the big change in their lives. They're about to become women, ready or not, and most aren't. They grow up almost overnight even if they don't want to. We help them where we can."

She smiled slightly. "We slip and call them girls from time to time but 'residents' is what we prefer. Just like the bells, you'll get used to it."

Through the open door, I saw uniformed women bringing in a coffee service.

"They're preparing a welcome to Booth Memorial for you," she said. "It'll give you a chance to meet the staff."

9

We entered a large room with a huge fireplace. The couches and chairs around the hearth looked just as uncomfortable as those in the entryway.

"We call this the Great Room," she said. "You'll find our furniture is catch-as-catch-can donations. All Booth hospitals operate this way."

"There's more than one?" I asked.

"Oh, my, yes," she said. "We have thirty-five hospitals in the U.S. There are fifty residents in each Booth home, and we could take more if we had room."

That's an awful lot of sinners, I thought.

"Would you like coffee or tea?" an officer asked. She was pushing a cart with silver coffee pots and teapots and matching cream and sugar containers.

"Oh, this is sterling," my mother whispered, "and that looks like good china."

Major Ellen winked. "Some hand-me-downs are better than others. The coffee pot has a small dent in it, but I see we didn't use the chipped Rosenthal this time. This is Captain Gertrude Svensen," she said. "We tease her because she's Norwegian and most of us are Swedes. There's a little rivalry there." Captain Svensen stuck her tongue out.

"Have some Norwegian *sandbakkels*," she said, motioning to the cookies, "and call me Trudy. Gertrude is old fashioned, and we're trying to get modern here."

I reached for a handful of cookies. A quick look from Mom reduced it to two.

"This is Captain Berthe Karlsson," Major Ellen said. "She's our administrator for supplies and purchases. I call her our 'window on the world' because she deals with people outside the Corps."

Captain Karlsson was old, at least in her forties. She was slim with sharp features and also wore her mouse brown hair in a bun. Half glasses, connected to a chain around her neck, perched on the lower part of her nose. She reminded me of a librarian, or at least the glasses did. When she looked at me, her smile became tight-lipped and sour. No question, a male wasn't welcome here, no matter what his age.

"Captain Berthe is new to Women's Social Services," Major Ellen said. "She's here as part of her career development, but I'm not sure if she considers it a promotion or punishment yet."

"Oh, I'm learning to enjoy it" Captain Karlsson said unconvincingly. "There's a new experience every day."

I recognized a funny formality between them, like their differences in rank really meant something. Major trumped captain, I remembered from World War II lessons.

"I have to check something before supper," Major Ellen said. "Captain Karlsson, would you please answer any of their questions about the Corps and our beliefs?"

Mom and I looked at each other. We never had a thought about the Salvation Army, not as a religious group or as a shelter for unwed mothers. Questions? We had none, and being strict Catholics, we didn't know if there was anything we wanted to know.

Captain Karlsson was determined to educate us. At one end of the room, I saw a small lectern with a Bible on it. Behind that was a stained glass window. With the afternoon sun shining through, it had the look of a chapel.

". . . and that's how the first Booth Memorial hospital started," Captain Karlsson said. "It was for women who had no place to go. Mostly beggars . . ." she paused, looked around and whispered to my mother, ". . . and prostitutes."

Captain Karlsson didn't know I'd heard that word before, including variations like streetwalker, call girl and whore, but I wasn't about to say so.

"We never seem to run out of residents," she said, "only officers."

We learned that officers were ordained ministers, but unlike Catholic nuns and priests, they could marry and raise families. Officers working in Booth hospitals, however, had to remain single. I looked around the room. No men.

"Major Ellen mentioned something about New Years Eve and Prom Night," Mom said, "but I didn't understand."

"Actually it is a bit deceiving. Our two busiest times of the year are the result of New Year's Eve and Prom Night. The New Years' are delivering now, and we expect Prom Nights to arrive three or four months after conception, which is also about now." She shook her head. "I really don't get the connection. I'm always in church on New Year's Eve and I've never been to a prom. No matter, can't these girls just say no?" This was all new to me, and I kind of sided with Captain Karlsson. What was so special about those two days? How could I find out?

A woman standing in the doorway rang a small silver bell. I hoped this was a signal for dinner because all the cookies were gone.

"Come and get it before it cools," she said.

We entered a large room with a cut-glass chandelier that hung over a large oval table. A white linen tablecloth, the silver setting with matching napkin rings and a large vase of fresh-cut flowers in the center, made it look like something from a glossy magazine. What really caught my eye was the food—steaming hot and ready for the taking.

"Mind your manners," my mother whispered. "Be a gentleman and don't get greedy."

I knew the gentleman part had to come first, but was I supposed to seat all the women in the room? Fortunately, they weren't as concerned with manners as Mom. They'd already seated themselves.

"I'll finish introducing the others after the blessing," Major Ellen said.

We bowed our heads, but instead of hearing the standard Catholic, "Bless us O Lord for these thy gifts," the grace I knew, I heard a rambling list of things for which to be thankful including the arrival of my mother in their time of need. I knew it was over when I heard

"Amen." I'd just been introduced to the world of "make it up as you go" Protestant praying.

"Before we go any further, I want to propose a rule," Major Ellen said. "We're bringing in someone new, so this is a special day. Just this once, no shop talk."

I would soon learn that "shop talk" was an invaluable way of learning how things really worked in this unusual world we'd entered. I could barely take my eyes off the plate of roast beef slices making its way around the table.

Major Ellen raised her voice. "Colonel Thomas, this is our new head nurse, Josephine Dardenne, and her son Rene."

An elderly woman who was picking at the food on her plate suddenly looked up.

"Are you talking to me?" she asked.

Colonel Thomas, at age eighty-five, could barely hear a thing. Her face looked like an apple doll and her hair was so thin the scalp shone through. Her uniform hung loosely on her body.

"It's a waste of time and money to get a new outfit," she said, "God will have to take me as He finds me."

"Colonel Thomas has been retired for quite some time," Major Ellen said, raising her voice again. "How long has it been now, Esther, ten, fifteen years?"

"You'll have to ask my daughter," the colonel said, pointing to the woman on her right. "She won't let me do anything for myself anymore. Can't even wind my own watch! Ask her."

"Now, Mother, please behave," her daughter said. "We have guests. Besides, you always drop your watch."

She looked at her mother and then to us, as if to say, what can you expect?

"This is her daughter, Brigadier Ruth Thomas," Major Ellen said. "Her job is residents' counselor but also she's near retirement."

Brigadier Ruth was a prim woman, thin with slender hands and silver hair pulled back so tight it stretched the corners of her eyes. She wore granny glasses and tilted her head down to look over them. They were attached to a chain around her neck just like those of the other librarian lady.

"Captain Karlsson told us that women working at Booth hospitals were all unmarried," I whispered. My mother whapped her knee on mine.

"Colonel Thomas joined the Corps after her husband died in Cuba in the Spanish-American war," Major Ellen said. "That was in 1898 wasn't it, Colonel?"

The old lady nodded. "He charged up San Juan Hill with that damn Teddy Roosevelt," she said. "He'd be alive today if he hadn't followed that show-off."

The room got quiet, and I had the feeling they'd either heard this story before or were shocked to hear a former president cussed.

"Mother," Brigadier Thomas said, "please don't swear. Remember our guests."

"Pass the boy some potatoes," the colonel said and waved her hand dismissively.

In front of me was a serving dish filled with waterlogged green beans laced with floating pieces of boiled bacon. Vegetables of any kind weren't my favorite, but I felt pressured to put some on my plate.

Minding my manners was tough. Where I grew up, we never worried about passing to the left or right; the platter might be empty by the time it got to you. The rule was, don't drop anything in the soup when reaching for the potatoes. It was hard to be patient. I settled back to wait for the potatoes while Major Ellen continued the roll call.

"You've already met Lieutenant Olson," she said. "Among many other duties, she's in charge of checking in new residents and assigning them to dorms."

"I'm so sorry about the mix-up," Lieutenant Olson said. "I noticed you wince when I called you Renée. My name is Margit, and that's a bit of trouble too."

Mom jumped in to explain. "Rene was a fairly common name in our hometown," she said. "We've found that others don't know that Rene and Renée are pronounced differently, and that takes some explaining."

She didn't mention some of the explaining was delivered by fists and rolling in the dirt. My name was best suited for a hot-tempered, physically able boy, which I wasn't. I dreaded the first day at my new school. As I looked around the table at all these strange faces, I wondered if I would ever tell them apart. That they all dressed in uniforms and wore their hair in buns was no help, but I figured if I could learn how to tell nuns apart I could probably handle this too. It would just take some time.

Just as the mashed potatoes reached me, there was a polite knock on the door. When Major Ellen returned, her face was pale. She motioned to Lieutenant Olson, and they left the room. Through the open door I saw two policemen standing in the Great Room. One was holding a small cardboard suitcase, the other a winter coat, bright blue with fur trim on the collar.

Dessert was finished and coffee poured before they returned. Major Ellen's calm, serene look had changed to one of deep sadness. Lieutenant Olson's eyes were red, and with her owlish glasses off, she looked like a shattered little girl. No one knew what to ask or say. Just minutes earlier they had been celebrating our arrival, and now a deadening silence settled over the room. Major Ellen just sank into her chair.

"This morning a young girl came to us as the last resort for shelter," Major Ellen said with a quiver in her voice. "She wanted to keep the baby, but her boyfriend changed his mind and didn't want any part of it. Her family turned her out. Didn't even give her money for bus fare. She had our number and called today. We told her advance notice and consent were usually required, but since she was over eighteen and could admit herself, we told her to come ahead."

Major Ellen paused to wipe her eyes as Lieutenant Olson began to cry softly.

"We were going to put her in the newly painted dorm, but the odor was so strong we were afraid she might get sick, so we gave her enough money for a room at the little hotel near the bridge. Margit wrote out the directions." Her voice choked.

"It was just down the street two blocks."

I shifted in my chair. Maybe I wasn't supposed to hear this stuff. Should I excuse myself to go to the bathroom? My mother hit my knee again.

"The girl seemed so disappointed that I asked Margit to fill out preliminary paper work to show some progress."

"We did that, and she seemed okay," Lieutenant Margit said. "She put her coat on and said we'd see her tomorrow."

"At noon something suspicious was reported on the Snelling Avenue Bridge that goes over the railroad yard," Major Ellen said. "This afternoon police found a small suitcase with a blue coat folded over it. There was money in the pocket and directions to the hotel. They also found my card. She had no other identification."

No one at the table said a word. Major Ellen didn't come right out and say it but this must have been the girl who jumped off the bridge. Captain Trudy got up and put a comforting arm around Major Ellen's shoulder.

"Ellen, it's not your fault," she said.

"I didn't know," she sobbed. "If I'd only realized she was desperate, I would have given her my room. I should have known. That's my job. That's what God put me here for, and I failed." Raising a napkin to her eyes, she stood and left the room.

"We'll see her tomorrow after all," Lieutenant Olson said, tears running down her cheeks. "The police asked us to identify the body."

It was well after dark when we left the dining room for our new residence, the nurses' home, just across the street. There I would finally have a room of my own, but I was too tired to appreciate the moment. I pulled on my pajamas, brushed my teeth and fell into bed. Before I fell asleep, I tried to review the new people I'd met, but I just couldn't shake thinking about the girl in the blue coat. I pictured her climbing over a rail to jump, but in my imagination she never reached the tracks below. I wondered how many of the girls I saw today considered the same thing. How often did this happen? Before today, unwed mother was just another term to me. Today it had expanded to mean sin, shame, misery, and death.

I'd always depended on my mother to make decisions affecting our life even though, sometimes, she had no choice. She had to go back to nurses' training. We had to move to Arizona. The decision to return to Illinois made sense; I'd been cured. But this? We moved to a new state to live in a non-Catholic environment where young girls killed themselves out of desperation? What was Mom thinking?

When she came in to say goodnight, I asked some questions. Instead of answers to what I thought were simple inquiries, she became quiet and sat on the edge of my bed. Her eyes were moist.

"Well, it's like this," she said.

Moist eyes and those words were signs I recognized as the beginning of a long, emotional story with no simple answers.

"When I was in training at Sisters of Mercy Hospital, a young girl came in to deliver," she said. "She had a difficult labor because the baby was in a breech position. After several hours, she went from moaning to screaming. Her chart showed she hadn't been given medication. I started to give her Demerol when the nun in charge snapped at me. 'Don't you dare. That girl isn't married,' she said. 'She's broken the seventh commandment. She deserves what she's getting. It's God's punishment. No pain killers.'"

"I couldn't believe my ears," Mom said. "She wanted the poor girl to suffer."

Tears were trickling down my mother's face. I'd never heard this story before.

"What happened to the girl?" I asked.

"When the doctor came, he asked the nun why no pain killer had been given. She made an excuse and told me to go ahead," Mom said. "When I administered the medication, the girl thanked me over and over again. She was lonely and scared and started to cry between the spasms. "I didn't know," she said. "I was raised by a grandma from the old country. When I asked where babies came from she said, 'They come from under cabbage leaves. Now shut up.,' and I believed her," she sobbed. "I didn't mean to sin. I just didn't know."

Mom's eyes welled up with tears as she said, "My mother told me the same thing. I was sixteen and in high school before I learned the truth. There and then I vowed that embarrassment would never happen to a child of mine" That explained a lot because where babies came from was never a mystery to me. How they got there still is.

Mom stopped to dry her eyes. Her tears made me uncomfortable because the birth of a baby was usually a happy occasion for her.

"What'd she have?" I asked.

"She delivered a baby boy," Mom said. "When they put the baby in her arms, she started crying again because she knew she'd have to give him up."

"What did the nun do to you?" I asked.

"There wasn't much she could do without raising questions about her own behavior. We never spoke to each other again except as the job required. On my student nurse evaluation, she wrote, 'Can be insubordinate.' Because of that, I decided God wanted me to help people in pain no matter who they are. That's why I wanted to be a nurse."

There was no doubt about Mom's dedication to nursing, but she still hadn't answered my question.

"You could be a nurse anywhere," I said. "Why here?"

"You remember how I met Major Ellen in Chicago? I told her that I was Catholic, had a teenage son and didn't know a thing about the Salvation Army."

I also remembered Major Ellen's response. It was just short of pleading.

"But you know obstetrics," she said, "and there are so many young women that you could help. The rest of it isn't a problem."

Mom threw her hands up. "I'd run out of objections," she said. "I told her I'd give it some thought but figured once we were on the train that would be the end of it."

"So what happened?" I asked.

"She called about a week later, begging me to reconsider. You were with your dad for the summer, and we couldn't talk it over. When Major Ellen said, 'Rene will have a room of his own.' I told her we'd be there by September."

She kissed me goodnight and said, "I have to meet Major Ellen for breakfast. Get plenty of sleep because tomorrow we have to enroll you at school."

As I lay in bed and reviewed the coincidental train platform meeting that brought us here, I remembered how mom's sisters used to tease her. "Jo Jo, you have a need to be needed. That's why you're a nurse," they'd say. Tonight, for the first time I finally understood what they meant. Mom just couldn't resist taking this job, but it created a problem for me I hadn't anticipated. When school started, what would I say to my new classmates? How could I ever explain fifty pregnant girls?

~4~

A loud squealing noise woke me up. I looked through the curtains and saw a streetcar come to a stop right outside my window, my introduction to big-city living.

A note was taped to the dresser mirror. "Gone to the hospital for a breakfast meeting with Major Ellen. Come over after you've washed up. Brush your teeth! Lunch at noon. Love, Mom."

It was nine twenty, time enough to look around my new room. The furniture wasn't a matched set. The metal twin bed might have been in a hospital at one time while the steel dresser had a phony wood grain with a long scratch. The other piece was a small nightstand with a plastic table lamp. This was the first-ever room of my own so, to establish claim, I moved clothing from my suitcase to the tiny closet.

Mom had her own bedroom, a first for her too with a small anteroom that separated us. A door that opened to the street made it seem like our own small apartment.

Next to my bedroom was a tiny half-bath—sink, toilet—that was it. As I brushed my teeth, washed up and combed my hair, I heard noises behind the other door in the bathroom. I opened it carefully and came face to face with a woman I hadn't met.

"I'm sorry," I said. "I didn't know anyone was here." I started to close the door.

"You must be Rene," she said. "I was on duty all night, but I've heard about you." She held out her hand. I wasn't used to shaking hands with women so was careful not to squeeze. Lieutenant Corliss Johanssen was a registered nurse who'd be working with Mom in OB. Corliss was quite different from the other officers, mainly because she was out of uniform. Instead she wore a thin baby-blue robe and pink scuffies.

"I'm fixing a cup of tea," she said. "Let me pour one for you."

Her honey blonde hair wasn't in a bun but fell over her shoulders. She appeared to be in her twenties with a face that was beautifully pink, her skin, smooth with no blemishes. She wasn't a looker but maybe it was the lack of lipstick or makeup. Even though the robe covered her body she looked slim. With her long legs, she stood over me by two inches. Lieutenant Corlis had a soft voice and spoke with a slight accent I didn't yet recognize. It turned out she was raised on a farm in northern Minnesota. As she bent to pour my tea, her robe fell open, and I noticed her curving cleavage. This bothered me because I'd become aware of things about women I'd had no interest in before. The first time was in eighth grade when I saw girls pull on the front of their blouses, which left ink smudges around the buttons. As the school year went on, the blouses pooched out, and the outline of a brassiere shone through the starched white fabric. The girls were getting tits.

"Did you sleep okay last night?" Lieutenant Corliss asked. "Sometimes there's a problem with a new bed."

Her question startled me out of my daydream about girls' tits.

"I woke up and didn't know where I was," I said. "I still don't. Is this a house?"

"It used to be," she said. "Booth Memorial bought it years ago to house some of the officers. They call it the Nurses' Home, but I'm the only nurse here."

The kitchen was used for making coffee or tea and not much else because most of the cabinets were empty. What dishware there was didn't match. The tile countertops were bare except for an old-fashioned front-loading toaster. The refrigerator was pre-war with a milk bottle, butter dish, and a box of baking soda the only things inside. The oven door of the gas range was antique yellow after years of flame-ups. A narrow cabinet door hid a drop-down ironing board.

"Counting you and your mother, there are six of us living here," she said. "Captain Tucker is in the old dining room." She pushed on the door and, sure enough, it swung back and forth just like in the movies.

"There's only one full bathroom and it's upstairs," she said.

I followed her up the back stairs to the second floor.

"Up here we have three bedrooms. One is mine, one is Lieutenant Margit's, and the other is Captain McTavish's."

Glancing in the rooms, I saw simple furniture, not much different from mine but with a few feminine touches like flowers and frilly pillows.

"And this is the bathroom we all share," she said. "I prefer a shower, but you'll have to make do with a bathtub like the rest of us."

I wasn't prepared to find things most men didn't see. Every hook and handle was covered with pink or white panties, brassieres, hosiery, garter belts, and belts I didn't recognize. I knew my mother wore underwear but this was the first time I'd ever seen other women's. I felt a heat rushing up my face since I was alone with a woman I barely knew.

If I can keep her behind me maybe she won't see my face, I thought. *Just keep looking around like you're inspecting the room. No, no, don't look at the toilet. There's a big box of Kotex on the tank. Look at the towel rack instead. No, there's a brassiere there. Look at the size of those! They could hold cantaloupes. I don't think I've met her yet.* I was trying to find some way to back out of there.

"As you can see, we're not used to having a man around the house," she said. "We didn't even think about that when we agreed."

What did she mean, "agreed," I wondered. *Did they vote on letting us live here?*

I looked in the mirror and saw I wasn't the only one who was uneasy. Her face, which started out pink, was now beet red.

We went down the main stairway to the entry hall. Off to one side was a large living room.

"This is the only room in the house that's never used," she said. "If we're not in our rooms, we're at the hospital. It's not a very comfortable room anyway."

To my untrained eye, she was right. Two large sofas had ugly floral designs woven into their dark-brown fabric. Their stuffing must have been horsehair or cardboard because they were both hard as a rock. The fireplace hadn't been used recently and had no screen. The one standout piece of furniture was a baby grand piano whose varnish was crazed and cracked. The legs were thick, ugly columns topped by Corinthian curlicues. I'd heard the expression "piano legs," but never expected to see the piano that inspired it. I lifted the keyboard cover and saw a row of blotchy keys, some chipped, some yellowed and one with missing ivory. I poked at a few of them as if I were testing the tune of the piano. I'd seen it done in the movies. I pretended I knew what I was doing.

"Oh, do you play?" she asked.

I shook my head, "No." But inside I heard a voice. It said, *not yet.*

Lieutenant Corliss looked at her watch. "It's almost lunchtime," she said. "Go out your side door, and you'll see the hospital just across the street. Watch out for the streetcars."

I stepped out into a picture postcard. The sun had burned the dew from the lawn, and the wind rustled through the maple trees. It was the first day of September, and Minnesota was showing itself off. Booth Memorial didn't look as sinister as it had yesterday. It sat well back from the street surrounded by a large lawn, and I could smell freshly cut grass in the air. I crossed the busy street and walked up the long driveway that led to the side entrance of the hospital.

A car with Wisconsin plates was parked near the stairs. It was a '46 Ford two-door sedan, its black paint stained with mud half way to the windows. It reminded me of Saturdays in my hometown when farmers drove in to do their shopping. Many country roads in Illinois weren't paved, and I guessed they weren't in Minnesota either. A man wearing a John Deere ball cap was sitting behind the wheel and reading a newspaper. As I approached, he slowly slid the paper up high enough to cover his face until I passed. I nodded "Hello" but he didn't respond. Not very friendly for a farmer.

Inside the building, the smell of fresh paint and varnish immediately brought back yesterday's drama. If the girl in the blue coat could only have waited, the odor was bearable today. Walking down the long hallway I glanced sideways into some of the rooms. Several were simply furnished bedrooms for the officers, another one a sparsely stocked library with a reading table in the center. No one was in there but I heard female voices coming from the room next to it. Several girls were talking and working on their knitting projects. Another was busy at the sewing machine. It looked as if she was copying one of those shapeless maternity smocks that almost all of them wore. She had patterns pinned to a dress form with a pillow taped across the stomach. It caught me off guard. *Even the mannequins are pregnant in this place,* I thought. Their conversation stopped as they looked up in surprise. Just as quickly, their eyes dropped, and they went back to their work, only this time in wary silence. I did notice yesterday they all looked close to my age.

The stencil on the office door read, "COUNSELING." As I walked by, I saw Brigadier Thomas at her desk speaking with two women. One was mature, wearing her Sunday best, including a hat, and the other was younger with a small suitcase at her feet. Without really trying, I overheard Brigadier Thomas say . . .

". . . Finally we will need your name and an address in case there are complications. Don't worry, all information is confidential . . ."

I wondered if she was a prom girl and was with the man wearing the John Deere hat. Then Captain Trudy popped out of the Administration office.

"Hello, kiddo. Just in time for lunch," she said. "Your mother asked you to wait for her by the stairway."

I plopped on an uncomfortable couch and began idly thumbing through a copy of *War Cry*, the weekly magazine published by the Salvation Army. It was about the size of a comic book but full of dull news about the Corps. There were black-and-white pictures of strangers in uniform and little else to hold my attention. Frankly, I was more interested in the distant echo of Brigadier Thomas's voice spelling out the conditions.

"Your stay here will cost seventy five dollars a month plus an additional fifty dollars for your delivery," she said. "The fifty includes postnatal care for you and your baby."

The mother interrupted. "She'll be here six months," she said. We don't have that kind of money. We had a bad crop last year, and milk prices are down this year."

I turned the pages of *War Cry* quietly, hoping no one would notice my eavesdropping as I strained to hear every word.

"Perhaps you can ask the father to contribute," said Brigadier Thomas. "If that doesn't work out, you can always apply for aid from the state. They'll pay the bills and give her some pocket change, but you'll have to prove need."

There was resignation in the mother's voice. "Well, we'll just have to make do somehow," she said. "That no-good isn't going to help us now that he's left Wisconsin."

There was a long pause, the silence broken only by soft sniffling.

"If we want to pay on time, do we have to sign something?" the mother asked.

"Nothing at all," the Brigadier said reassuringly. "We trust you to pay us back when you can. We don't profit out of the misfortune of others. The money will be used to help other girls in her same situation." She must've said those words hundreds of times and knew how to deliver them with little or no emotion.

The shrill ring of a bell ended the mini-drama. It signaled lunch —or dinner as they call it here—and triggered the sound of shuffling footsteps. Down the stairway came that never-ending line of pregnant girls working their way toward the basement.

They passed by in the same mix as yesterday, some giggling, some laughing, and some pouting. This time a few offered a faint smile and the more venturesome wiggled their fingers at me. At the end of the line was Mom, acting like a mother hen shooing her chicks. She was talking, laughing and had a glow about her that I'd never seen before.

"You were sleeping so well I didn't have the heart to wake you up," she said to me. "I didn't think you'd mind."

She was right about that, but the food smells from the kitchen were a strong reminder I had missed breakfast.

The dining room was set for fourteen again, but we were less than half that. Major Ellen and Lieutenant Olson were still at the morgue and wouldn't be joining us. Mom and I found our napkin rings where we sat the previous evening and assumed those were our designated seats. Captain Trudy re-introduced herself since things had been so chaotic yesterday.

"I'm the creative and spiritual leader around here," she said. "My first job is to keep the residents busy with arts-and-crafts projects so they won't get bored. That's their embroidery and knitting in the display case outside."

I nodded but didn't want to say I didn't remember them.

"Because TV is new, no one's donated a set yet. Our residents are tired of the radio," she said. "Boredom is a big problem with teenagers."

To my eyes, Captain Trudy, at least in her mid-forties, was an old lady. I wondered if, at one time, her silver hair had matched her black eyebrows. It was so coarse there wasn't one hair out of place. At first, I thought she might be shy, but her blue-grey eyes had a sparkle that gave away a mischievous personality. I couldn't forget that she stuck her tongue out at Major Ellen yesterday.

"I'm also in charge of chapel services on Wednesday and Sunday," she said. "We don't require much of the residents, but chapel attendance is mandatory. You're welcome at any time."

I guessed she didn't know the Catholic Church wouldn't allow us to attend any other church service. We were told it was a sin.

"Do you sing?" she asked. "I direct the choir, and we've never had a male voice."

Without waiting for my answer she said, "Probably yours hasn't changed yet, but that's okay. My best soprano just gave birth this week. Maybe you can fill in."

I was dumbstruck. Just the idea of singing with a group of unwed pregnant girls would be enough for a priest to make me get on my knees and recite the rosary. She must have been kidding, but, if so, I couldn't tell. I looked at my mother, assuming she would offer a polite refusal to this ridiculous suggestion. Instead she was all smiles. Before I could come up with an excuse, Brigadier Thomas came in with her mother, the Colonel.

"Sorry we're late but I had to admit a resident by noon," she said. "Her father had to get back to milk the cows. He wouldn't even come in to say goodbye."

"What's her name and when is she due?" Captain Trudy asked.

"June A. is what she chose. She'll probably deliver in March."

"They don't use their own names?" I asked.

"Oh, no," Brigadier Thomas said, amused at my question, "nor their hometowns. They typically choose their names from movie stars. She probably chose June Allison. Isn't she popular now?"

"Yes, as well is Myrna Loy," Captain Trudy said. "I think we have two Myrna's now." She turned to Mom and me. "When a new girl comes in, the other residents always ask three questions. 'What's your name, when are you due, and where are you from'? They're always relieved when the hometown isn't the same as theirs. That way they won't have to answer any questions about the area because they aren't from there in the first place."

I must have looked confused so she explained. "Even though we tell newcomers all personal information is confidential, they still feel the need to lie about their names and hometowns," she said. "That's why they rarely receive mail or get a phone call. Some of them are really homesick."

"But there's a phone booth in the lobby," I said. "Don't they use that to call home?"

Before Captain Trudy could answer, Brigadier Thomas jumped in. "Most of our residents are from small towns where everyone knows everybody else's business."

This must have been her favorite topic because she leaned forward and lowered her voice like she was telling a secret.

"In those places long distance phone calls are always handled by the operator whether you're calling in or out." She paused to let me take that in. "It doesn't take too many calls to figure out that little Suzie did not go to live with her Aunt Clara in Keokuk like her parents said."

"And the same with the post office," said Captain Trudy. "They read addresses and postmarks and might make a comment to your neighbor at church. Then the cat's out of the bag for sure."

"They don't need a truck to deliver the mail here and I doubt you'll ever hear that phone ring," said Brigadier Thomas. "Once their confinement is over, the residents won't worry about someone disclosing where they've been the last six months. Life outside can be very cruel if they're ever discovered."

"In all my time here," Captain Trudy said, "I can't recall a resident who claimed Minneapolis or St. Paul as home, or even the state of Minnesota. I also don't remember anyone who called herself 'Mary' even though, according to the *Farmer's Almanac*, it's been the most popular female given name since 1900."

That makes sense, I thought. I doubt anyone would want to take a chance in choosing the name of the Virgin Mary. It could be sacrilegious.

The old Colonel made a loud "ssshhh" when two residents came in bringing the food. Apparently, what was said in this room was meant to stay in this room.

The noon menu was chunky beef stew over rice with a side dish of Brussels sprouts and a promise of dessert to come. It was worth missing breakfast. I had just put the first juicy bite of beef in my mouth when I heard the cry of a woman in pain. Without chewing, I swallowed the mouthful and hurriedly looked around the room. The officers were making small talk about the morning and took no notice. I know I heard a woman moan, but it looked as if no one else had. Maybe it was just some girls clowning around in the hallway. Once again, I took a forkful of meat and began to chew. This time a loud groan was followed by a piercing scream that caused even hard-of-hearing old Colonel Thomas to look up. I turned to my mother. She was looking at her watch.

"That must be Rita H.," she said. "She's about ready. I'd better go upstairs."

She left and I looked around the room, not knowing what to say. The officers seemed embarrassed and nervously toyed with their food. Brigadier Thomas cleared her throat . . . twice. Only the sound of silver clinking on china pierced the silence. Then came another scream, this one longer and higher-pitched, followed by gasping. Then more silence.

"That must be it," Captain Trudy said. "I wonder if it's a boy or girl."

I couldn't believe it. I had just heard a baby being born while I was having lunch. There must've been a strange look on my face.

"This hospital is somewhat unusual in its design," Captain Trudy said. "The architects, the design group and the approval committees were all made up of men."

"Of course," old Colonel Thomas interrupted. "Who else would put the labor and delivery rooms over the dining room except a damn committee of men?"

"Mother, please," said Brigadier Thomas. "Don't swear at the table when we have guests."

"Pass the boy some food," the old lady said. "He's barely eaten a thing."

* * *

As I walked down the hallway, I thought, *so, that's labor*. I'd heard Mom talk about it but didn't know it involved screaming. Was every meal going to be like that? Captain Trudy said she was giving Mom a complete tour of the hospital this afternoon and asked if I wanted to come along.

"It's not something we normally do," she explained, "But we're going to make an exception for you. Be back by the staircase at 3:00 p.m."

I opened the side door and almost tripped over the recently admitted girl. The muddy Ford was gone, and she was sitting on the brick steps, crying. No, it was more than that. She was sobbing—deep, heaving gulps of air followed by trembling exhales. She looked up at me before I could slip by. Tears were streaming down her face.

"He wouldn't even say goodbye," she said. "He just got in the car and drove away. I've never been away from home before. What am I supposed to do?"

This was the first time I'd ever experienced anyone so emotional. Her face might have been attractive in any other situation but now it was all red and splotchy. Tears cut through her powder and makeup. I guessed she was embarrassed at losing self-control in front of a stranger who, by now, must know her terrible secret.

It was an awkward moment for me because she was hurting badly and I didn't know what I should say or do. That's not exactly right. On my way out, Captain Karlsson stopped me in the hall and advised me what not to do. "The new girl is probably crying outside the door," she said. "Don't try to help her because you can't. I know it sounds callous, but we've all had to learn it. Believe me, for the sake of the girl, don't get involved."

Those sobering words were still fresh in my mind when I came face to face with June A. but I couldn't just walk by.

"I'm not a bad girl," she said, pleading. "He lied to me. He told me he loved me. I'm not a bad girl like they say."

I was looking for the right words but they wouldn't come.

"June, I'm sure you aren't," I said with no great certainty.

Hearing her new name came as a shock. She stopped sobbing and looked at me with eyes wide, realizing that in a quick moment her life had changed. She was no longer the girl who had walked in the door with her suitcase barely an hour ago. There were no more questions to ask and none to answer. From now until she left, she must live a new life—as June A. I glanced up at the side door. Standing there, slowly shaking her head was Captain Berthe Karlsson.

* * *

"Man on second. Man on second."

With the loudest volume she could muster, Captain Trudy announced our progress up the stairway to the second floor.

"No residents are supposed to be up here at this time of day, but you never know," she said in a gentle voice. Then with an even more commanding tone, "Man on second. Cover up girls."

I thought this over for a second. The idea of an uncovered pregnant girl was not very appealing. At age fourteen, however, I was impressed at being called a "man." Captain Trudy guided me down a highly polished hallway to a room with six neatly made beds. A wall locker and a small table flanked each. The walls were painted a lackluster industrial green and were also naked of pictures.

"It's kind of plain, isn't it?" I said.

"We discourage the residents from putting personal effects on the wall," she said. "A small picture on the table or in their locker, that's okay. Otherwise, when they leave there would be tape marks or nail holes and then we'd have to paint the room again. It's rather stark but better this way." She pointed to a doorway with no door.

"That's the bathroom for this floor. It's pretty big and usually no waiting for anything. We run on a schedule here, as you know. Bells,

31

buzzers . . ." A metallic voice interrupted. "June A., please come to the Administration office."

" . . . And the ever-present intercom."

We looked into one last dorm. June A. sat on a bed, still sniffling while carefully unpacking her clothes. Captain Trudy's voice changed tone.

"June, you're wanted at the office," she said. "Remember the rules. You're not to be in the dorms in the daytime."

June looked up suddenly, surprised to hear her new name called.

"I'm sorry," she said. "I didn't hear my name. When did they call me?"

"It doesn't matter but you'd better get downstairs," Captain Trudy said. "You can unpack later and then take your bag to the storeroom in the basement." Still sniffling, June left.

"They almost always miss the first intercom calls because they're not used to their new name," she said. "It takes a day or two for them to adapt to their new situation."

"Why aren't they allowed to stay in the dorms in the daytime?" I asked.

"It's not good for them to be alone. The two biggest things we have to worry about are boredom and depression. One leads to the other, and then we have bigger problems."

Captain Trudy explained that all the residents had assigned duties. Some worked in the kitchen, some in the laundry, some did housecleaning in the building and others served in the dining room. They kept shifting chores to avoid boredom and as they got further along in their pregnancies the work got lighter.

"At least fifteen of our residents are still in high school," she said. "They attend classes every day just down the hall."

She led me to a room outfitted just like a regular classroom with blackboards, student desks, bookshelves and pull-down wall maps. The instructors were part time and supplemented with student teachers from the university.

"The girls will go back to high school at the same learning level," she said, "but they'll have earned credits so they can graduate with their class. We are very proud of this room."

During this time I was trying to picture how pregnant girls used a school desk. Did they sit sideways?

The intercom blared, "Captain Svensen. Please go to the nurse's office."

"I guess your mother's ready for us. OB is just down the hall."

We skirted the main staircase and followed our noses to an open door.

"We're passing the special-diet kitchen," Captain Trudy said. "It's for mothers and babies that need special food, which is actually prepared in the kitchen and comes up by dumbwaiter. The residents really hated it when they had to hoist it up by ropes. Now it's electric."

The door with Operating Room stenciled on the frosted glass opened into a room with desks, chairs, medical paraphernalia and an office marked NURSE. Mom was just finishing some medical charts. When she stood, I saw bloodstains on her shoes, which had been sparkling white at noon. That meant I'd have to polish them that night same as I'd done since I was a little boy.

"Let me show you around my new domain," Mom said. "Over there is the examination room. If she's close, each girl, I mean resident, comes in on Monday to be examined and weighed."

She led us down the hall to a room full of equipment. The overhead light looked like a reflector. Directly under it was an oversized table with chrome stirrups set at a really high angle.

"This is really my office," Mom said. "It's the delivery room where all the babies are born. We've already had one today, and another's on the way."

The room smelled of something peculiar. Not quite body odor but something personal—not as offensive as the paint down the hall but close.

"Across the hall's a nursery with three babies in it," she said. There's a big ward for the residents who won't be keeping their babies and a much smaller one for those who will. These two doors are to the labor rooms."

I looked inside one of the labor rooms and saw nothing more elaborate than a bed, a chair and a small side table with a shaving cream brush and a man's razor on it.

Captain Trudy interrupted. "We'll have to cut the tour short because the residents are coming upstairs to clean up before supper," she said. "The third floor is nothing but more dorms anyway."

From the next room I heard a sudden gasp followed by a plaster-penetrating scream capped by a loud moan. Startled, I turned toward Mom, who was looking at her watch.

"Sounds like Claudette C. is right on time," she said. "I might be late for supper but save me some dessert."

From below drifted girls' voices and the tinkling of silverware being set. I must have been standing right over the dining room. If so, that meant another meal with screaming and, if old Colonel Thomas was right, it was because of that damn committee of men.

~5~

ON THE FIRST DAY OF SCHOOL, my stomach was full of butterflies. I'd come up with a plan to keep my connection to Booth Memorial hidden. I would leave the hospital after breakfast, go back to the nurses' home for my books, leave by the back door, walk down the alley and circle back on Como Avenue to the streetcar stop just in front of the nurses' home. A group of kids about my age were already waiting. We boarded together. So far, so good. They eyed me over during the trip, and a few put a hand over their mouth to whisper to their pals. That was always followed by a laugh. I noticed that some of the girls looked my way and then turned away giggling. They couldn't know about the hospital so it must have been a girl thing. In a few weeks I'd probably know them all but at that moment I felt pretty lonely. To look busy I leafed through my new textbooks and wrote my name inside the covers. It was strangely quiet except for the kids whispering, the sound of steel wheels on the rails, and the bell's "*ding, ding ding.*"

The bell at Murray High School had a different sound. The ring was stronger with more authority—almost an industrial urgency to it. My task was to reach my assigned homeroom before the bell sounded again. The hallway teemed with teenagers facing the same challenge, bumping and shoving to get by. I was about to lose my personal race.

Murray High was unlike any school I had attended. A three-story brick building, it was almost a block long. Inside was a constant flow of students that moved from class to class every fifty minutes. In Arizona, junior high was a buffer from elementary to high school. Students stayed in the same room while the teachers did the moving. In St. Paul, there was no junior high. With one year of high school experience, my new classmates already had a sophomore swagger. I didn't.

My homeroom was the woodshop classroom. I tried to sneak in unnoticed. The instructor, wearing a sawdust-spotted shop coat, was taking attendance on a clipboard. Unfortunately, he'd already reached the D's.

"Dardenne. Renée Dardenne," he said, using the female pronunciation. "Anybody seen her? What's a girl doing in here anyway?"

"That's Rene," I said, trying to emphasize the difference. "Rene Dardenne, and I'm here, sir."

The instructor looked up from his clipboard and shouted, "Did you goof-balls hear that. He called me 'sir.' I haven't been called that since I was in the Army."

He motioned me to an empty stool. "You must be new here," he said.

The room grew quiet, and I looked around just in time to duck a small piece of scrap wood thrown directly at my head.

"Where you from Dardenne?" the instructor asked.

"Arizona, sir," I said.

Someone shouted, "Ride 'em cowboy," followed by "Hi Yo, Silver."

This wasn't going to be easy. My plan to blend in had been shot down. The whole day was a blur of bells, endless parading from class to class, new faces, new teachers, locker combinations, and finding the boys' toilets. A funny thing kept happening. Wherever I went, I heard remarks about cowboys.

One guy looked at me and said, "Howdy, amigo." Someone behind me said, "Giddy up, cowpoke." I heard, "Hey, Roy, where's Trigger?" a couple of times. The most popular was, "Unh, Keno Saber" from *The Lone Ranger*. It puzzled me all day until gym. A guy walked up to me and said, "Hey, Tex, where's your boots?"

"What do you mean?" I asked.

"You've got your cowboy outfit on but no boots. What did you do, leave 'em in the bunkhouse?"

A couple of his buddies grouped around me and laughed at his joke. He acted cocky because now he had an audience.

John Bittolini, better known as "Johnny B.," was bigger than the other guys and had a shadow on his face that was the start of a beard. By comparison, I had a couple of short, fuzzy hairlings poking through my baby-smooth chin. Well, maybe there were a few zits in the way but it was mostly smooth.

Suddenly it hit me. I was the only student in the whole high school wearing a complete western outfit—cowboy shirt, genuine Levi's with matching jacket and a hand-tooled leather belt with a longhorn steer buckle.

In Arizona, it was what we wore every day, but here no Levi's were in sight—not even a pair of Oshkosh b'Gosh jeans. I had committed the sin of not wearing the peer-approved male student uniform . . . chino cotton pants (tan or gray) and a long-sleeved gabardine shirt. Shoes weren't important as long as they weren't boots. As Johnny Boy leaned in close, a shrill sound cut through the tense atmosphere. I was saved, literally, by the bell that ended class.

The next bell I heard was the familiar "*ding, ding, ding*" of a street-car taking Mom and me to correct my wardrobe mistake. She didn't see anything wrong with my coordinated Levi's outfit. After all, it was almost new, bought just before we left Arizona. New clothing created a bigger problem. She had spent most of her meager savings on bus fare to start this job, and she had yet to be paid. Without asking, she reasoned my request must be very important—especially since I'd never before shown much interest in what I wore.

The streetcar turned onto Snelling Avenue and headed over a long concrete bridge that spanned a wide valley with railroad tracks running down the center. We went by the Happy Hollow Motel, and I thought of the young girl in the blue winter coat who must've passed here on the way to her death.

Was she still crying? I wondered. What spot did she choose? Did she climb on the railing or just jump over? Snelling was such a busy street, why didn't anyone stop her. I remembered when Major Ellen and Lieutenant Margit returned from the morgue. No one wanted to extend their pain by asking details and the subject never came up again—at least at the dining table.

"*Ding, ding, ding*," sounded the bell as the motorman announced, "University Avenue transfer point. Watch your step."

We got off in the middle of the busiest intersection I had ever seen. University Avenue was a wide boulevard with several tracks down the center, the main connector between the downtowns of St. Paul and Minneapolis. It was dusk, and traffic noise compounded our confusion as we clutched our transfers and pushed through the rush-hour crowd. Just then, a brand-new St. Louis PCC streetcar threaded its way through the intersection and coasted to a stop. The doors opened to a whole new world. No more Toonerville Trolley, no more clanking and jerking, no more worn handrails and varnished benches polished by thousands of bottoms. The seats were of a brand new material that looked like leather, the handrails were polished chrome. The paint was fresh and the interior smelled new. The only tie to the past was the "*ding, ding, ding*" of the bell, but even it was sharper and brighter sounding.

Now, this was more like it. We were in the big time, I thought as we glided away. The heady pleasure was all too short as the operator called our stop. We stepped onto the traffic island in the center of University Avenue where, directly in front of us stood the largest department store I had ever seen. It was at least six stories and ran for a whole city block. In the center was a tall tower with a sign in big red letters telling me I had come to the place that could solve my wardrobe problem: "Montgomery Ward."

As we approached the main entry, the large door slowly swung open. *Boy,* I thought, *this place has automatic doors!* Then I saw a man in uniform, wearing white gloves, whose job it was to provide that service.

"Boys' clothing please," Mom asked. The doorman looked me over carefully and said, "Men's clothing, first floor by the escalator." I couldn't believe my ears. I had been upgraded right in front of my mother and was now recognized as a man by another man. I led the way so fast Mom had trouble keeping up. When we reached the escalators, I said to Mom, "Let's go up. I've never ridden one before." Apparently neither had she, and we both stumbled over the stairs as they moved under our feet.

The second floor was like a fairyland. I had never seen as many things for sale in one place. We rode the escalators all the way to the fifth floor (farm machinery, power tools, snow shovels) and back down to the first. It was like we had stumbled into the Montgomery Ward mail order catalogue. Mom reminded me that we'd miss supper if we didn't hurry, so my first visit to a grown man's world went by in such a hurry I didn't have time to enjoy it. When we passed the doorman on the way out, I was clutching two new pairs of cotton twill pants, two new gabardine shirts and a receipt for a winter jacket on layaway. This was not to be my last visit to the wonderland of Montgomery Ward.

The next day I followed my plan and met the same group waiting for the streetcar. This time I paid attention to what they were wearing. My new clothes fit right in. The same girls were giggling but not staring at me anymore. Can't imagine how I hadn't even had a clue yesterday. One of the guys sat down next to me and said, "My name's Eddie Henderson. Saw you in homeroom yesterday. Thought I'd welcome you to the neighborhood."

Eddie had that wholesome look of kids raised in the northern states, kind of ruddy and a little beefy, certainly bigger than me. By his last name I guessed he was Swedish.

"You live around here?" he asked. I had sort of rehearsed an answer for this question, but it came up too fast, and I was caught off guard.

"Yeah, just around the corner and down the street," I fibbed. "Don't know the neighborhood too well, but it's over there somewhere." That seemed to satisfy Eddie for the moment.

"If you want to come over, we play football on the vacant lot next to my house," he said. "They play football in Arizona? I couldn't tell by that outfit you were wearing yesterday." He smiled and said, "I saw you gettin' worked over by Johnny Boy after gym. Watch out for him. He likes to pick on new guys."

Today, I thought, there'd be no more reason for Johnny Boy to call me "Tex."

~6~

BY LATE OCTOBER, THE GIRLS from Prom Night 1949 were in place and those from New Year's Eve 1948 were gone. It was like being inside a moving puzzle. Everyone came in from nowhere and used names not their own. Those who departed went nowhere, leaving behind their identities and their babies and disappeared without a trace. Cardboard suitcases came and went from the lockup downstairs. The stories told were all similar, but a few stood out.

One afternoon a 1941 Ford coupe pulled up. It was metallic blue, had fender skirts, snazzy hubcaps and Laker pipes. This was not a farmer's car. It carried Iowa plates, which meant it had come some distance. A young couple got out. She was wearing a poodle skirt and saddle oxfords, and he sported a letterman's sweater with a big "W" on it. From my favorite overhearing point in the anteroom, I got the story.

She had just graduated from high school, and he'd graduated the year before. They wanted to get married, but her parents weren't in favor because he didn't seem to have a future. It didn't help that he was from the wrong side of town and his parents were divorced. After graduation, he took a job at a local bakery and spent his first check on a down payment for a used car.

By the time she discovered her pregnancy, he'd already enlisted in the Army for two years to avoid the draft. Their plan was for him to report to duty and go through basic and the second eight weeks training. After that, he would be eligible for dependents, and she would be eighteen. They'd marry, no matter what her parents said.

"I see you've already been here with your parents," Captain Berthe Karlsson said to the girl. "They have signed the papers, but you will be paying the expenses. Is that correct?"

"I'll be covering that, ma'am," the boy said. "I've got some savings from the bakery, and I'll use my Army pay. We'll make it through."

Not a perfect plan, they admitted, but they had few choices. She looked sad as he drove away but didn't cry. She had a future with the guy she loved, and this was just a brief stopover. Her Booth name was Corrine C.

In the same week Booth had an unusual admittance. When I came home from school, a cab and a Railway Express truck stood in the driveway. I thought a new officer was moving in but that wasn't it. I quickly went to my spot in the anteroom to thumb through the latest copy of *War Cry*. The voices speaking to Captain Karlsson sounded more mature. The man had a northeastern accent, maybe from Boston. Hers was southern with a bit of mountain twang.

They were in the road show of the latest Broadway hit musical, *South Pacific* that was appearing downtown. He was the assistant conductor of the orchestra and she was in the chorus. Her other role was as first understudy to the lead character, Nellie Forbush, the part sung on Broadway by Mary Martin. She admitted it was a wonderful career opportunity gone sour.

Captain Karlsson asked the approximate date of conception to estimate her delivery.

"I think it was opening night in Philadelphia," the woman said. "You'd celebrated too much and I told you to be careful." There was a painful silence.

"And that was when?" asked Captain Karlsson.

"Three months ago," the man said.

"And have you done any strenuous activity since then?" she asked the woman.

"Well, I'm a dancer so I do a lot of high kicks and bumps and grinds every night."

I wish I could have seen Captain Berthe Karlsson's face when the woman mentioned the bumps and grinds. I'll bet she looked as if she'd sucked on a lemon.

"I was doing just fine but the assistant producer said I was beginning to show," the woman said. "She got kind of nasty about it and said they wouldn't hold my spot."

"Honey, Della was just doing her job," the boy friend said. "We've been through this."

Captain Karlsson listened to their story patiently and set out the terms for the stay at Booth Memorial. She reached the part about possible state aid.

"We don't want charity," the man said. "I'll send money every month. How much do you need right now?"

While they signed papers I moved into the Great Room to wait for supper. On the way out, the couple stopped in the anteroom.

"I'm going to hate it here," she said. "They want me to work and everything. I didn't even do that at home."

"Well, honey, it's the best we can do on short notice," he said. "You can't go home, and you can't go back to New York like this. It would ruin your career."

"I want to go with you," she said. "Don't leave me here."

"It's only six months," he said. "By then the show plays San Francisco, and it'll be over. You and the baby can join me there."

"What about your wife?"

"I'm going to ask her for a divorce tonight. Then I'll be free and we can get married in Frisco."

"Promise you won't forget me?"

"Honey, I'll write every day and call long distance on Sundays. Everything's going to be okay. Now I gotta rush to catch the train. Give me a kiss and walk me to the cab."

It was quiet in the anteroom. I stopped holding my breath.

"Rene Dardenne, please come to the Administration office. Rene to Administration."

The sharp intercom voice startled me. I'd never heard my name called before.

Lieutenant Margit was behind the office counter.

"Somebody told me you were in the anteroom," she said.

Was I seen eavesdropping, I wondered. Instead of saying anything, I just waited.

"Our newest resident has some large baggage Max can't handle by himself. Can you give him a hand?"

So, I wasn't discovered. "You bet," I said, using enthusiasm to cover my relief.

"And Rene, the new resident's name is Jonna J."

The cab and truck were gone. In their place was a large trunk covered with labels. It looked like it had been around the world. It also looked heavy. Max, the building superintendent, was figuring out how to move it. Jonna J. stood next to two small suitcases. She looked irritated and I knew why.

Jonna appeared to be about twenty, much older than I was, and quite mature. *Man, she's really good looking and better dressed than most new girls*, I thought. She was wearing a tailored suit and high heels. Even the seams on her hose were straight. Her makeup looked professional, and her hair was perfect. To top it off, she wore a bright red beret. Right away she reminded me of my favorite movie star, Claudette Colbert. The only thing that spoiled the image was a slight bulge at her waistline. *She'll be wearing one of those shapeless dresses before long*, I thought. I didn't even want to picture it.

"Thank you so much for helping out, darlin," she said.

I recognized the distinctive voice with a slight twang.

"My trunk's so big this poor man can't move it."

When she leaned over and gave me a kiss on the cheek, I got a sudden feeling I could move it by myself. Max and I grabbed the trunk and began lifting and shoving it toward the basement. The labels showed all the cities where it had been, but there was nothing but black ink where her name should be. *She's crossed out her past, just like the others*, I thought. *She isn't that different after all.*

Between the heaving and scooting, I got to see Max close-up. We had waved to each other from a distance but never met. He was a smallish man, in his forties, I would guess, and had a scraggly beard that was starting to drip sweat. He spoke in heavily accented English. We made space in the suitcase room and wrestled the trunk inside.

Finally, I recognized his accent. He sounded just like my grandparents. "Sveikas," I said using their word for hello.

His mouth dropped for a moment, and then formed a big smile.

"Sveikas, sveikas," he shouted. "You are Lithuanian?" He began pumping my hand. He seemed overjoyed that I knew at least one word in his language.

His name, Mordecai Sheferis, had been Americanized to Max. During the war, the Nazis had imprisoned him for the unpardonable crime of being Jewish. He survived the death camps, but his wife and children had not. Friends in Minneapolis sponsored him and found this job to give him a chance to build a new life. For now, his whole world was a small room next to the laundry. He was responsible for maintaining the furnace, the boilers, the laundry equipment, and numerous tasks in the building. The job did call, in some small way, on his mechanical engineering degree.

I'd never been in the basement, so he insisted on a quick tour. In one room, residents were shoving laundry into big washing machines. Others ironed sheets and tablecloths on a mangle. Because of the heat and humidity, these jobs were the least popular and assigned to girls early in their pregnancies. The laundry was the domain of Captain Cora McTavish, an ample woman and owner of the cantaloupe brassieres hanging in our bathroom. She was always on the alert, since new girls tried to get away with as little work as possible. They discovered it was not a good idea to cross the captain who spoke with a Scottish burr.

Supper smells came from the next room. Kitchen work, staffed by soldiers in the Salvation Army, was a paid job, but residents assisted them by doing dicing and slicing for meal prep. Max said the paid people were not sympathetic to the girls' situation and lectured them with Bible verses, most having to do with sin and the evils of fornication. This job was almost as unpopular as the laundry.

The residents' dining room was adjacent. It was bright for a basement room and had curtains on the high windows. The two long tables were covered with red-checkered oilskin tablecloths. Residents had just finished setting the flatware when the bell sounded for supper. From a distance, I could hear the shuffling of feet heading in our direction.

The last room had a strong, stinky smell.

"They call it the Den," Max said.

The officers held off for years, but women's smoking became too popular, and they finally gave in. The decision coincided with converting to heating oil. Since there was no more need for a coal room, the residents swabbed a coat of Kem-Tone green on the walls and shoved in some furniture. With only a hanging light and a small window near the ceiling, it was still a dingy room. A small table held a writing tablet and fountain pens so the girls could write home, but they hardly ever did. The sound of "Mule Train," the latest hit by Frankie Laine, came from a table radio. The girls sang along, smacking their hands together to mimic the crack of a whip. The smoke was so overpowering, it burned my eyes. They didn't even cough.

Jonna J. came out of the resident's dining room. "Just one little minute, darlin," she said. "I need to put something into my trunk. Could you help me?"

I was expecting clothing, but the trunk was packed to the brim with all sorts of odd items—well, odd to me. Wigs, uniforms, makeup, colored fabrics, and more. She closed the lid, locked it, dropped the key inside the front of her blouse and winked. That sexy move would capture my imagination for several weeks. At supper, Major Ellen thanked me for helping.

"I hope Jonna J. will fit in," she said.

I was hoping the same thing.

"Rene, I notice you've been reading *War Cry* a lot," said Captain Karlsson. "If you'd like some back issues, I have several in my office."

Does she know I have no real interest in War Cry, *I thought. Does she suspect?*

~7~

MY INTENT WAS TO REMAIN A GOOD CATHOLIC when we moved to St. Paul, but it turned out to be more difficult than I thought. A few months earlier, I was under the all-watchful influence of priests and nuns. Now I spent time every day with ordained ministers of the Salvation Army and fifty girls who had tasted the immoral side of life. To be truthful, I enjoyed making daily choices without someone looking over my shoulder. Were they the right choices? I wasn't used to this kind of freedom, and I couldn't tell. My first inclination was to do what I knew best—go to confession on Saturday and attend mass on Sunday.

Our Lady of the Lake Catholic Church was only two blocks from Booth Memorial. Latin was the universal language of Catholicism. Neither Mom nor I spoke it, but hearing it made us comfortable in the new church. On Sunday we attended eleven o'clock mass, and, while I went up to the rail for communion, Mom sat in the pew sniffling. Years ago a priest refused to give her communion because she was divorced. He even quoted a dead pope as his resource. Mom was a fighter, but the priest stood there with the power of the Almighty behind him and, she had been intimidated. That bothered me because he didn't know the story. Mom didn't ask for the divorce yet she was the one who was punished. It didn't seem fair, but I learned not to say anything when she cried during Communion.

Father Peter McGowan, the pastor, had the rugged look and reddish, curly hair of the Irish. His ruddy complexion turned out to be a barometer of his beliefs. During sermons, you could gauge his passion for

48

the subject by the color of his face. Any kind of sin lit him up, but he saved his best glow for sins of the flesh. I realized I might be the one he was aiming at, though I couldn't figure where I was on his sin list. It didn't look good. I was consorting with Protestants daily, sharing their food and housing. To make it worse, they were sheltering unrepentant sinners. On the other hand, I did my best to avoid their worship ceremonies, though I had a tiny slip when Captain Trudy insisted I hear her choir at Wednesday service. I listened to the hymns, and then she followed with a verse from the Bible. Before I knew it, they were reciting the Lord's Prayer. By reflex, I joined in. To my surprise, it was the same as ours, with a few more words at the end. What were they doing with our prayer?

Now I had to decide. Had I committed a sin by reciting the words to the Lord's Prayer in a Protestant service? I wasn't sure how to explain it in confession.

Soul-searching produced even more questions. After a month of daily contact with the Salvation Army women, I'd found them to be decent people honestly caring for and about others. To me, they didn't appear to be instruments of the devil. It was hard to believe they were going to hell just because they weren't Catholic. Same thing with the residents. Most were nice-enough girls who tripped on their way into life. The sad part was they were doing the penance while their boyfriends were nowhere in sight. Not all Catholic girls were fountains of purity either. It was a shock to learn there were hospitals for Catholic unwed mothers—lots of them. After a lifetime of confessing my little sins, I couldn't imagine what it would be like to confess that to a priest.

I was stuck on figuring out what amounted to an adult sin. Confession was something I had to do on Saturday whether I'd sinned or not. Now, I was getting into bigger stuff, like my thoughts about girls. I wasn't doing anything about it, but did those count as sins? Even worse, I was confused about confession itself. What good was it? In Catechism we learned, God forgives and then forgets. I confessed my sins each week, did the penance and committed the same old sins again. When was God going to catch on? He was not dumb.

I was afraid to put these questions to Father McGowan. He might launch into one of his "Faith and Fear" sermons that put the blame back on me. As a little boy I was taught that Jesus loved me. As I got older the real message came through. Yes, Jesus loves me, but if I really mess up God'll get me.

~8~

I SAT IN THE LAST SEAT OF THE STREETCAR and stared intently out the window at the passing landscape. In the window's reflection, schoolmates glanced toward me and turned away to whisper and then laugh. This moment was never supposed to happen, but what could I have done?

My plan to avoid discovery of my relationship with Booth Memorial had worked. Every morning, after breakfast, I'd go to my room in the nurses' home. Then I'd leave by the back door, go down the alley and stroll back to the corner as if I lived somewhere else in the neighborhood.

The process had become routine, but today was a little different because we'd had the first light dusting of snow. It had already melted on the sidewalks but still covered the lawn. Breakfast was a treat as usual because there were choices. If I wanted eggs, any style, all I had to do was ask. There'd be a selection of fruits and an option of breads, toasted or not. Hot chocolate was my usual drink. If a well-balanced breakfast was the gateway to a healthy life, I was on the right path.

The staff was used to me by now and the conversation was usually shoptalk or politics, both church and state. I didn't own a watch but kept an eye on the clock over the door. The streetcar arrived at seven thirty-five. Major Ellen excused me, and I headed for the side door. As I passed the main entry stairway, I heard loud, convulsive sobbing. Ever since my first clumsy encounter with June A., I made it a point to walk by quietly when this happened to avoid getting involved. The sound was from someone in great pain, emotional more than physical and came from Joan C., a girl I met when she cleaned the nurses' home. She was a quiet girl who hummed hymns as she dusted. When we did talk, she usually asked questions about

51

what it was like to be a Catholic. Apparently, she'd never met one before and was curious. As her due date got closer, they took her off housekeeping, and I hadn't seen her for a while. The shoptalk around the table was that she'd delivered a healthy girl and was one of the mothers who chose to bathe, dress and feed her baby before making a choice. Joan C. had a maternal instinct and seemed to enjoy the duties of a new mother, but the truth was she had no choice at all.

During her pregnancy, Joan C. had led a very quiet life. No phone calls, no mail, and no family connections nor concern. One day someone came to take her home to celebrate her birthday, and she left in pretty high spirits. On her return, her attitude was completely different. She told the girls that, as they got closer to her hometown, she had to lie on the car floor until they were in the garage and then had to pull a coat over her head to walk to the house. During the visit, she wasn't allowed to leave or answer the phone and had to stay away from the windows. Her parents' concern wasn't hard to understand. Her father was head pastor of the Lutheran church in their little community. It would be difficult for him to mount the pulpit each Sunday and rail against sin while he was sheltering the most grievous of sinners under his own roof. While she knew how others would treat her, she was unprepared for the reaction of her parents. Not only was her faith in her family shaken, she felt deserted by God.

Tuesday was the day the social worker collected babies for adoption. Joan C. had just given up her baby, and her life was at its darkest point. She had no self-esteem, no future, and now no baby girl. Even with Captain Karlsson's "Don't get involved" warning, I just couldn't walk by without doing something. I put my arm around her shoulder and felt a shiver from deep inside her body. Again I had a feeling of inadequacy with no experience in what to say or do.

"They just took her away," she said. "I hadn't made up my mind yet. I just needed a little more time."

Her eyes were red and swollen.

"I didn't even get to kiss her goodbye."

While I was full of compassion, it had gotten late and to miss the streetcar meant I'd be late for school. When I gently slipped my arm away, Joan grabbed my hand as if it was a lifeline. Major Ellen came to my rescue. She motioned me away, sat next to Joan and offered some comforting words.

I looked up at the big clock in the hallway. Seven thirty-four. One minute left. No time for my nonchalant walk to the corner. I bolted out the big front door, ran across the lawn, hopped the hedge and leapt onto the rear platform just as the streetcar pulled away. As I looked back, I saw my footprints in the new-fallen snow. They left no doubt from where I had come. I pretended not to notice the stares of my classmates as I grabbed a seat in the rear. The streetcar, normally filled with school chatter and laughter, was quiet—except for the murmur of low voices and whispering. Eddie Henderson slid into the seat next to me and brushed the snow off my shoes.

"I've known for a long time," he said quietly. "Just waitin' for you to say something."

~9~

I T'S NOT WORKING, ELLEN. She doesn't belong here."

Captain Berthe Karlsson's voice echoed down the hallway. Major Ellen burst into the dining room with the captain right behind.

"She's distracting the residents and upsetting procedures," the captain hissed in a tirade aimed at Jonna J. Normally, the officers waited until I was gone to say how they really felt. Not today. I was hearing this morning's shop talk unfiltered.

"She's a disruption," said Captain Tucker. "And she can't do kitchen work."

"She's no help in the office," Lieutenant Margit said. "The others see her getting away with it, so I can't get them to work."

"She's taught them all the lyrics to *South Pacific*," Captain Karlsson steamed. "Have you heard them? Some are downright filthy."

I heard those songs on the radio and didn't remember any dirty words. I wondered if Jonna made them up. Captain Karlsson turned to Major Ellen.

"What are you going to do, Ellen?" she said. "She's a bad influence and a detriment."

"Give her to me," said Captain McTavish, the laundry officer. "Then we'll see how loud she sings."

I cringed at the thought of Jonna J. stuffing sheets into those big washing machines. After a week of that, her seams wouldn't be straight but her hair would be.

"The girls seem to like her," Captain Trudy said in quiet defense.

"Of course. Wouldn't you?" said Lieutenant Margit. "Getting out of work."

I'd never heard such a buzz. There was very little Christian kindness going around the table that morning.

"Just ask her to leave, Ellen. Then it'll be normal again," said Captain Karlsson.

Mom listened in silence. "What about you, Mrs. Dardenne?" Major Ellen asked. "What's your experience with Jonna?"

"Things are a lot livelier on second," Mom said. "Lots of happy noises. I'm hearing more singing in the halls."

"It's from the devil's mouth," said Captain Karlsson. "They're evil words."

Old Colonel Thomas put her false teeth on the table. "Who's this?" she said. "Who are you talking about?"

"It's the new girl, Mother," said Brigadier Thomas. "The one from show business. Her name is Jonna J."

"What kind of name is that? Is that some new movie star?"

Major Ellen raised her hand for quiet. "What's the real issue here?" she asked. "Is it because she doesn't work or because she creates problems?"

"It's both and more," said Brigadier Thomas. "She raises dust sweeping a floor."

"She claims she can't slice and dice carrots," said Captain Tucker. "And she's proved it in the kitchen. She's no use to us."

"I found fingerprints on my knife at supper," said Lieutenant Margit. "I'm sure they were hers. She set the table."

"Max complains that the bathroom sink drains are all clogged," said Captain McTavish. "No wonder. They're all running around singing about washing men out of their hair."

Jonna's name flew across the table like a ping-pong ball and everyone wanted to take a shot. Major Ellen listened carefully.

"She must have some good points," she said. "Let's think on the positive."

"Her voice is beautiful," said Captain Trudy. "I wish she was in the choir."

"And she does seem to be a good organizer," said Lieutenant Margit, "but we don't need any more bosses around here." A big smile told them she was only kidding.

"She doesn't seem to mind helping around my office," Mom said.

"That's because you have a mirror where she can look at herself," Brigadier Thomas said.

It was time for my streetcar, but I hated leaving before they decided what to do.

Major Ellen turned to Colonel Thomas. "Esther," she said. "Surely you've faced these kinds of problems before. What do you recommend?"

The old lady put her teeth back in. "Put her in the laundry for a while," she said. "That place could stand some brightening up."

~10~

DAILY MAIL CALL AT BOOTH MEMORIAL never drew a crowd. All the residents had taken great care to hide where they were living, therefore, they weren't expecting any. They took the same care to hide where they came from because a return address could say a lot. Only two residents could count on daily mail.

Corrine C.'s boyfriend was lonely, and he poured out his dislike of the Army and its exhausting routine. His complaints had to do with marching miles with a heavy field pack. She shared his gripes with the others while knitting a pair of socks, not knowing he wouldn't be allowed to wear them because they weren't khaki.

Jonna J. didn't share her letters so freely. Occasionally she would mention *South Pacific*'s audience response in a city but not much else. She read the letters quickly and put them in the pocket of the shapeless smock she now wore. Duty in the laundry had taken its toll. Her nearly perfect hair now drooped from daily exposure to heat and humidity. Her songs did manage to brighten the laundry room, but only when Captain McTavish was gone. Like the others, she had begun to count the days.

One day a letter came for Mom with a return address I didn't recognize. She read it to me after supper. It was from a friend she'd met years ago when he was in the hospital and she was the nurse on duty. He'd searched for her through the Nurse's Registry and uncovered our move to St. Paul. He would be attending a convention in Minneapolis at the end of November and would like to visit us while he was here. Only two weeks away. Mom remembered him as a nice guy with a wife and young son. She planned to answer his letter that night.

At 9:00 p.m., there was a knock on our apartment door. A resident said Betty H.'s baby was in a breech position. Lieutenant Corliss said a doctor from University Hospital was on his way, and she wanted Mom there. She put on her uniform and said not to wait up. I had heard enough about breech deliveries to know it could take all night. It must be serious though. They rarely called a doctor.

I woke up to the smell of coffee and the low murmur of voices coming from the kitchen. I listened through the bathroom door and could hear my mother's voice and that of a man. Just then, the door opened, and the kitchen light spilled in.

"I was just coming to wake you," Mom said. "You have school today."

I rubbed my eyes from the sudden bright light and saw a man sitting at the table.

"Rene, I want you to meet Dr. Hickman," she said. "He delivered a beautiful baby boy this morning, and we're celebrating."

Dr. Hickman shook my hand with a firm grip. He was a tall man with dark, wavy hair and a thin moustache. I guessed him to be about forty. I thought, *one hour ago, the hand I'm shaking must've been covered in blood.*

"Your mother was just telling me she's worried about you and the Minnesota winter," he said. "You can't avoid it so always wear your hat and gloves. Also, don't put your tongue on anything metal." It seemed to be unusual advice, but he must have had to unfreeze kids' tongues all the time.

He spoke in a rather breezy manner. Not very serious for a doctor, I thought.

"The next time you have a breech, I'll bring along an intern," he said to Mom. "They don't see a lot of those."

His comment defined the role of Booth Memorial in the medical teaching world. It acted as a lab for the university for anything beyond normal births and was regarded as an even trade. Booth Memorial got professional service free of charge, and interns got practical experience.

"I have to go, Mrs. Dardenne," he said, getting up. "Nice meeting you and thanks for your help on the breech and for the coffee. Call me anytime."

Mom, all smiles, thanked him several times and said the coffee pot was always on. On his way out, he offered me more advice.

"Rene, don't ever walk on ice with your hands in your pockets," he said. "And, if you must fall, always fall forward."

Mom and I watched from the kitchen window as he drove away in a 1947 Oldsmobile. *Not a bad car for a doctor*, I thought.

"Rene," she said. "Have you ever thought about becoming a doctor?"

I looked down at her shoes speckled with the blood of Betty H. and then I lied. "No, Mom," I said. "I really haven't."

~11~

EVENINGS WERE A QUIET TIME at the nurses' home. After supper, Mom and I would get together in the kitchen. She always had ironing, and I always had homework. Shows on the radio made the time pass. We had a television station in town, but no way could we afford a TV set. The cheapest one cost $125 at Dayton's Department Store. We had to be satisfied with taking a streetcar downtown and watching TV through the store window. That was out of the question tonight. Temperatures were below freezing, and native Minnesotans swore the first substantial snow was just around the corner.

It didn't matter because it was a good radio night. George Burns & Gracie Allen led off followed by *Fibber McGee and Molly* and then *The Shadow*. Bob Hope, sponsored by Pepsodent toothpaste, was next and last was a brand new program, *Dragnet*. Who needed television? The pictures in my head were better, and they were in color.

Mom usually liked to talk back to the radio, but she was quiet the whole evening. She kept sniffing, and I asked if something was wrong. When she wiped her eyes I knew I was in for a story.

"I was in the office today when a girl and her parents came in," she said. "I don't like to eavesdrop, but sometimes you just can't help it."

I was tempted to tell her it helped to have a copy of *War Cry* handy. Mom said the girl was just starting her senior year of college when she discovered her pregnancy. Before she signed the papers, the girl insisted her boyfriend must not find her, but she didn't say why. When asked to pick her Booth name, without a pause she chose Eudora W.

"I was thinking how this poor girl has to go into hiding," Mom said, "And she's going to protect the guy who did it. It just doesn't seem fair."

After unpacking, the girl reported to Mom's office for the admission exam.

"She's about three months gone and completely healthy," Mom said. "She should deliver at the end of May."

"Did she tell you any more?" I asked.

"I didn't want to pry," Mom said. "Even though she insisted on secrecy, I sensed she wanted to talk. I asked if Eudora was an old family name. It was as if I had pulled a plug."

She was careful not to give the name of the college, but her major was literature. She'd been reading a new author, Eudora Welty, whose stories had inspired her to become a writer as well. "It's something she wants to work on while she's here," Mom said.

"But what about her boyfriend," I asked. Why won't he marry her?"

"He doesn't know she's pregnant," Mom said. "She didn't say why."

Instead, she told Mom about him. During the war, he had been a medic. If he got out alive, he swore he would become a doctor. The G.I. Bill paid for most of his undergrad years, but it couldn't cover the expense of med school. A job in the cafeteria gave him free food and time to study between meals.

"We met when I was a freshman," Eudora said. "He was pre-med and I fell for him right away. We've been going steady ever since. We tried to wait but just couldn't."

"But why haven't you told him?" Mom asked. "Surely he would understand."

"If he knew I was pregnant he'd drop out," she said. "He couldn't possibly support us and go to school. He's come too far to quit now. I decided if someone had to drop out, it would be me."

"What did you tell him?" Mom asked.

"I wrote a letter telling him that I wanted a career too," she said. "I was going away for a year to try it on my own. If I didn't do it now I would always wonder so I asked him not to try and find me."

"Did he believe you?"

"I don't know, but what else could I do?" she said. "I considered abortion but didn't want someone fishing around inside me with a coat hook. I do want children. Just not now."

"What are you going to do when the baby's born?" Mom asked.

"I don't know yet," she said, her eyes filling with tears. "I can't stand the idea of giving our baby away, but what are my choices? I love Jack Howard so much that I just had to do it this way. I don't want his future ruined too."

Mom's tears dripped onto the ironing and sizzled when the iron passed over them. The story made me uncomfortable. Until now, the stories I'd heard were only about the girls, never the guys. This one had complications like love, careers, and a baby. I felt Mom told me more than she should have about Eudora W. Why, I don't know.

"Why couldn't they wait?" I asked. "What's so hard about that?"

Mom had probably been dreading this moment, when my questions about life couldn't be deflected with simple answers. I was at the age where mothers begin checking underwear to see if their sons have been experimenting. The age when they tell the father it's time to have that talk. That option wasn't open, nor did Mom seem to want that responsibility. Since the divorce, she heaped all her affection on me, and I fed it back. It was an almost perfect world.

Now that it was time for me to become more adult, I think it was Mom who wasn't ready. Instead, she chose the real-life drama passing in front of us as a substitute, hoping I would somehow get it. I hadn't. Unfortunately, the story highlighted the pain and punishment of having sex. Mom never mentioned any pleasure or benefits. It probably wasn't her intention to focus on the penalties of sins of the flesh, but Father McGowan couldn't have done it any better.

~12~

THE FIRST REAL SNOWFALL OF THE SEASON came in mid-November, the most snow I'd seen in four years. It was pretty, but snowy weather meant something else to the staff. Booth Memorial was at capacity with fifty-seven residents waiting for their turn on the table with the funny stirrups. Life inside would become more restrictive, the rules more objectionable, the girls more irritable. They couldn't walk to the drugstore for cherry cokes and ice cream cones when they wanted, and ice on the sidewalks would decide if they saw a movie. Winter also meant finding enough bulky coats to cover their swelling stomachs, which made it harder to get a group together. Even in summer, no one would walk alone, but it wasn't just for safety. If there were several girls, it was easier to suffer the stares of the housewives and crude remarks from teenage boys. Once outside their protected world, the herd mentality still worked best.

Back before winter arrived, boys in the neighborhood played football on a vacant lot next to Eddie Henderson's house, and he asked me to join them. As the new guy, I had to play center, which meant I spent a lot of time with my nose buried in the grass. There were suspicions I had a connection with Booth Memorial, but the guys never mentioned it until the day I had to run for the streetcar. My secret was exposed to the world by simple tracks in the newly dusted snow that left no doubt from where I had come. No one on the streetcar spoke to me that morning except Eddie, but news traveled fast. By the time I got to Murray High, it seemed everyone knew. I expected razzing, especially from the guys in homeroom, but it wasn't that bad. Somebody yelled out about "gettin a piece of ass," and "havin some nookie." Boys my age talked a lot about sex but were short on experience. Suddenly there was someone in their midst who had gone beyond the secret door—they thought. Because I was such an unlikely choice, they didn't know what to say.

The girls were another matter. Most had had that talk with their mothers when they started menstruating. Their actual experience was limited to measuring cramps, comparing flow and exchanging tips on how to hide Kotex odor. They acted as if I knew what they knew, or maybe even more. That I came off as naïve only confused them. One well-developed girl I had my eye on threw me a sly smile and then winked. It took me a while to realize she had aimed it at the guy next to me.

I suffered through the day until the last class—gym. During basketball, Johnny Boy and his buddies kept peppering me. Comments like, "I hear you're gettin' some," and "Sounds like you're in pussy heaven."

It got worse in the locker room. Since I'd made no progress on pubic hair, I always made it a point to dress facing the corner. Johnny B, already with a dark shadow on his face, sported a fine crop. He enjoyed showing it off and massaged himself until he raised a good-sized boner. Then he would challenge anyone to match it. There were no takers.

After my experience with the cowboy clothes, I learned to stay away from Johnny Bittolini. His story was that his family left Italy to escape Mussolini, but the rumor was his father was sent here to expand the Mafia out of New York. I'd heard about the Mafia on *The FBI in Peace and War* on the radio. They were into bootlegging, gambling, prostitution, and something called dope. When Italy entered the war, the police, and even their neighbors, gave the Bittolinis a rough time. They didn't even fit in with other Catholics. Johnny and his older brothers were in a lot of fights, some of which they started. Johnny learned early on how to bully and intimidate.

I hurriedly tried to put on my underwear, but he wheeled me around.

"Come on, Tex. Let's see your pecker," he said and pulled my shorts down.

"Well, looky there," he said laughing. "He ain't got nothing. Bald as a cue ball."

I pulled my shorts up, but it was too late. Johnny Boy's buddies took his cue and began to laugh.

"No wonder they let you in that place," he said. "That's just a toy. Get me in there. I'll show them girls what a real dong looks like."

Then he got a grin on his face I didn't take as friendly. A couple of guys from my neighborhood saw I had a problem and drifted over just in case.

"I'm going to help you out, buddy," Johnny Boy said grabbing my arm. "Let's rub some liniment on that crotch of yours. You'll raise a patch in no time." He turned to his buddies. "Hey, somebody open that first-aid box. We're gonna have some fun."

Eddie Henderson stepped forward.

"Okay, Johnny," he said. Fun's over. Let him go."

I prayed for the bell, and it rang, but the damage was done. The worst day of my life was almost over. Earlier that day, I had an undeserved reputation of being sexually savvy. The coy attention of girls and begrudging envy of boys was heady stuff. The facedown in the locker room stripped that away and exposed a closer truth. Sex was a mystery I had yet to solve. My limited experience, coupled with Father McGowan's sermons, proved it could be dirty and dangerous. Was there a reason for sex other than to have babies? If so, I didn't know it. It gave me something else to consider during the long streetcar ride home.

Our football game that day ended when a group of Booth girls walked by.

"Hi, Rene," they said in chorus, waved and went on. The guys didn't say anything, but out of the corner of my eye I saw them snickering. Eddie, who stood up for me in the locker room, whispered, "You sure you're not gettin' any of that?"

~13~

MOM RECEIVED ANOTHER LETTER from her friend, the one coming to a convention in Minneapolis. He'd be here over Thanksgiving, and Major Ellen invited him for dinner. His name was Carlton Allison, and he owned a lumberyard in a small Indiana town not far from our Illinois hometown.

Thanksgiving morning was bright and sunny, but, with no leaves on the trees, it had that cold look of a winter day. A brand new 1950 Buick Roadmaster, the one with four portholes in the fender, pulled into the hospital driveway. It had to be Mom's friend because it had Indiana plates. Mom was taking curlers out of her hair, so asked me to bring him to the house.

I tore out the side door and almost tripped over a big French poodle with his leg lifted on our stairs. The startled dog jumped back and barked.

"He won't bite, son," a man's voice said, "but you'd better be careful. You could get hurt running out like that." It was Father McGowan out for a morning walk.

If your dog wouldn't piss on my porch it wouldn't be a problem, I thought, relieved that I hadn't said the words out loud. Instead, I thanked him for his concern and wished him a Happy Thanksgiving.

"Is this where you live?" he said, pointing to the nurses' home.

"Yes, Father, it is," I said.

"Doesn't it belong to them?" he said, pointing toward the hospital.

"Yes, Father, it does," I said, hoping he wouldn't make me kneel down and do confession on the spot.

"There's a boy at Booth Memorial, I've heard. Are you that boy?"

"I guess so, Father,"

He had a quizzical look, like something didn't quite figure.

"If I was you, I'd be careful, son," he said. "See you on Sunday, and God bless you."

There it was again, that "God bless you" thing. It meant something was going to happen, especially when it came from a priest.

As I ran across the street, I wondered if coming out of a Salvation Army house was a sin. What about his peeing dog? Would I have to confess I was about to use a nasty word? Did he mean it about seeing me on Sunday or did he say that to everyone, kind of like drumming up business? Saturday was only two days away, and I was going to have to decide what I had to confess.

Almost out of breath, I reached the hospital just as Mr. Allison was going in the side door. I introduced myself and checked out his car.

"Just got it," he said. "I'm breaking it in on this trip. So far it's great."

It was light blue and painted with the new metallic paint. On the trunk, in chrome script, was the word "DynaFlow" which meant he didn't have to shift it.

"The turn signals are on the inside," he said. "No more sticking my hand out the window."

I could even smell new rubber from the whitewall tires.

"You'll have to drive it sometime," he said.

His casual comment excited me. Just the thought of sitting behind the wheel of a new car was a thrill but it also implied I looked old enough to drive. I had grown an inch and my voice was changing but nobody had noticed. This guy spotted it right away.

He sat down on one of the hard couches in the living room and a puff of dust came up. I remembered Lieutenant Corliss's remark about the room we never used. Apparently, we never dusted it either. Mr. Allison and I talked about the weather and the World Series. He was a Cubs fan, but, of course, they weren't in it. This gave me a chance to size him up. He was about Mom's age, but his hair was completely gray and combed straight back, just like in the thirties movies. He looked successful, meaning he wasn't skinny or even trim, just what you might expect from someone who owned his own business.

I smelled Mom before she came into the room. Morning Glory was her favorite cologne for special occasions, and this must be one because she was wearing her best dress. He stood up so fast it startled me.

"Hello, Jo. It's been a long time," he said. "You look great."

His words went through me like lightning. It was the first time I viewed my mother through the eyes of another male. I couldn't disagree. She did look great. Mom had a pretty face and a great shape topped off by an ample bosom. "Buxom" was the word she used to describe herself. If that meant conspicuous breasts, she was on the money. My Catholic "pain and punishment" background kicked in, and I suddenly felt guilty because I looked at my mother in an impure way. How could I ever confess a thing like that? I felt something else strange too—a twinge of jealousy.

"I just looked at Mr. Allison's new Buick," I said, redirecting my mind. "Wait'll you see it."

"Call me Carl. That's what I go by," he said. "Why don't we go for a ride?'

We had a wonderful morning, driving grandly down University Avenue to downtown St. Paul. We went past lakes and through city parks whose names I had only heard on the radio. The University of Minnesota campus was larger and prettier than I ever expected. We drove through the deserted State Fairgrounds all the way to my high school. It didn't look as important without students around. We came back on Como Avenue, the way I went to school every day. Instead of the musty odor of an old streetcar, I inhaled the smell of a brand new Buick all the way. I made believe we were an ordinary family out for a drive, maybe to Grandma's house for dinner. It wasn't true, but it was fun to pretend. I wished somebody I knew saw me now.

Major Ellen arranged an informal get together in the Great Room, and Mom introduced Carl all around. He smiled a lot, but I think all the names and titles confused him. Captain Tucker's little bell called us to the dining room. She, and the kitchen staff, had gone all out. They prepared mashed potatoes, sweet potatoes, rutabagas, cut corn, cooked carrots, stuffing, cranberry sauce, and green beans swimming in bacon-flavored water. Major Ellen's prayer gave special thanks to the donor of the biggest turkey I had ever seen.

My image of Thanksgiving dinner came from Norman Rockwell illustrations on the cover of *The Saturday Evening Post*. Grandpa stood at the head of the table with a large fork and carving knife. The family looked toward him in anticipation and waited for that first slice of turkey to come their way. Reality was a bit different. The head of our family was a matronly major in the Salvation Army. She faced a group of officers and others who waited for that slice. I was curious how this was going to play out because she wasn't holding a knife or fork.

Major Ellen looked toward her guest. "Mr. Allison," she said. "Would you please do us the honor of carving our turkey?"

I watched him closely. What if he doesn't know how? I sure didn't. How could he back out of it? Instead, he didn't flinch an inch.

"Why, of course, Major," he said. "I'm pleased to be asked."

He took that knife and fork and proceeded to carve the life out of that bird. I mean there wasn't anything left but a pile of bones and some scraps. I asked for a drumstick, and he dished it right up. Dessert was pumpkin pie with real whipped cream or mincemeat pie with hard sauce topping. I had both. It was the best Thanksgiving meal I'd ever had.

The officers liked to sit around after dinner and talk over their coffee. I always got restless about this time. Eating was what I came to the table for, not to talk. To be well mannered, I sat and sort of listened. Major Ellen, making polite conversation with Carl, asked if he had a family.

"I used to," he said. Suddenly I was alert. "After the war, my wife wanted to go back to where she was raised. She moved to Florida with our son while I stayed on with my business in Indiana."

I checked Mom's reaction to this news. She sat still as a stone, her face in a frozen smile.

"We divorced a few years ago, but we're still friends," he said. "I have my son during the summer months."

A light bulb went off in my head. That's why he's here. It wasn't a convention he was interested in. It was my mother. Damn that "God bless you."

"DID YOU KNOW HE WAS DIVORCED?" I asked Mom the morning after Thanksgiving. She and I sat in the kitchen.

"Well, yes and no," she said. She was good at giving that kind of answer, and it always left me frustrated. I didn't know much more than before.

"I answered his first letter saying we'd be happy to see him," she said. "In closing, I wished his wife and son well. His return letter told me about the divorce. He said he hoped it didn't matter."

"Why didn't you tell me?" I asked. I'd tossed and turned about this all night and had already formed an opinion.

"I didn't think I needed to, Rene," Mom said. "He's an old friend, and I looked forward to seeing someone I knew since we have no friends here."

"Is he Catholic?" I asked, thinking of what Father McGowan might say.

"We never talked about that, but I don't think so," Mom said. "Didn't you like him though? Isn't he a gentleman?"

I had to admit he made a positive impression on me, especially with that new Buick. I needed some time to process this new information. My knee-jerk reaction was he could be competition for my mother's attention, a problem I never had before. I tried to think positive, but my under-riding emotion was, she's mine.

"It's almost time for the mail," Mom said. "I'm expecting a letter from Aunt Mary telling me what to get her for Christmas. Go see if it came, and then we can take off."

Mom had the day planned. We'd take the streetcar downtown to see the Christmas windows and then shop for presents because stores had some good sales today. We might even watch a little TV in the store window. To me, it seemed she was trying to take my mind off this new situation.

I hiked to the hospital with my shoes disappearing under the fluff of new snow. Remembering Dr. Hickman's advice, I walked with hands outside my pockets and would fall forward if I had a choice. I wondered what he told the Booth residents. They certainly shouldn't fall forward should they?

I almost collided with Major Ellen as she rushed out of her office. "They're coming," she said, waving a letter. "We have to get ready."

This atypical display of emotion startled Lieutenant Margit and Captain Trudy.

"Who's coming?" they said.

"The Northern Region's Review Board!" Major Ellen said. "They're coming to review our hospital. They'll be here just before Christmas, of all times."

Several residents stood around the desk after mail call. Corrine C. had just read her army boyfriend's letter and was looking for someone to share his news.

"What's going on?" she asked.

"Looks like we're going to be inspected," Lieutenant Margit said. "You girls better get ready for a big cleaning party. We've got to be spic-and-span."

71

"And they like to be entertained too," said Captain Trudy. "We're going to have to come up with something special for Christmas Eve. It's almost too late."

Jonna J. stood off to the side reading her mail. "Could you use an extra hand?" she asked.

"Why, yes," Captain Trudy said, obviously surprised. "We could certainly use someone with your experience."

Since her arrival, Jonna hadn't taken part in any activities. She'd served her time in the laundry room without complaint but nothing more. Her pregnancy was far enough along for lighter duty, but Captain Mc-Tavish seemed determined to squeeze the last bit of stubbornness out of Jonna J.

"I might consider it," she said, "but there'll have to be some changes."

"Like what?" Captain Trudy said, her guard coming up.

"This sounds important," Jonna said, "and since there's a short deadline, I might have to work on it full time."

"You want out of the laundry, don't you?" Captain Trudy said.

"Well, I can't do that and do a good job for you," Jonna said in a voice filled with southern sweetness not recently heard. "I'm talking about a really good job."

Captain Trudy must've had a vision of a celestial choir singing carols in the Great Room while a narrator recited the Christmas story to an enraptured audience. It had been her dream since becoming activities director.

"I can't make that decision," she said, in a dispassionate voice that hid her excitement. "I'll bring it up to Major Ellen and Captain Mc-Tavish. They might not be in favor."

Through her open door, Major Ellen heard the give and take. She got up, cleared her throat and tapped on the desk. When she caught Captain Trudy's attention, she signaled a big okay.

"I'll let you know, Jonna," Captain Trudy said. "Suddenly I have a good feeling about it."

I'd been watching the whole time and figured out this was how things worked around here. Problem girls didn't get yelled at or receive punishment. They were just given assignments that gave them time to think things over. It looked like Jonna had gotten the message.

Major Ellen had a quick meeting with Captain Berthe Karlsson, Lieutenant Margit, and Captain Trudy. "This is no ordinary inspection," she said. "They're bringing somebody in from national headquarters. I don't know what, but something's up. We've got to look sharp."

"When can I have Jonna so we can start on the music?" Captain Trudy asked.

"Right now, but be sure you keep an eye on her, Trudy," Major Ellen said. "She's a clever girl. I want "O Little Town of Bethlehem," not "Bali Ha'i" with snow."

"Especially watch the lyrics," said Captain Karlsson. "I heard a song about someone named Bloody Mary coming from the laundry. That could be misunderstood. We don't want trouble with New York."

"And the program should be a little . . ." Major Ellen paused.

"Slick?" Captain Trudy said.

"Yes, that's the word. Some New Yorkers think we live in igloos up here. Make it slick," she paused again, "but not too slick."

"I'll talk it over with Jonna. She'll know what you want."

The Christmas season at Booth Memorial officially began that day. Captain Trudy started a search for sheet music while Jonna began recruiting a choir. Before she started her new job, Jonna made one last request—to have her hair done.

~14~

W HAT'S GOING ON?" BRIGADIER RUTH THOMAS asked. "We've been expecting December depression, but I haven't seen it yet."

Everyone around the table agreed. December was usually a difficult month at Booth Memorial. For most residents, it was their first Christmas away from home. No mom baking cookies in the kitchen; no dad chopping wood for the fireplace; no presents piling up under the tree. Some hoped to go home for the holidays, but it would depend on the weather and if they could travel. Others weren't welcome at home and pretended it didn't matter. The staff knew that December depression, if not on time, was inevitable.

"It's our Christmas program," Captain Trudy said. "Ever since Jonna's been out of the laundry there's music in the hallways."

"Not Broadway show tunes, I trust," Major Ellen said.

"Oh, no, these are Christmas carols, and they're singing in parts. Oh, Ellen, it's wonderful."

The officers cautioned Mom that this month brought out the most conflict among residents. Feelings were easily hurt and depression followed even minor disagreements. If she spotted those telltale signs, she should call an officer. They knew how to handle the problems.

"Is Jonna keeping up her end of the agreement?" Captain Berthe Karlsson asked cattily. "I still don't trust her to be for anyone but herself."

"She's doing even more," Captain Trudy said. "She rehearses the choir every day and is working with Eudora to write a narration to read between the carols."

"I see she's charmed Max into building something," Captain Mc-Tavish said. "Every day he's over in the corner pounding and sawing away. He says he's making a manger. The poor man is Jewish and doesn't even know what a manger is."

I could just hear Jonna's honey-dripping voice sweet-talking Max into building a set for the program. She probably batted her eyes and tugged playfully on his beard until he gave in. My own experience was a good example of what a persuader she could be.

"I hear you might be in it, Rene," Lieutenant Margit said. "What part would you play?"

"She wants me to be Joseph," I said. "I told her I'm too young, but she says the real Mary was only fifteen when she had baby Jesus. I'm still thinking it over."

"What are you all talking about?" old Colonel Thomas asked. "I heard something about baby Jesus."

"It's for Christmas, Mother," Brigadier Thomas said. "They are planning a musical program for Christmas Eve."

"Well, whatever they do," she said, "I hope it's good and loud."

As I left the building, Dr. Hickman's Oldsmobile was parked on the snowy driveway. That usually meant a girl was having trouble with delivery, but not always. In the last few weeks, he'd made several non-emergency visits, usually accompanied by an intern. Mom said he was trying to give them wider experiences, but these visits usually ended up with him and Mom having coffee in the Great Room.

It gave me a chance to check something unusual about many Minnesota cars. The windows in the driver and passenger doors had an extra pane of glass glued on the inside and I didn't know why. Dr. Hickman came out the side door and I asked him.

"That's to keep frost from forming on the windows," he said. "The windshield has a defroster but the side windows don't. You can't keep scraping frost off while you're driving, so the double thickness prevents it." It was a good solution, but, for the first time, it made me wonder just how cold it got here in the winter.

On the way to my room, I looked across Como Avenue and saw heads moving up and down on the vacant lot. Too much snow on the ground for football so I walked over to check it out. The bobbing heads were from an intense game of hockey. The neighborhood kids were on ice skates, hockey sticks in hand, chasing a puck across a frozen surface.

"Where did this come from?" I asked, pointing to the ice.

"Fire department," they yelled as they skated by.

At the first freeze, the Fire Department came around and squirted water on school playgrounds and vacant lots. What a great idea, I thought. Football was over, and the lot would stay frozen until baseball season. This was how Minnesota kids passed time in winter. I watched my buddies hustle after the puck. They used their bodies to check and block, skated backward as fast as forward, turned on a dime to go the other direction. It looked a lot more exciting than baseball or even football. I could hardly wait to get in the game. Someone yelled, "Put on your skates." Only then did I realize I was probably the only kid in Minnesota who didn't know how to skate on ice.

THERE WAS A NOTE ON MY DRESSER. "Rene, Max needs you. Love, Mom."

It wasn't hard to guess Max's need as I tracked a trail of pine needles up the stairs into the hospital's side door. Every year Olaf Jorgenssen's grocery store, at the corner of Snelling and Como, donated a Christmas tree to Booth Memorial. When Major Ellen got the call, she made a big to do and acted like it was the first time, but she had primed the pump so to speak. She knew Captain Tucker had already been to Olaf's to buy Scandinavian specialties for Christmas dinner. The free tree offer followed in a few days so today's call was right on schedule.

As I followed pine needles down the hallway, I heard noises in the Arts and Crafts room. Usually it was just a couple of residents knitting or making an ugly smock. Now it looked like a small sweatshop. Girls held up old sheets, draped them on live models, pinned folds, took tucks and spoke in that funny way of a mouth full of pins. Nimble fingers fed yards of material into the sewing machines and churned out choir robes for the Christmas Eve program.

Two residents sat in the corner, cutting and forming pieces of white construction paper into cone circles. I must have looked confused because a girl mouthed, "Halos" and arched her eyes as if saying, "I hope God can take a joke cause we're no angels." In the middle of it was Jonna J., who pointed to where she wanted darts to create an empire waist. She pronounced it "om peer" but they seemed to know what she wanted.

"Rene, can you come in for a fitting tomorrow?" she asked. "Your robe should be ready then."

I nodded, but still wished I had said no when Jonna sweet-talked me into playing Joseph. At least none of the guys would see me. I had to explain a lot that day we played football and the Booth girls' cheered me on. Mom needed a job I told the guys. She hadn't given much thought to the living arrangements and certainly didn't expect we'd take our meals at the hospital with women who were like nuns. I downplayed the girls as much as possible and even said they weren't all that attractive when their stomachs got big. A couple of the guys said they felt sorry for me and that was just the way I wanted it. If they saw me being fitted for a robe, the jig would be up.

The track of pine needles ended in the Great Room where Max was struggling to put a base on the tree. We tipped it up in place alongside the stained glass window, just where Captain Trudy pointed. It was a big Minnesota Balsam fir with a beautiful shape, just like the trees in the picture books. She sent us down to the suitcase room for the boxes of lights and ornaments.

"Jonna wants that too," Max said, pointing to her huge travel trunk.

"Where does it go?" I asked.

"In the big room behind that thing she calls a manger," he said, pronouncing it like "banger." Then he said a few words in Lithuanian. I remembered my grandfather using those words whenever he bumped his head.

After supper, the residents gathered for what Captain Trudy called an old-fashioned tree trimming party. My chore was to take the lights out of the box and hand them to the girls. To string the lights was a job for girls six months pregnant or less. After that, they were too big to grab the ladder, let alone get on it. To stretch the evening, Captain Trudy would bring an ornament out of the box, give a little of its history, and then let someone hang it.

"This ornament was on our Christmas tree when this building was dedicated in 1913," she said. "We always hang it first." She handed it to Mae W., who looked like she was about to pop.

"We honor the resident who has been waiting longest," she said, "and Mae looks like she could go anytime now."

Mae waddled to the tree and hung the ornament right smack in the center. Everyone went "aaah" and broke into applause. Captain Trudy tried the history approach on the next ornament but the girls were already bored. Anything made before nineteen forty one was pre-war and of no interest. They reached into the ornaments box and bickered about who would hang them where. This must be what a big family was like, I thought. To calm things down, Corrine C. played Christmas carols on the piano. The girls, by now well rehearsed, sang along in two-part harmony. Captain Trudy almost cried.

The officers stayed at the back of the room but watched everything closely. At supper, Major Ellen reminded them that decorating the tree could be the most emotional event of the year for the residents.

"Be on guard for any girl who starts sniffling," she said. "If she runs out of the room, go after her and just listen to her story."

Today, June A.'s parents called to say they were not bringing her home for Christmas. She accepted it without emotion, but everyone knew she hurt inside. When Corrine played "O' Little Town of Bethlehem," June took several deep breaths and headed for the door. Lieutenant Margit was right behind her.

Unlike the other girls, Corrine had a reason to look forward to Christmas. In his last letter, her Army boyfriend wrote that if he fired Expert on the rifle range, he'd get a medal and a chance for Christmas leave. He'd be shooting for both of them.

With the last ornament in place, it was time to hang the icicles. These were survivors of many Christmases past because they were made of pewter, not flimsy aluminum. No one knew how many trees they'd graced, but they were wrinkled enough to be at least pre-war. When this tree came down, they'd be carefully folded over pieces of cardboard and used again next year. The girls disagreed whether they should hang the icicles neatly on the tree or fling them with abandon, like nature gone crazy. They chose to do both.

When Corrine played "O Tannenbaum," I plugged in the lights. Everyone oohed and aahed and waited for the final decoration. Captain Trudy gave me the honor, probably because I was the only one who could climb the ladder to the top safely. I slipped the star over a white bulb, and it gave off a soft glow. From that perch, I had a view of the lights twinkling, the ornaments glowing and the girls sitting around the tree looking like presents. I looked for the officers who sat in the back, but they had gone to comfort the girls who couldn't take it. It was a reminder that not everyone had a good time that night.

Everybody in the room joined in to sing "Silent Night, Holy Night." When someone sang "round, non-virgins," they all laughed, and the tree trimming party was over for another year. As I returned the boxes to the basement, I looked back on that strange evening. The only child of a divorced Catholic mother, surrounded by pregnant girls and Protestant spinsters, who all sang carols to the same God on Christmas Eve. What was so wrong with that?

"There are three of them. No, wait, there's a man too," Lieutenant Margit said, looking out the window. "Looks like he's a colonel."

"Well, go meet them, Margit," Major Ellen said. "I'll get the staff together, and we'll have coffee in the dining room."

It was the Northern Region inspection team from Chicago. They came in, stamped the snow off their feet and left their galoshes at the side door. Melting snow dripped from their coats as Lieutenant Margit led them down the hall. At the Arts and Crafts room, they did a double take. Sewing machines were going full tilt, and the halo makers were still at it. Jonna J. made the final adjustments on my Joseph's costume as I stood on a table in the middle of the room.

"Damn it, Rene. Hold still for one minute," Jonna said. "I'm almost done."

I put a finger to my lips to shush her. Jonna could swear like a sailor when upset, but now was not a good time. The inspection team looked at me and then back at Lieutenant Margit. They seemed confused. I wasn't a girl and I wasn't pregnant so why was I here?

"Major Ellen has coffee waiting," Lieutenant Margit said. "She can explain everything." As they walked away, she shot a backward look that clearly said, "Why the hell is Rene standing on the table in a robe?"

Following the fitting, I went to the Great Room to help Max assemble elements for the manger. June A. stood by with paint and brush. We'd get a piece in place and she was on it doing something artistic. Jonna J. breezed through, made a small suggestion and dashed off to her choir rehearsal in the library.

The dining room door opened and Major Ellen brought the inspection committee through. "This is our Great Room," she said, surprised at the construction mess. "Looks like we're preparing a little Christmas program."

Max stopped working and took off his hat, just like in the old country.

"This is our superintendent, Max," she said, "and this is Rene, who is helping him."

"We just saw Rene helping someone else," the Colonel said. "He was wearing a sheet then."

While they continued the tour, Max and I went to the basement to wrestle Jonna J.'s trunk up the narrow stairway. He used several of his Lithuanian words as we hoisted it a step at a time. We were almost at the top when Major Ellen and the inspection team started down.

"This must be a prop of some sort," she said as they squeezed by. "I'm told it's going to be a wonderful program." Major Ellen had a fixed smile, but her eyes clearly said I hope you know what you're doing.

"Max, when you're available, please show the team around the laundry," she said. "They have some equipment questions."

As I waited for Max, I wondered what was in Jonna's trunk that could be worth all this effort. I examined the marked out labels, looking for a name or home address but she had done a good job covering her past. I tried the lid to see if it was locked. It was.

My imagination took command. I visualized Jonna as she approached the trunk, reached inside her blouse and removed the key from her brassiere. She winked as she handed it to me. It was warm to the touch, almost hot. My hand quivered slightly. Just as I was about to insert it, the intercom blared, "Mail call. Mail's at the front desk." My little dream ended suddenly.

The usual group of girls was standing around the desk. Corrine C. was already reading her letter, and Jonna's was waiting on the counter.

"Here's something for your mother," Lieutenant Margit said to me. "It's from Indiana." Her innocent remark reminded me why hardly any mail arrived at Booth Memorial with a return address. She handed me the letter. It was from Carl Allison.

81

CHRISTMAS EVE DAY HAD A STORYBOOK start with fresh snow sticking on the trees. The skies were dull and grey, heavy with overcast. In Arizona, it was what we missed most at Christmas time. There, every day was sunny and clear—every day. Now, a world away, Mom and I walked to the hospital for breakfast. She liked to kick the snow with her boots, making it fly up to her knees. My fun was to run and slide along the icy parts of the driveway trying not to land on my butt. On the way, she told me about her letter from Carl.

"He would like to come here next week," she said. "He wants to know if I have plans for New Year's Eve." This was something I didn't expect. New Year's Eve was sort of special for us. We would listen to the celebration in Times Square on the radio and then wait for midnight in Chicago. By the time the New Year reached the Mountain Time zone, we had gone to bed.

"Do you have plans?" I asked.

"No," she said. "Not for years. Do you mind if he comes up?"

I couldn't think of any good reason why not, and it would be a chance to ride in his Buick again. After all, it was still almost new.

"No," I said, lying only slightly.

At breakfast, I met Colonel Paul Payton from headquarters in New York. With the rest of the team going over the books and doing inventory, we were the only ones in the dining room. He said he was here to check out the building and make sure it was still up to the job.

"This place is thirty-six years old," he said. "It's been at capacity for years, and I have to decide whether to add on or build a new facility somewhere else. Major Ellen has been after us for years for more space."

He went on to explain things like cost of land in the suburbs versus property values in town. I appreciated being spoken to like an adult, but it was really boring. To be polite I nodded my head and even agreed once or twice. I was more curious about him since he was the first man I'd met wearing a Salvation Army uniform. He appeared to be in his fifties with dark-brown hair turning gray. His wire-rim glasses made him look like he could be a teacher.

"Are you like a priest?" I asked. He looked startled, and then chuckled.

"Well, not really," he said, "but I have dedicated my life to Christ, similar to a priest."

"Are you married?" I asked.

"Not now," he said. "My wife died of cancer two years ago and now I'm available. Know any prospects?"

I was embarrassed that he would ask me something personal, especially since a quick review came up with no one except Mom. He saw I was uneasy and laughed and then said he could probably find someone on his own. Since I was in this deep, I asked if he had children.

"No," he said. "We married late and were never blessed. I volunteered for this assignment so my staff can spend Christmas with their families."

All in all, I liked this guy. He had a sense of humor and cared about others so, in my eyes, he was a kind of priest. There was a knock, and June A. stuck her head in and said Jonna wanted me for dress rehearsal.

The Great Room was still a mess. Max had completed the manger and June A. had painted everything. She even did wood grain that made it look like a stable. Several residents had been to the fairgrounds and gotten straw from the cow pens to put on the floor.

Jonna helped me into my Joseph's costume. Mae W., the one about to pop, would play the part of the pregnant Mary. As the choir rehearsed "O Little Town of Bethlehem," Jonna talked us through our moves. Captain Trudy read from her script, speaking softly because of a sore throat. Even though I had no previous experience, I was impressed by how professionally Jonna directed us. She was all business, but I was distracted. For the first time I was close enough to notice the color of her eyes. They were gold.

"Here's where I sing 'O Holy Night,'" Jonna said. "When the light goes off, Mae goes off stage, and Veronica takes her place. Mrs. Dardenne puts the baby Jesus in the crib and the choir will sing "Away in a Manger."

Veronica L. had just delivered a boy two days ago, which meant she had the freshest baby and the flattest stomach of the residents. As she sat there looking at the empty crib, I wondered if she had made the decision to give him up or not.

"Next we'll sing "We Three Kings of Orient Are," Jonna said. "And girls, I want to remind you not to slouch when you sing. People do notice, so just remember, 'knockers up' at all times."

Captain Trudy frowned, but even if she had wanted to say something, she couldn't.

"Next, Max comes in and stands next to Joseph," Jonna said.

Max? I couldn't believe it. Jonna had been after him for weeks because he had a real beard. She used her every southern charm but he would not give in.

"I'm Jewish," he said. "I don't belong up there."

Her winning pitch was that Jesus was Jewish, and Max would be an important king from the East carrying rich gifts. He finally agreed but only if he could be a Jewish king. My thought was he's lucky he's not Catholic. I didn't know how I was going to confess this. The penance was going to be huge.

We couldn't complete the rehearsal because Eudora was still working on the narration. It was just as well. Captain Trudy's voice was barely above a whisper. Everyone had a home remedy but she went upstairs to Mom for treatment.

Jonna went over her list. "Max, we need a royal looking headdress for you," she said. "Rene. You look too young. Come early tonight and we'll give you a beard."

Well, that was more like it. I was going to get something out of this. I half wished that Johnny Boy could see me with a full beard, but knowing him he'd pull my shorts down and show everyone that I was still bald as a baby's ass.

IT WAS ALREADY DARK, AND A LIGHT SNOW was falling when I climbed the stairs to the side entrance. The hallway buzzed with activity. Residents ran in and out of the Arts and Crafts room for final fittings of their robes. In the middle was Max, who stood on a table and wore what was once a sheet. The girls had tied it in knots and dyed it with four different colors. When they untied it, the patterns looked exotic, like those in stained glass windows. They called it tie-dye. His costume was the most colorful of all, no doubt. All he needed was a headdress to look like a visiting king.

Jonna was waiting for me. "Put your robe on first, sweet thing," she said. "Now, sit on this stool and don't move." At her elbow was a kitchen bowl filled with hair for my beard. "I need some spirit gum from my trunk," she said to June A.

Right in front of my eyes, she reached in her blouse, searched for a moment and removed a key, just like in my imagination. She handed it to June, who didn't seem to notice that it was burning hot. Jonna leaned down and, with her face close to mine, smeared on spirit gum and began applying the beard. A small bump appeared in my pants.

"Damn," she said, breaking the spell. "We're not going to have enough hair. I might have to put it on your left side only, Rene. Just don't turn toward the audience."

Shirley T. came in with a blanket for the crib. "Did you hear?" she said. "Margaret's water just broke."

"Oh, just in time," Jonna said. "June, honey. Would you rush upstairs and get me some more material, please. Make sure it's dry."

Max came backstage in his tie-dye outfit. Jonna went to her trunk, returned with a multi-colored cloth and wrapped it around Max's head like a turban.

"It's a sarong I wore in *South Pacific*," she said. "I think it's perfect." It certainly was an odd mix of colors and patterns but I didn't feel qualified to comment. "Besides," she said, "who knows what a Magi looks like anyway."

We could hear people gathering in the anteroom. Captain Tucker had set out a coffee and tea service using the least dented silver and un-chipped china. Major Ellen had invited the director of the Northern Region and other local corps members, which meant the room would be nearly full. Even Doctor Hickman promised to stay after he finished his rounds. As Jonna's fingers raced across my face, pasting bits of hair over bare skin, Eudora rushed backstage with a bad news look on her face. "Captain Trudy has no voice," she said. "Can't even whisper."

"Oh, shit," Jonna said, emphasizing the T. "It's stage fright. Rene, do you have any ideas?"

I thought for a moment. "How about Colonel Payton?" I said. "He's the guy with the inspection team."

"Will he do it?" Jonna asked.

"Probably," I said, with confidence based only on my short time with him. "Have Eudora ask him."

June came back with a bowl of new material. Jonna looked at it and her smile dropped. "We forgot," she said. "Margaret is a redhead."

Jonna's brain went to work. "June, sweetie," she said. "Get the eyebrow pencil and a brush out of my trunk. We can make this work."

As she pasted the new material on my face, June followed right behind with pencil and brush coloring the red hair. When she finished, Jonna looked at my beard critically.

"We've got a pretty good match," she said. "Don't scratch your face and don't let your mother see you. I want her to be surprised."

June looked at my face closely and began to giggle. Jonna gave her a hard look, and she stopped.

Captain Trudy, reduced to hand motions, moved the choir onto risers. Twenty-five girls volunteered to sing. Usually there are only ten so it meant it was a tight fit. They looked beautiful in their white robes, but without question they were all with child. As a final touch, they wore halos that made them look angelic, even if they weren't. Jonna ducked behind stage to change into her robe. In her never-ending effort to be different, she emerged with a sarong over her shoulders, sort of like a shawl. Since she would be standing out front conducting the choir, the extra color would be insurance that no one would miss her.

When the doors opened, the sight of the Christmas tree, the manger, the stained glass window, and the twenty five-voice choir impressed the audience. Backstage we could hear "ooh's and aah's" as they took their seats. Major Ellen made welcoming comments and opened with a prayer. It was a rambling one that thanked everyone but especially God for providing Colonel Payton as a last minute narrator.

I was getting nervous. Not only was I about to take part in a Protestant service, but I was also playing Joseph, someone I had only seen as a statue in church. I could imagine Father McGowan's face if he found out. Mae W. waddled backstage and stood on her mark for our entrance. She took one look at me and let out a loud laugh. Several people said "Shh," which shut her up, but I could see her struggling to stifle another laugh. The choir sang "O Little Town of Bethlehem" and Colonel Payton began his narration of the Nativity Story. We walked slowly into the manger scene. Mae sat on a box painted like a wooden bench, and I stood facing her. It was supposed to be a solemn moment but Mae's stomach kept jiggling like a bowl of Jell-O. At first, I thought it was her baby kicking, but then it stopped. When she looked at me, the jiggling started all over again, and it was hard to keep a straight face. Only Captain Trudy's "Ahem," followed by a stern look, kept us under control.

When the music ended, Colonel Payton resumed his narration. The light in the manger went off, Mae W. shuffled out and Veronica L. took her place as post-baby Mary. All we needed was baby Jesus.

Jonna turned to face the audience. Never having heard her sing solo, I was more than curious. She performed "O Holy Night" with the most beautiful soprano voice I had ever heard. Her tone was clear, her expressions and hand gestures clearly said "professional." The audience was visibly moved, Captain Trudy most of all. She sat in the front row using her handkerchief to dab away tears. The applause was loud, long and well deserved. Jonna, smiling modestly, took two bows before cueing the light for the manger.

On the first notes of "Away in a Manger," I looked down and saw a baby in the crib. I was so fascinated with Jonna's solo that I hadn't noticed Mom sneak in with the infant boy. Veronica stared at this wonderful thing she had done, and tears ran down her cheeks. I wondered if that meant she had already made the decision to give him up. I couldn't tell by the look on her face, but that wouldn't count anyway. It was when that Tuesday arrived, the day she handed her baby over to an expressionless social worker, that we'd know what was really behind that detached look she'd worn all during pregnancy. I was glad I didn't know. It meant I could delay facing my own difficulty with emotional situations. Ever since my experience on the stairs with Joan B., when I heard a girl crying I just walked the other way. Was that what I'd do the rest of my life? Fortunately, I didn't have to solve my problem now, but she had only a few days to decide.

The program was going perfectly until Veronica glanced up at me. She looked away quickly but I saw her stomach begin to quiver and shake, just like Mae's only without the bulge. I riveted my eyes on Captain Trudy, determined not to spoil the moment. I couldn't figure out why these girls behaved so immaturely, especially since they were older than me.

Colonel Payton was doing a great job with the narration despite no rehearsal. With the choir singing behind him, he recited the visit of the Magi. Max entered the manger scene bearing a gift, a sterling soup tureen on a platter. We hoped the audience would imagine it filled with frankincense or myrrh. When Max saw my face, his eyes grew wide, and he started to smile. I cleared my throat and shot him a hard glance, and he got the message.

Colonel Payton began the final narration. Jonna had said she wanted it "tweaked a little" to make the message more contemporary. Since Eudora had just finished writing it, the "tweaks" hadn't been read or approved by Captain Trudy or Major Ellen, and they both were on the edge of their chairs.

In a solemn voice, Colonel Payton described the dream of the wise men and their decision to return to their own countries without reporting their findings to Herod.

"Ancient records show that one of the wise men traveled to the end of the Roman Empire," he said. "He settled in what is now England where he married, raised children and spread the story of the birth of Jesus, especially emphasizing the humble surroundings in which our savior was born. This story passed through their family from generation to generation until it reached William Booth, the founder of our Salvation Army. His ingrained care and concern for the downtrodden, dispossessed and destitute is what brings us together tonight."

Colonel Payton paused for dramatic effect. "By providing nurture and shelter in their hour of need for these unfortunate young women under our roof, we maintain a direct connection with the events that happened in Bethlehem almost two thousand years ago this very night. It is a connection that must never be broken."

After these emotional words, the choir sang its final carol, "Joy to the World." The audience joined in and sang at full volume through the two encores that it demanded, followed by applause that wouldn't quit.

I saw tears on the faces of Captain Trudy, Major Ellen, and Jonna, each for a different reason. For Captain Trudy they were tears of accomplishment; for Major Ellen, relief and for Jonna they were for being back in the spotlight.

For me it was an evening to remember. I'd never been a part of anything so emotional, and it gave me a feeling of family. In addition, it was my first beard, odd reactions and all. I looked for Mom, but she had returned the baby to the nursery. Jonna broke away from the congratulations and handed me a small bottle.

"This is spirit gum remover," she said. "Go home and take that beard off."

I complained that I wanted to show it to Mom.

"Go right now," she said firmly. "Get it off before it causes a rash."

I enjoyed the attention of walking around in costume dressed as Joseph, but I sure didn't want a rash on my face and left reluctantly. I had just opened the bottle of spirit gum remover when Mom came home. She was excited about the performance and especially my part in it.

"I want to see what my boy looks like with a beard," she said. When she came closer, I expected her to break out laughing like the rest. Instead, her eyes got bigger than Max's.

"Get that off your face and do it right now," she said in a very loud voice, emphasizing each word. I didn't think she was worried about a rash. "I'm going back to the hospital," she said. "I want a word with Jonna."

That certainly wasn't the response I had expected, as I'd never seen Mom so mad. I went in the bathroom, looked in the mirror and saw a stranger with a short, curly beard. Reaching up, I ran my fingers through the coarse hair and realized why everyone found it so funny. It was my first close-up look at real pubic hair—only it wasn't mine.

~15~

I T WAS CHRISTMAS MORNING, and I could hardly wait, but it wasn't the lure of presents that woke me up. I jumped out of bed, ran into the bathroom and examined the mirror. No rash. My face was pale red, but I wasn't sure if it was from the spirit gum or embarrassment. I was in bed when Mom came in last night, and I had no idea what she said to Jonna and wondered if I should even bring it up. It had been such a great evening that I played it over and over in my mind until I fell asleep. Jonna's parting words were still ricocheting inside my head.

"You were wonderful, darlin'," she said, and gave me a big kiss. That and the slight peek at where she kept her key would keep my impure thoughts busy for quite some time. What my mind couldn't visualize would be filled in by the women's underwear section of the Sears Roebuck catalog.

I opened the door to our anteroom quietly. On the corner table was the small Christmas tree we had bought at Olaf's Grocery for a dollar, trimmed with a single strand of lights that made it look almost over decorated. Our Christmas would be pretty skimpy since money was still tight. Using my meager allowance, I'd bought Mom's favorite dusting powder and tied it with a bow. It was all I could afford. Under the tree were two presents for me. One was good-sized, bigger than a shoebox. The other was smaller than a book. I was tempted to shake them but had to get ready for church. It was Sunday, and that meant eleven o'clock mass, Christmas or not.

I was dressed when Mom finally came out of her room. I gave her a kiss and wished her Merry Christmas. She gave me a hug and then held me back at arm's length. She was blinking back tears, and her face had that, "I'm so sorry you had to go through that without your Mother to protect you," look. Frankly, I was feeling just the opposite and was on cloud nine about how it worked out because I felt a little more grown up. Mom didn't want to talk about it then and handed me a present.

The card on the smallest package read, "Love, Mom." It was a hockey puck, much softer and warmer than the ones I was used to in a game. The second gift was heavier and made bumpy sounds when I shook it. The card read, "Love, Dad." I ripped the paper, lifted the lid and saw a pair of hockey skates from Montgomery Ward. They were maroon-and-black leather with yellow laces, and the colored tree lights reflected in the chrome blades. Dad lived in Florida, which meant there was no way he bought them there. When I looked up to thank Mom, she was holding a hockey stick with a red ribbon on it. The little card said, "Go get 'em. Love, Mom."

This gift was my ticket to peer acceptance. Till now the guys allowed me to join them reluctantly, but with no skates, the only position I could play was goalie. I wasn't good at it because my leather-soled shoes had no grip on the ice. That meant I spent as much time on my back as on my feet and stopped very few pucks. With these skates, I could stand at my position and block every puck that came my way. There was only one thing; I still didn't know how to skate. Well, one thing at a time. With those gifts, I was on my way.

On our walk to church, Mom opened up a little about her conversation with Jonna.

"I was really mad at her," Mom said. "I asked what she was thinking when she put that beard on you." I could tell, Mom was still mad, no doubt about it.

"She said that she was just trying to do a good job for Major Ellen," Mom said, "and you looked too young to be believable. She said it was all she could think of in a hurry."

I'm not sure Mom bought that excuse completely but she was giving it some thought. My feeling was that Jonna would have to be careful around Mom, especially during Monday's pre-natal exam.

"She did offer to help me in the nursery," Mom said, "but I think it's because she'll be keeping her baby and doesn't know a darn thing about them."

It was a nice gesture on Jonna's part, but I'd overheard enough talk at the dining table to know her motives weren't always trustworthy, especially if it kept her from going back to the laundry.

"You have to keep your eye on Jonna," Mom said. "I'm sorry you have to learn these things so young, but I can't protect you forever."

I knew she didn't mean it literally, but the truth was, I could barely take my eyes off Jonna, and I was tired of being protected. Maybe Mom lost track of time. After all, in nine days I'd be fifteen.

Father McGowan's Christmas sermon let up on sins of the flesh and concentrated on love and family, deemphasizing gift giving whenever he had a chance. My thoughts were on the new ice skates I'd gotten, exactly the sort of thing he was condemning. Just as his face reached full flush about the evils of Christmas commercialism, his black poodle showed up at the side of the pulpit and started whining. Father McGowan glanced at the dog and tried to ignore him, but it was no use. I hoped he would lift his leg on the pulpit just to see how Father McGowan would handle a dog pissing on his own property. The priest stopped in mid sentence and chuckled, like a parent might do when a cute child misbehaves.

"He gets lonely back there," he said, and led the dog back to the sacristy. At first the parishioners didn't know what to do. Then some girls began to giggle, and it spread like a grass fire until the whole church was talking and laughing at the same time. When Father McGowan reappeared, his face was the reddest I had ever seen, even redder than when he gave his sermons on fornication. When he tried to get the momentum restarted it didn't work. He got to a convenient spot, made the sign of the cross, said some words in Latin and headed back to the altar. Mom laughed so hard, that when it was time for communion, she forgot to cry. It was the most entertaining Mass I'd ever attended and to think, all it took to liven things up was a dog.

ON OUR WALK BACK FROM MASS, we saw a car turn into the hospital's driveway. It was a 1949 Cadillac four-door, the new one with taillights that looked like fins. An older couple got out and opened the door for a man in an Army uniform. He was on crutches.

"That car has Iowa plates," I said to Mom. "I'll bet its Corrine C.'s boyfriend home on leave." The last time I saw him he was wearing a letterman's sweater with a big "W" on it. My deduction was it stood for Waterloo, Iowa, a town that wasn't too far from St. Paul. This guy looked thinner, but Corrine said he'd lost weight in the Army because they had to march every day. I'd hoped to see his '41 Ford coupe with the Laker pipes again, but the Cadillac was okay. As they went into the Great Room, we heard the intercom. "Corrine C., please come to Administration."

Christmas lunch could have been mistaken for a meager meal day. Most of the officers were at church services and many residents had gone home or were at the movies. A plate of sandwiches was on the table along with some canned fruit and chocolate cake for dessert. Lieutenant Margit said the prayer and Brigadier Thomas and her mother, the old Colonel, said, "Amen." I hoped there would be more of a crowd because I was anxious to get feedback about last night's program. Lieutenant Margit was more than enthusiastic and couldn't stop talking about how wonderful it was. When she made a comment about my beard, Mom quickly changed the subject. Brigadier Thomas was concerned about the historical accuracy of the ties between the Magi and General Booth but felt it fitted the moment. Old Colonel Thomas complained the music wasn't loud enough and, as proof, she'd slept through at least half the program.

Our conversation was interrupted by a loud, "Oh, no." It was a girl's voice. "No, it's not true," she screamed.

I looked at Mom, wondering if Mae W. was in labor. She was bewildered because the labor room was empty. We heard the sound of heavy sobbing from the Great Room where Corrine and her parents and boyfriend were. Whatever the reason, it wasn't good news. Lieutenant Margit left the table and slipped into the Great Room. Corrine was on the edge of losing control, and we could hear the parents trying to calm her. My appetite disappeared with her first cry, and I asked to be excused. As I walked down the hall, I wondered how things could change so fast. At one moment I enjoyed compliments about the holiday program and, in the next, I walked away from dessert. Selfishly, I felt relieved that Corrine's parents were there to help her through the pain. Maybe they had more experience in knowing what to say or do. I waited for Mom to walk back to the nurses' home together.

The guy in the Army uniform was sitting on the side steps puffing on a cigarette. When he looked up, he had tears in his eyes. I went into my look-straight-ahead mode, but Mom sat down next to him and asked how he hurt his leg. I got a closer look at him. Corrine's boyfriend was taller, stockier and had blonde hair while this guy was about the same age but slim with dark hair. A plaster cast stuck out of his right pants leg.

"It was an accident, ma'am," he said. "I got hit by a bullet." Mom asked him if it had any connection to the bad news that Corrine just received.

"Yes, ma'am, it does," he said and, looking away from her, he began to cry.

"Can you tell me about it?" Mom asked. "It may be useful in helping Corrine get through it."

Even though I was only watching, I got that helpless feeling again. This was worse because, in the movies, soldiers never cried. Maybe it's because he was new and not toughened up yet. Whatever the reason, it must be serious. Jimmy was his name and Corrine's boyfriend, Rick, was his best friend.

"Her name ain't what you call her," he said. "It's Joanne. I just can't call her Corrine."

Jimmy and Rick graduated from Waterloo High School in Iowa. They went to work in the same bakery and when the Army offered a buddy enlistment instead of the draft, they went in together.

"They sent us to Fort Leonard Wood, Missouri," he said. "We were in the same company and shared a bunk bed in the barracks."

I listened carefully because the draft was still in effect and I knew, someday, I would be draft bait. Of course, that was three long years down the road.

"Near the end of first eight weeks training we were on the rifle range," he said. "Rick and me did real well and fired Expert and that qualified us for Christmas leave."

He threw his cigarette down, ground it out and lit another. He was smoking Camels.

"When we come off the range they make us put our rifles in the air," he said. "When the Range Officer says 'fire,' you pull the trigger. They don't want anybody sneaking rounds off the range so all they expect to hear is clicks."

"A round. Is that a bullet?" Mom asked.

"Yes, ma'am," he said. "Some guys like to send them home as souvenirs."

"Why?" I asked. He just shrugged.

"In the barracks we stack our rifles in the rack at the door," he said. "You've got to leave your weapon cocked and ready to fire, even though it's empty."

"Why do you do that?" I asked.

"After lights out, the CQ goes around to every barracks and pulls the triggers to make sure they're empty. If you're awake you hear the "click, click, click" until he's done. Our bunk was at the top of the stairs, just above the rifle rack, and we could hear the clicks real good."

He stopped for a moment, his shoulders shaking and began to sob. Mom put her arm over his shoulder, partly for comfort, partly because it was so cold.

"I heard a "bang" and felt pain in my leg," he said. I turned on my back and saw Rick's mattress starting to turn dark. Then I felt liquid dripping on my stomach. I held my hand up and saw it was his blood."

Mom couldn't comprehend. "Weren't the rifles empty?" she asked.

"Somebody sneaked a round off the range and put it in his weapon," he said. "He just forgot to pull it out before bedtime. Some son of a bitch . . ." he paused.

I flinched but realized that Mom must have heard this kind of language at one time or another.

"Pardon me, ma'am," he said, "but some SOB killed my best friend. They say he died instantly, but they didn't hear him moan like I did. I'll never forget that sound as long as I live."

He stopped to take a drag. His nicotine-stained fingers trembled when he put the cigarette to his lips.

"I've been sick ever since cause I knew I was going to have to tell Joanie," he said. "She didn't take it too easy, what with the baby comin' and all."

Lieutenant Margit leaned out of the door and asked Mom if she could administer some form of sedation to Corrine.

"Rene," she said. "Would you please go into the luggage room and bring Corrine's suitcase upstairs. She'll be leaving us for a few days."

I brought the suitcase to the anteroom where several girls waited to use the payphone. The old-fashioned wooden phone booth stood in the corner by the stairway. With the door closed and the light on, I saw Jonna on the phone with her boyfriend. Her face was animated and she waved her free hand around as if describing last night's program. When she broke into an open laugh, I supposed she told him about her creative solution with my last-minute beard. As I passed the phone booth, she smiled and threw me a kiss. Whatever Mom said to her last night didn't seem to slow her down.

I knocked on the door of the Great Room and handed the suitcase to a man I assumed to be Corrine's father. As I looked around the scene of last night's triumph, I saw a much calmer Corrine drying her eyes. How quickly things changed, I thought. Her well-planned future, overturned in a second by the act of one stupid person. Not only would she have to handle the loss, she'd have to decide what to do about the baby . . . a choice she thought she'd never have to make.

~16~

THE SUN WAS BARELY OVER the horizon as I made the short trek to the vacant lot. Man it was cold, but I was anxious to try out my new skates, especially before any of the guys showed up to play hockey. None of them could remember not knowing how to skate. It was like a Minnesota birthright. From my lonely position as goalie, I watched as they glided back and forth, dug their tips in and suddenly headed in another direction. It looked easy, and I wanted to find out how they did it.

I laced up and, using my hockey stick as a crutch, got up off the snow bank. Immediately my feet went forward, my legs spread apart and I landed back in the snow on my butt. Fall forward I told myself, but the ice looked too hard for that. I tried again with the same result, so I turned around and tried it in reverse. Suddenly, I was on my feet but the ice was now behind me. I stuck my hockey stick in the snow and pushed hard. Away I went across the ice backward. When I tried to change direction, the skates went out from under me, and I landed on my stomach. I crawled back to the snow bank hoping no one saw my clumsy attempt. I kept at it until my fingers were too cold to grip the stick and snot began to freeze on my upper lip. It was hardly a total success, but at least I could stand up on a pair of ice skates. Rewards, I learned, came a little at a time.

When I came in the back door, Mom was in the kitchen. I guess she hadn't gotten over her anger about the beard because she lit into me again. "What are you doing staying out in the cold?" she said. "Why do you think we had to move to Arizona?" Mom always asked those kinds of questions in threes. The last one was, "Do you think we lived there for four years just so you could catch your death in St. Paul?"

I didn't think she expected answers, and I didn't bother to make anything up. Instead, I wanted to tell her about my success in standing up on ice skates, but right then didn't seem the right time. She stuck a thermometer in my mouth and put some water on the stove.

"Take off those cold clothes," she said. "I'm heating some water for your feet. You've got to learn to take care of yourself."

I appreciated Mom's concern, but we left Arizona because I was cured. Her treatment of me like a little boy began to bother me.

"I don't want you going outside for the rest of the day," she said. "You can find something to do on your own."

Her words put me in a sudden crisis because I had put off an announcement for several days.

"I can't do that," I said. "I have a date."

Mom went rigid, as if I had just said "shit." Then she wheeled around with her hands on her hips.

"What do you mean, you have a date," she said. "When did you get a date? Who do you have a date with?" She finished her usual three questions in a row, and I tried to answer, but then she started on the next three.

"How do you know this girl?" she asked. "Where does she live? Where are you going on this date?" When she paused I jumped in.

"She's a girl I met in my English class," I said. "She sits across the aisle, and we both laugh at the same things, so I asked her if she'd like to go to a movie."

"Where is this movie?" she said, "and what's it about?" I stopped her before the next question.

"It's the *Wizard of Oz* and it's at the Como down the street. They've just re-released it, and I hear it's pretty good even though it's kind of old. The first time they showed it was before the war."

I didn't think Mom was ready for this moment in my life. Even though I had had several girl "friends," this was the first time I had ever

100

asked one out. Mom's idea of a first date was going to a dance or the prom—something she could build up to. I'd caught her off guard.

"Well, you'll have to get busy on your speeches," she said. "You're going to have to think of things to talk about."

That puzzled me. Why would I have to think up things to say to Carolyn? I talked to her every day in class. Maybe it went back to when Mom was courting. She told me guys came to her house and sat on the front porch swing and talked about things. None of it must have been very personal because one of my grandparents was always there knitting or reading the paper. I'm not sure if she was ever alone with my father except at a dance or the prom. My grandparents must've known what could happen at a prom, therefore, it was no surprise they were there on the front porch.

As I trudged the two blocks to Carolyn's house, my mind wasn't on what to say but how to avoid looking like my mother had dressed me. It was a short walk, and I'd be home before dark, but Mom insisted I wear a heavy jacket, thick muffler, wool hat, and ear muffs. At least I won the battle against rubbers or worse, galoshes. By the time I reached Carolyn's house, I'd ditched the muffler, the hat, and earmuffs in a snow bank. I'd pick them up on the way home.

Sitting in Carolyn's comfortable living room, Mrs. Lautner seemed as curious about me as my mother was about Carolyn. She didn't ask much, but her questions were carefully designed to gather information. Things like, "How long have you lived in this area?" and "Are you active in youth groups at your church?" Luckily, we had to leave before she could ask exactly where I lived. A truthful answer might have ended the date before it started. She promised she'd have hot chocolate ready when we got back, and we could tell her all about the movie.

On the way, Carolyn was really talkative and laughed a lot, wanted to know what I got for Christmas and things like that. It got me over my nervousness right away. She took me by her grade school and the Lutheran church her family attended. She'd lived in the same house and neighborhood and attended the same church her whole life. It was a stability I could only imagine. Hopefully, some of it would rub off.

We reached the Como Theater in time for the matinee and sat through the newsreel, cowboy serial, previews, and cartoon that ran before the main feature. We'd heard the picture would change from black and white to color but didn't know when. The magic moment came with Dorothy's arrival in Oz, and we were impressed. Neither of us had seen the movie since we were four years old when it was released in 1939. Back then no one spent Depression money just to entertain little kids.

Halfway through the movie, I decided to make it a real date by trying to hold her hand. From the corner of my eye I checked her lap. No hands. It was like she'd left them at home. Finally she scratched her nose, but before I could make my move the hand was gone. During one of the bright scenes, I saw she was sitting on her hands and sat on them for the rest of the movie. I wondered if it was her mother's idea.

As we left the theater I took a calculated risk and said, "Let's go to the drug store soda fountain for a malt." The residents would still be doing their chores at Booth Memorial. If we didn't stay too long, we'd be gone before any of them chanced to come in.

"As long as we're home by four fifteen," she said. "I don't want to miss *Stella Dallas*. Mom and I listen every day." Perfect timing, I thought.

Over our chocolate malts, we talked a bit about the movie, mainly wondering how they were able to find so many little people. Still, there were some awkward silences. In class, there was only a short amount of time to talk, and it was easy to have something clever to say. Now I was stuck. She didn't know much about sports and didn't care about cars. I had no interest in her collection of Shirley Temple dolls, and neither of us wanted to talk about *The Tale of Two Cities* from English class. Now I wish I'd spent some time thinking about things to say like Mom had suggested.

This was the first chance I'd had to look at her face to face because I'd seen her mainly in profile across the aisle. She wasn't movie-star pretty, but her skin was nice and peachy and she used color on her cheeks and lips. I even saw a little bit of eye shadow, something I'd never noticed on a girl before. Her cashmere sweater was a bit tight around her breasts and made them look pointy. I wasn't sure if she wore it to be sexy or she'd just grown out of it. She even had on a pearl necklace, which Mom said was a sign of refinement. I was having a good time and was about to ask her for another date.

"Do you have the time?" she said. "I don't want to miss the program." I was embarrassed because I didn't own a watch but spied a neon-lighted clock over the soda fountain.

"Five minutes after four," I said, like I was used to getting my time from it. "We'd better get going."

I paid for our malts and, for the first time in my life, faced having to leave a tip. Math wasn't my best subject but I figured ten percent would do it and flipped the tip onto the table like I did this every day.

Waiting at the stoplight at Snelling and Como, I saw several Booth residents walking in our direction.

"Let's cross now," I said grabbing her by the hand and pulling her across the street. "Don't want to miss *Stella Dallas*." Finally I was holding her hand, but now the residents would tell Mom they saw me doing it. She placed great importance on proper behavior and holding hands on the first date wasn't it.

"What kind of girl is she?" she'd ask.

I decided to drop her hand and act casual but there was no way to ignore the girls.

"Hey, Rene," they all shouted and waved at me from across the street. "We loved your performance. You looked so cute with your curly beard." They broke out laughing hard and a couple of them grabbed their stomachs. Carolyn and I walked along in silence for what seemed forever.

"How do you know those girls?" she asked finally. "They certainly seemed to know you."

Her question really put me on the spot because I couldn't claim I didn't know them. On the other hand, I didn't want Carolyn to know how well. This was what I should have worked out before going on a date in the neighborhood.

She didn't wait for my answer. "I'm surprised you even speak to them," she said. "Do you know what they've done?"

I did know what they'd done, but I was still unclear on exactly how they'd done it. It was something I didn't want her to know.

"What about those people who take care of them?" she said. "I hear its some sort of religion, but we'd never do that in the Lutheran church. And what is this about a beard? I've never seen you with a curly beard . . . or any beard."

I stumbled my way through an explanation of how I was in a Protestant pageant about the birth of Christ, wearing a beard applied by a woman who swore like a trooper and used to do bumps and grinds on stage. None of the story made sense without an explanation of how Mom and I ended up in St. Paul and there was no time for that because we were in front of her house.

"I had a nice time," she frostily. "Thanks for the movie and the malt. I'll see you in class." With that, she headed up the sidewalk for her date with *Stella Dallas*. She must've forgotten about the hot chocolate her mother promised.

On the way home, I tried to figure out how I could have handled the situation better. At least I was smart enough not to tell her the beard was made of pubic hair. I wondered if she had any of her own yet. I bet not, but after today there'd not be much chance I'd ever find out.

~17~

A SNOWPLOW ROARED DOWN THE STREET, and its blade hurled waves of new snow onto the sidewalk. My buddy Eddie Henderson and I jumped off to the side to avoid getting buried. Eddie's house was next to the vacant lot, and after he watched the struggle of my first attempts to skate, he gave me a call.

"You're never going to learn on that little patch of ice," he said. "You've gotta have some room. Let's go to Lake Como tomorrow."

I didn't want to tell him Mom gave me hell for staying out in the cold, and I made up some weak excuse. He was surprised that evening when I called to ask if his offer was still on. After I had a talk with Mom about my first date, and she didn't seem upset at all.

"I'm sure you did your best," she said. "Don't worry. You have a lot of time, and there'll be plenty of other girls."

She seemed almost relieved, but it was the opposite for me. My date had been going great until the Booth girls came by. Then everything went to hell. Was this what growing up was going to be I wondered. No control on what happens in your life.

"Why don't you just forget about her and concentrate on learning how to ice skate," Mom said. "Go out first thing tomorrow. Before you know it, you'll be playing hockey with the boys."

This was a real shocker. What happened to all that yelling about four years in Arizona? Why was my sudden interest in girls a greater danger than catching my death of cold in St. Paul? I decided not to bring it up. Instead I called Eddie.

When we got to the lake, the snowplow was already there clearing away big patches for the waiting skaters.

"Isn't he driving on ice?" I said, trying not to sound stupid. "What happens if he falls through?"

"No chance of that. The lake's frozen a couple of feet down by now," Eddie said. "It's when we get snow in May that he has to worry but we're plenty tired of skating by then anyway."

We sat on a snow bank and put our skates on while flocks of small boys swarmed past us as they hit the ice at full speed. They were like little ducklings scooting around, skating forward and backward, stopping suddenly and taking off again just as fast. Some of them chased after the snowplow as it made its monotonous back and forth sweep across the lake, stopping only to dump a load of snow onto a huge pile at the end. The girls were just as numerous but more delicate. They made large figure eights followed by nice spirals and had absolutely no interest in the snowplow.

A girl in a bright blue skating outfit came onto the ice. About my age I figured. She wore a matching hat with white fur trim around the edge. What I couldn't believe was that her legs were bare, or looked like it. She had to be practicing for competition because she did a series of turns that cut perfect circles into the ice. Then, while everyone watched, she made some beautiful jumps and did spins I had only seen in a Sonja Henie movie. She skated to a snow bank and sat next to a woman who threw a blanket over her red legs. Everyone tried to applaud but all I could hear was the muffled sound of mittens slapped together. After watching the figure skater and seeing all the boys as they bounced off each other like pool balls, I was ready to take my skates off and go home. Instead, Eddie jerked me to my feet, and we started off across the ice at a helluva clip. Skating backward, he held onto my hands and shouted instructions.

"Lean forward. You're not gonna fall," he yelled. "Lift your left leg and push with your right. Okay, weight on your left, lift your right and push." I got confused immediately and fell, taking us both down. Eddie showed a great amount of patience.

"I went through this last year with my kid brother," he said "and now he's a great skater. I know you can do it. Lean forward and push."

By noon, I launched myself from a snow bank, crossed the lake, turned around and came back without any help from Eddie. I was even able to do a little sideways skid to stop. We did one circuit with our hockey sticks, and he showed me some tricks to use when I could finally take to the ice in a game. My real goal, even though I didn't announce it, was to be able to skate backward just like him, but for now this would have to do. The whole morning I never once thought about my disappointing date with Carolyn. Mom was right after all.

I barged into the kitchen, eager to share my skating accomplishments and startled a resident who had been sent to clean the nurses' home. I knew she was new to Booth Memorial because she was wearing street clothes and had only begun to show.

"You scared me," she said, grabbing her stomach. "They said no one would be here."

"It's Christmas vacation," I said. "Usually I'm in school at this time."

She was plain looking with long stringy hair and crooked teeth. Her figure was beanpole thin, which meant the swelling at her waistline was even more obvious. Many of the residents had the wholesome look of cheerleaders, but this girl wouldn't have made the squad.

"The name is Rene," I said. "My Mom's the head nurse here."

It was her turn, and she thought for a moment, searching for the name that she'd picked for herself.

"Cass D.," she said with a big smile that emphasized her crooked teeth. "You can call me Cassie."

Like most of the others, she had chosen the name of a movie star. Usually they picked names of glamorous, sexy or mysterious women in a fantasy effort to be someone they could never be. Instead, she chose the name of an actress best known for a gangly body, pratfalls, a crazy way of singing and a memorable set of buckteeth. Sure, Cass Daley was a big star, but I'd never met anyone who wanted to be like her.

"They told me to mop the kitchen floor," she said, "but I can't find the bucket."

"All that stuff is downstairs," I said pointing to the basement door. "Careful, the stairs are steep."

To clean the nurses' home was not a popular assignment. Even though they were unsupervised and could take their time, many girls didn't like the idea of working in an empty house. Most of all, they were afraid of the basement. It was my get-away place because it was warm in the winter. There was an old couch where I could lie down and read and next to it was a ping-pong table for exercise. The problem was finding a partner. Lieutenant Corliss came down and challenged me to a game when she didn't work the evening shift. She grew up with older brothers and skunked me regularly. I blamed it on not being able to back up and get a good swing because of the V-8 juice boxes. A large corporation recently purchased the V-8 company and donated thousands of cases with the old label to the Salvation Army. They advertised it as a healthful, nutritious drink perfect for mothers-to-be. Several hundred cases were sent to Booth Memorial and ended up stored in the nurses' home basement, right by the ping-pong table. When Mom saw them, she thought she'd stumbled on the fountain of eternal life. Eight vegetables in one can—perfect to help her young son maintain his health through a cold winter. She gathered an armful of cans, stuffed them in the empty refrigerator and insisted I begin each day with a glass of V-8. Unfortunately, after the second day the juice took on the metallic flavor of the opened can, changing a tolerable health drink into something that tasted more like medicine. After several weeks of this method of iron intake, I could hardly wait for winter to be over.

Since Mom wasn't home to hear my skating exploits, I decided to spend time learning how to play the piano. Last semester I'd taken typing and was really good at it. The piano couldn't be that much different I thought because they both had keys. When I lifted the cover, my fingers left marks in the dust. The girls must've figured the piano didn't need daily dusting since no one ever played it. I ran my fingers over the stained and broken keys and made plunky sounds but nothing came out that resembled a tune.

Sitting there took me back to a party the previous year in Arizona. Joanne, the birthday girl, was just about the prettiest thing I'd ever seen. I tried to impress her with my knowledge about airplanes, but a guy pounded out a popular tune on the piano. She didn't even say, "Excuse me," but sat down next to him, and they played a duet. Since that day I had a hidden goal to play the piano and that's what was on my mind as I tried to coax a melody out of the keys. Cassie stuck her head in the room.

"Is that you making that racket?" she said, shattering any pretense I had of playing music. "If I was you, I'd be looking at some lessons."

It was a good suggestion, but lessons by a piano teacher were out of the question financially. Mom was still paying off my Christmas gifts.

"Look in the bench and see if there are any books on beginning piano," she said. "Maybe you can teach yourself."

I found two books on piano instruction. The title of the first one, *A First Piano Book for Little Jack's and Jill's* turned me off. After all, I was a high school sophomore. The other one, *Sixty Progressive Piano Pieces You Like to Play*, was more like it. As I thumbed through the book, words like etude, sonata and scherzo kept popping up. The people who wrote the exercises had names like Bach and Brahms and others I'd never heard of. I recognized the name Beethoven because he composed a symphony that started with the "dit-dit-dit-DAH" that was played a lot on radio during World War II. Mom told me it was Morse code for V, the first letter of Victory. That sounded pretty neat to me, using music to send signals to spies behind enemy lines. I tried to play the notes but couldn't find the right keys and to look in the book for a clue didn't help. The written introduction was hard to understand and everything after that was in musical notes. Maybe this was something I should look at in a week or two.

I made sure Cassie wasn't around before I opened the other book. It had titles like, "Fluffy Kittens," "Little Princess Waltz" and "Pop, Pop, Pop, Goes the Popcorn!" The musical notes were simple and the exercises easier, but I couldn't stand the titles. Maybe I'd wait till I was alone to start my musical career. I put the books back in the bench, making sure the Jacks and Jill's book was on the bottom, facedown. The biggest disappointment was that my typing experience didn't seem to help one bit.

~18~

ON MY WAY TO BREAKFAST ONE MORNING, I saw fresh sets of tracks in the snow that led to an ambulance at the side door. The empty 1946 Packard sat with its motor on idle, the defroster on full. Emergency equipment was in the back, but the stretcher was missing. Parked next to it, covered with a layer of new snow, was Doctor Hickman's Oldsmobile. There was a problem.

At the front desk, Lieutenant Margit was on the phone, her voice tense.

"That's right," she said. "They'll be on their way in a few minutes. The doctor says to prepare for surgery." She gave me a wave and a faint smile.

"Mae W. has complications," she whispered. "It's twins and she's having trouble delivering."

I remembered Mae's huge stomach jiggling like Jell-O when she played Mary in our Christmas pageant. I guessed twins wouldn't be a surprise.

"They're worried about Mae," she said. "It's been a hard labor and she's very weak."

I thought baby delivering was cut and dried. Some screams, some blood, and then a baby cried. Kind of messy afterward but nothing serious.

When she heard noise on the stairway, Lieutenant Margit motioned me to hold the hallway door open. Ambulance attendants brought Mae down the stairs on their stretcher. Her hair was matted, her face bone white, and she gritted her teeth to block the labor pains. Mom followed, wiping the sweat from Mae's forehead while Doctor Hickman spoke softly to an intern. As the attendants carried Mae past, she gave

111

me a slight smile, maybe remembering my Christmas beard. I tried to smile back but couldn't. It was another one of those awkward moments where I didn't know what to say or do.

"I know there are two in there," Doctor Hickman whispered to the intern, "but something's wrong. I can't move them separately. They might be joined." The young man looked startled.

"Are you sure?" he asked.

"No, I'm not," Doctor Hickman said, "but this matches everything I've read in my medical books." He fished in his pocket for a set of keys.

"Take my car to the hospital," he said. "They're expecting a Cesarean, but tell them there's a possibility the babies are Siamese. They'll know who to call."

Snowflakes landed on Mae's face as they rolled her to the idling ambulance. With Mom and Doctor Hickman aboard, the driver switched on the red emergency light and siren for the trip to University Hospital with fresh tire tracks in the snow as the only reminder of how quickly Mae's life had changed.

The hallway was jammed with residents who strained to get a look at the drama. Usually full of smiles and laughter, now they were serious, sobered by the possibility that it could happen to any one of them.

Lieutenant Margit motioned me into Major Ellen's office.

"Don't say anything to anyone about a Siamese birth," she said. "The doctor isn't sure, and we don't want to alarm the other girls. Their imaginations are already overworked."

What she didn't know was that my own mind had already created some ugly images. My knowledge about Siamese twins was learned from cheap carnivals. Sideshows always had pictures of abnormal people painted on canvas but I didn't know freaks could be born to normal girls. I promised not to say anything.

"Hi, Sugar," Jonna said to me. "What are you doing on New Year's Eve?"

Still high from her Christmas Eve success, she was all bubbles and charm.

"Not much," I said, trying to sound cool. "Mom and I will probably listen to the radio for the dropping of the ball in New York and then maybe Chicago and—"

"Oh, I was there last New Year's Eve," she interrupted, "and it was so much fun." It seems Jonna wasn't really interested in hearing my plans after all.

"Times Square was just packed with people," she said. "We danced and kissed each other at midnight. I'm going to miss that so much this year."

The image of Jonna dancing with her boyfriend and kissing everyone in sight made my plans with Mom sound kind of dull. She liked to have a glass or two of wine to welcome the New Year and always bought a small bottle of "David Mogen." No amount of persuasion could convince her of the correct name. She thought they had just made a mistake on the label. Whatever Mom called it, she promised I could have my first glass when I turned sixteen. What she didn't know was that I'd sneaked a few sips last year and replaced them with water. I didn't think she ever noticed.

"Mail's here girls," Lieutenant Margit announced. "Rene, here's a letter for your mother from you know who."

The girls giggled and looked for my reaction. It was no secret that Mom had a male friend but I didn't know how to put it in words. He certainly wasn't her boyfriend since he was at least forty years old. What was it called when your mother went out with an old man I wondered?

"When's he coming back, Rene?" someone shouted. It hit me like a rock. The real answer to Jonna's question was I would be doing nothing. This New Year's Eve, Mom would be sipping her wine with Carlton Allison.

* * *

MID-AFTERNOON AND STILL NO SIGN of Mom or Doctor Hickman. I spent the morning practice skating on the vacant lot. After lunch, I opened the *First Instruction Book for Piano Written for Older Pupils* again. Maybe yesterday's poor start was just a fluke. It wasn't. I checked to make sure no one was around and pulled out the *Piano Book for Little Jacks and Jill's* and turned to page one. After an hour I had to admit learning to play the piano might take more time than I figured.

The back door opened, and I heard Mom offer to make coffee. She and Doctor Hickman took off their heavy winter coats. They looked beat. He sat at the table while she put a pot on the stove. I could usually tell what kind of a day Mom had by looking at her shoes. The more blood spatter, the tougher the day. Today they were covered with reddish-brown dried blood, and I knew what tonight held for me. My concern was about Mae and her twins, especially if they were Siamese, but I didn't want to be the one to bring it up.

"I don't think we could have done any more for them, Jo," Doctor Hickman said. "There's no real way to know and prepare for it."

Mom stood at the stove. Her back was to me, but her shoulders were shaking. Something was wrong. When she turned to pour the coffee I saw tears on her face.

"It's very difficult to survive a birth of joined babies, even if you suspect it," he said. "It's incredibly tough on all of them."

"Were they Siamese?" I blurted.

"Unfortunately, yes. They were joined at the breastbone and had only one heartbeat," he said. "The girl was dead at birth and the boy died shortly after delivery. I'm not particularly religious but thank God they didn't live."

"And Mae?" I asked.

"Even with the blood loss, she survived the surgery but was exhausted from labor," he said. "She just didn't have any strength left."

"I feel so responsible," Mom said through her tears. "That girl trusted me to take care of her through her pregnancy, and now she's gone."

Gone! I couldn't believe what she said. That meant dead. How could Mae be dead? She wasn't that much older than I was, maybe seventeen. Sure, she'd sinned, but was it that bad? Why punish her when so many others had done the same thing? I didn't understand how God thought and didn't know whom to ask. For sure it wouldn't be Father McGowan.

"Let's go break this to Major Ellen," he said. "Then we have some paperwork before the body can be released to the parents."

He looked at the kitchen calendar, and his shoulders sagged.

"Tomorrow is New Year's Eve," he said. "What a terrible time to have to tell them." He paused while Mom dried her eyes.

"Jo, if you have no plans, maybe we could get together for dinner tomorrow night. It might help if we talk about it."

Mom looked confused at his suggestion. I didn't think New Year's Eve was much on her mind right then.

"I don't know, Doctor," she said. "Rene and I usually—"

I pointed to the envelope on the kitchen table. She recognized the handwriting.

"I'm sorry. I forgot. I do have plans," she said. "An old friend is coming in town, and we're having dinner. Maybe a rain check?"

"I'm not surprised you're in demand," he said. "Some other time then."

Mom slipped the letter in her pocket.

"Let's go talk to Major Ellen," he said shaking his head slowly. "What a helluva way to end the year."

The bottle of shoe polish and a damp rag still sat on the kitchen counter when Mom returned. She'd been on this case since two in the morning, and it was now past eight in the evening. There was a look of tiredness in her I'd never seen before.

"Major Ellen's taking this pretty hard," she said. "They don't lose many babies and the death of a mother is rare. She says she'll never get used to it."

Mom slumped in a chair, and I took her bloody shoes off.

"Now I know how she feels," she said. "When I worked in a hospital, a stranger came in for delivery and, in a week, she left with her baby. It was all a happy time."

She started to cry, and it made me uncomfortable because Mom hardly ever cried.

"It's different here," she said. "I'm with these girls for months. I know their personalities. Mae shared her plans for the future."

I picked up the bottle of shoe polish and shook it hard. I really wanted to throw it against the wall but that wouldn't bring Mae back.

"There'll be a memorial service for her tomorrow afternoon at the hospital," she said. "Major Ellen wants the girls to know what happened so rumors don't get back to their parents. Other hospitals have been threatened with lawsuits over things like this. Can you believe it? Being sued for trying to help another human being?"

I needed to change the subject. "What about New Year's Eve?" I asked.

"I haven't had a chance to read Carl's letter," she said, pulling the envelope from her pocket. While she read it, I started cleaning her shoes.

"Carl's flying in tomorrow," she said. "He's rented a car and has a room at the Happy Hollow Motel on Snelling. He should be here around two."

I was disappointed but didn't say anything. That meant no new Buick to ride around in on New Year's Day. On the other hand, I'd never known anyone who rented a car. Even if it were just some old Ford, it'd be kind of special.

"Can we go to Minneapolis and look around?" I asked. "We've never been there."

There was no answer. Mom was asleep in the kitchen chair. A tap on the shoulder woke her and, zombie-like, she went to her room and fell into bed. I don't think she even undressed. I picked up her shoes and went back to the sad duty of removing Mae's blood. It would take almost an hour to get them white again. The laces were the toughest for me. They had the last traces of Mae's life.

~19~

THE FINAL DAY OF 1949 BEGAN cold and clear. After ten hours sleep, Mom felt rested but groggy and dressed for work. I hoped for a cloudy day with heavy snow showers, the kind that would make it impossible for planes to take off or land. The night before I had a lot of time to think about Carl's trip. Why was he spending money on a plane ticket, a car and a motel just to visit a friend? What else was he planning? The question of why so many girls got pregnant on New Year's Eve bobbed up in my mind. Now there was a new piece to the puzzle . . . my mother.

The winter sun cast long shadows of the naked trees along the driveway, and I jumped over them, like cracks on a sidewalk. I did until Mom reminded me of Doctor Hickman's warning about how to walk on snow and ice.

"You don't want a broken arm or busted head to start the New Year," she said. "It's bad luck."

The hallway was unusually quiet with only the sound of a piano in the distance. Lieutenant Margit was at the administration desk sniffling into a handkerchief. Then she sneezed.

"Sounds like a cold, Margit," Mom said. "Come upstairs and I'll give you a shot of penicillin. It's bad luck to end one year and begin another being sick."

I'd never heard either of those pieces of wisdom before from Mom, but they made sense, and I made a mental note of them.

"Rene, would you please set up some chairs for the memorial service?" Lieutenant Margit asked. "We'll need about forty, and Major Ellen will need the lectern."

Tears came to her eyes and she paused.

"Also, would you please bring Mae's suitcase up from the trunk room," she said. "We need to pack her things."

Jonna was in the Great Room rehearsing solos for the service. Joanne B., wearing street clothes, accompanied her on the piano. I watched her fingers fly over the keys, and her eyes followed the music like she was reading a book. With my new appreciation of the piano, I was impressed with how she made it look beyond easy. Captain Berthe Karlsson and Captain Trudy were there to talk with Jonna about her hymn selections.

"I've done a lot of memorial services," Jonna said, "and these hymns are the most requested. 'Abide with me' is an evening hymn. 'Oh God, Our Help in Ages Past' is a good, traditional hymn that's very appropriate if you eliminate the fifth verse. I'd like to finish with 'Amazing Grace.' It's becoming as popular for funerals as weddings because it has a message of redemption. We're lucky that Joanne knows all these."

"Because Major Ellen will be delivering a eulogy," Captain Trudy said, "we'll have time for only two hymns. We must finish before the supper bell."

"And I'm not sure 'Amazing Grace' is the right hymn for this occasion," said Captain Karlsson. "Some of the words in the verse might be inappropriate for someone who conceived out of wedlock. No sense taking chances of offending."

Joanne B. and Jonna looked at each other in a mix of amazement and amusement, like they were dealing with people from another century. Jonna tried to object but was cut off.

"In our meeting this morning, we selected 'In Heavenly Love Abiding,'" Major Trudy said. "It's probably old fashioned to you girls, but it was sung at our regional director's funeral. We don't get to hear it too often, so do it along with 'Abide with me.'"

"But I don't know it. In fact, I've never heard of it," Jonna said turning to Joanne. "Have you?" Joanne shook her head.

"You've got a couple of hours to learn it," Captain Karlsson said, handing her the music. "You're a professional, so it shouldn't be a problem. I'm sure you'll love it."

The rest of the morning, the girls worked on the new hymn while I brought chairs up from the basement. Captain Karlsson was right in one respect. After hearing it over and over, I did get to like it but didn't think I'd pick it for my funeral.

It was two on the button when Carlton Allison pulled into the driveway in his rental car, a '49 Chevy two-door, standard shift with a radio and heater. The driver and rider's windows had those double panes glued on to the glass so they wouldn't frost over.

"It's not a Buick Roadmaster," he said, "but it'll do." When Mom came in, he put his arms around her and gave her, what I thought, was a pretty long kiss. She returned it, all the while looking at me out of the corner of her eye.

"I had a perfect flight," he said. "It was in one of those new double-deck Boeing Stratocruisers with a lounge downstairs. I had a martini at three hundred sixty miles an hour." This all sounded pretty exotic to me. I had to say Carlton Allison seemed to be a man of taste.

"Let's have a cup of coffee, and I'll tell you what's been happening," Mom said. She seemed really glad to see him.

The bell rang promptly at three o'clock, and the girls filed down the stairs to the Great Room. They were somber as they took their seats. The staff was there, including Max, dressed in his best suit, rumpled shirt and tie. Joanne B. played a soft prelude before Major Ellen moved to the lectern. At the last minute, Eudora came into the room with her parents. They'd been at a winter resort for a few days and had no idea of what happened. If Major Ellen was bothered, she didn't show it even though she preferred to keep this news "in the family."

She opened in prayer but it wasn't one of those meandering ones. There was a formula for memorial services, and she stuck to the script.

The service was to celebrate Mae's brief life and not to focus on her death, but I didn't think she convinced those of us who were crying. I couldn't shake my last image of Mae smiling at me on the way to the ambulance.

As her first hymn, Jonna sang "Abide with Me." Her voice was beautiful and used just the right amount of emotion to draw a tear from everyone. As hard as I tried to focus on poor Mae, my mind kept slipping back to the day I met Jonna dressed in her fashionable New York style clothing. She was an absolute knockout. Now, even though she had to wear frumpy smocks, the image of her as she retrieved a key from her brassiere was still enough to get a rise out of me. I know I shouldn't have had those thoughts at a memorial service, but since there was confession tonight, maybe I should've just enjoyed them.

Major Ellen read passages from the Bible and I was surprised at how easy they were to understand. In our church, a priest read the gospel from the pulpit in kind of a flat monotone that bounced off the walls. It was the word of God, but because of the echo effect it was hard to comprehend and easy to ignore. Then she got into the sensitive part, why and how Mae and her babies died. She talked about the miracle of birth but there were times when things didn't go as planned.

"Mae was one in forty thousand women who have babies that are joined in the womb," she said. "We call them Siamese. They're usually joined at the hip, chest, or abdomen and sometimes survive although their lives are never normal. If they don't have separate organs, such as the heart or liver, they hardly ever live beyond birth. This was the case yesterday."

The audience, already quiet, became almost grim at the telling of Mae's bad fortune. Doctor Hickman slipped into the room and took a seat in the back row right next to Carlton Allison.

"The doctors and nurses at University Hospital did all they could to save Mae and her babies," she said, wiping a tear, "but God had other plans. We can be assured they are now with Him in Heaven."

Her words brought up a question. How does God judge someone who dies before they have a chance to repent? Maybe to have a baby before marriage wasn't the greatest sin in the world, but it was a pretty big one. Was her sin the reason she produced two babies who never had a chance to live? It was a puzzle I couldn't solve and I decided not to think about it.

"Please join me in the Lord's Prayer," she said. This time I listened closely because some words were different from our version. They were easy to spot. Protestants used "debts" instead of "trespasses" and they tagged a few words on the end about kingdom, power and glory. Not such a big deal.

As Captain Karlsson insisted, Jonna sang "In Heavenly Love Abiding" as a finale. Just to be safe she had the music on a stand. She and Joanne did a real good job with no mistakes that I could tell. Major Ellen finished the benediction just as the supper bell sounded. Captain Trudy was so pleased with her timing that she was ready to bust.

* * *

THE GIRLS FILED PAST ME slowly headed downstairs to their dining room— no smiles, no small hand waves and, strangely, no tears. The memorial service confirmed their worst fears: it could have been one of them. Who cared if the odds are forty thousand to one? It happened to Mae.

Mom introduced Carl to Doctor Hickman.

"So, you're the one who beat me out for New Year's Eve," he said jokingly. Carl looked startled since I didn't think he knew he had competition.

"Sometimes you just get lucky," Carl said, smiling, even though his eyes weren't. I guess he figured Mom would explain it all later.

"Where are you going for New Year's Eve?" Doctor Hickman asked.

"The St. Paul Hotel is having a gala," Carl said. "Dinner, dancing, champagne, party hats, the whole shebang."

122

It was the first Mom had heard of any of this, I was sure. She was expecting a quiet dinner at a nice restaurant and some conversation until midnight. Maybe even a glass of David Mogen.

"Good choice but don't keep this lady out too late," Doctor Hickman said. "She had a long, hard day yesterday."

"If you gentlemen will excuse me," Mom said. "I have to get ready for such a grand evening."

"Doctor Hickman, will you stay for supper?" Major Ellen asked.

"Thank you, Major," he said, "but I'm on call tonight to allow the younger doctors to celebrate. Maybe it'll be my luck to deliver the first baby of the New Year."

I thought meals couldn't get much simpler than Christmas dinner but the one for New Year's Eve matched it on every level—sandwiches and canned fruit again with tapioca pudding dessert as the only change. Doctor Hickman was lucky he didn't stay. For sure he'd think they starved the girls. The truth was that the kitchen staff had taken off after lunch and wouldn't be back until the next day. That meant canned peaches, cold cereal, and V-8 juice for breakfast.

All the officers were there for supper. There was some quiet conversation but silverware pecking on china was the dominant sound. They did discuss the New Year's Eve service they'd be attending downtown, but I heard nothing that would unravel the mystery of New Year's Eve. There'd be a new crop of girls in three months, so it was a safe bet they wouldn't spend New Year's Eve in church.

According to Brigadier Thomas, the increased availability of the automobile was responsible for pregnancies filling the gap between New Year's Eve and Prom Night.

"I read it in *War Cry*," she said. "They call it Joy Riding."

"That's nothing new," her mother said, suddenly coming to life. "We did that when I was young, only we used a horse and buggy. Try that in cold weather with no heater."

Everyone sat there in shock. The image of that old lady being felt up in a buggy was embarrassing to think of, but she was right about the weather. It seemed to me there'd be problems getting pregnant in a car on New Year's Eve in Minnesota. To begin with, your private parts might freeze, even with the heater on full blast.

"What are your plans for New Year's Eve, Rene?" Captain Trudy asked, quickly changing the subject. "Your mother said she'd be going out with Mr. Allison."

"Oh, nothing special," I said, trying to sound adult. "I'll probably listen to Times Square and then . . ." I paused when I realized there was nothing after "then." This was the first New Year's Eve I'd be on my own. I wondered if Mom bought a bottle of Mogen David and, if so, where was it. Brigadier Thomas broke into my thoughts.

"You're welcome to come to church with us," she said, seizing on a chance to bring in a new soul.

"Thank you anyway," I said quickly, afraid that just considering it would put me in more trouble with Father McGowan. "It's Saturday and I have confession tonight. Want to start the New Year off clean."

They tittered at my little joke but then the room got very quiet again. I had the feeling they wanted to talk but not in front of me. I wolfed down my tapioca pudding and asked to be excused. As the door closed, I heard the conversation pick up quickly. The group had given me a subtle hint I'd recognized even without Mom there to bump my knee. I must be getting mature. When I stopped by the front desk to check the mail, there were voices coming from the Great Room.

"When we got home Jack Howard was sitting on the front porch," a woman said. "He told us he wouldn't stop until he found you."

"What did you say?" Eudora asked. She must be talking with her parents.

"We told him what we agreed on," her father said, "but he sure is stubborn."

"We haven't seen him lately," her mother said. "He's in med school somewhere."

"Don't change anything," said Eudora. "I know I made the right decision."

* * *

IT WAS DARK BY THE TIME I took off for confession. Mom and Carl were already on their way for an evening on the town. She'd saved some Christmas money to buy a new dress and looked absolutely great. I still had difficulty looking at Mom in any other way than just Mom, but Carl couldn't take his eyes off her. I didn't know if I could ever get used to that.

I walked past the vacant lot where we played hockey. The street-light was bright enough that I could stay on the ice after the guys went home. That way I could learn how to skate faster and control a puck. After just a few evenings, I had improved even though I still couldn't skate backward.

Church was fairly crowded for a Saturday evening. As much as I disliked the restrictions and regulations of Catholicism, it felt comfortable to be back in that environment. The ceremony, the statues, the robed priests, the Latin, the holy water, and even the smell of incense must be part of me. Based on my minimal experience, the informal, free wheeling off-the-cuff attitude of Protestantism gave it the feeling of a "make it up as you go" religion. They confessed to themselves, didn't tell a minister or even do penance. How did they know their sins were forgiven? And yet, most of the Protestants I'd met were nice people. The Salvation Army women seemed as dedicated to God as any nun and not a one of them had whacked my fingers with a ruler yet. The strangest part was that we all seemed to worship the same God but in a different way. Were they going to hell just because they weren't Catholic?

I was taught that to confess to a priest was the only way to clear myself with God, and Saturday was the best day to do it. Usually there was no crowd, but tonight I saw lines at both confessionals. Father Mc-Gowan was tough because he asked questions and gave stiff penances. The other priest, Father Farelly, was tough also but had a softer side and seemed almost as sorry for your sins as you said you were. The best part was his penances were light. Which line to choose was always a gamble because they switched confessionals each week. The older kids called it Roman roulette. At least I think they were talking about confession. Two nuns were in line and that surprised me. I couldn't figure out what they had to confess except smacking hands of kids in school. Of course, that was their job, but sometimes it looked like they enjoyed it too much. It reminded me of a joke I heard a priest tell on the radio.

"Listening to nun's confessions is like being stoned to death with popcorn," he said. "It doesn't kill you, just wears you down."

It must be the same to listen to kids' confessions. Maybe they made kids go now in order to get comfortable with the idea when the real sinning started.

I stood in line, went over my sins, and tried to figure if it was best to start with the little ones and build up or mix them together. I wanted to do a list but realized I couldn't read it in a dark confessional. Besides, Mom might find it and then there would be hell to pay twice. As I sat in the darkness, the panel slid open.

"Bless me Father for I have sinned," I recited. "It has been two weeks since my last confession." I plunged on, reeling off all the young boy things that priests had endured for generations. When I got into the part about a Protestant service I got a reaction.

"Hold it, son. Where was this?"

It was Father McGowan. He grilled me on whether I had willfully gone into a Protestant church, if my lips moved when they prayed and if I knelt, sang out loud, raised my hands in the air or rolled on the floor. He made such a fuss about it that I decided to hold off the confession about swear words, boners, and impure thoughts about Jonna's brassiere until I was better organized. I didn't think I'd ever tell him about the pubic hair beard.

I remembered Mom's words. "Beginning the New Year in a lie is bad luck." I hoped she was wrong on this one.

* * *

ON THE WAY BACK TO THE NURSES' HOME, I felt pretty low. I'd failed my first attempt at confessing adult sins. I was alone on New Year's Eve. Couldn't skate like every kid in Minnesota. Couldn't play the piano. Messed up my first date. Didn't have any pubic hair. I could've continued, but I had another idea. Mom's bottle of Mogen David. Where would she hide a bottle of wine? Not in the kitchen or the basement. Certainly not in my room. I was headed for her dresser when the phone rang. It was a voice I didn't recognize, at least at first. It was Lieutenant Margit, who said she had the flu and must go to bed. She asked if I could take over for her tonight.

All the poor Rene thoughts were suddenly gone. Someone was in need, and they called me! My feet slipped and slid on the ice as I ran down the driveway and double-timed it up the stairs. Girls stood around the administration desk while Lieutenant Margit lay on the couch in Major Ellen's office.

"Why isn't anyone helping her?" I asked.

"She won't let us," Claudette said. "She's afraid we'll be infected, and then the whole hospital will get it." I felt badly for using a sharp tone.

"There was no one else to call," Lieutenant Margit said. "Lieutenant Corliss is upstairs with a girl in labor, and the rest are all at church and won't be back until after midnight. You only have to answer the phone, and it hasn't rung all evening."

It was strange for me to be on the other side of the desk and be in charge even though I wasn't. Jonna was in the phone booth and, by the sound of it, she wasn't happy. Her boyfriend had been faithful with his letters and always called on Sunday, but nobody thought those would last even as long as they had because they always argued. She slammed the phone booth door.

"Dammit, he's drunk," Jonna said, "and he still has a performance to do." She saw me behind the desk, but no words like "sugar" or "sweet-thing" flowed out of Jonna's mouth that evening. "I know that man," she said. "Some little chorus girl's gonna get it tonight, and here I am stuck in this damned ice box."

Jonna just gave me another part of the New Year's Eve puzzle. Whatever happens must have to do with sex and booze. No wonder Captain Karlsson didn't have a clue. She didn't drink, and she was in church every New Year's Eve. So far, Jonna was one of my best sources, and I wasn't unhappy about that.

The ten o'clock bell signaled lights out, but the girls still wandered around. In my most adult voice, I reminded them about the rules.

"Oh, no, Rene," they pleaded. "Lieutenant Margit promised we could stay up and listen to the radio till eleven. Jonna was at Times Square last year and is going to tell us what happens minute-by-minute right up to midnight in New York. It'll be just like being there."

Did they tell the truth or not? I was responsible for the rules but was not about to wake Lieutenant Margit when she was so sick.

"Please, Rene," they all said, in little girl's voices. "Just this once. We won't tell."

I tried to think it through. I couldn't tell them what to do anyway; it is a special night and staff wouldn't be back until after midnight, so what was the harm?

"Okay," I said commandingly, "but everybody in bed right after eleven."

They all cheered, and June A. gave me a big kiss on the cheek. From the desk I could hear the girls laugh and sing in the Great Room as they danced to Guy Lombardo and his Royal Canadians at the Waldorf Astoria. Jonna acted as Master of Ceremonies. She used a sterling silver peppermill as a play microphone and interviewed the girls about their New Year's resolutions and wishes. Mainly to tease me, I was sure, many of the girls wished really bad happenings on the guys who'd gotten them pregnant. Things like cutting off private parts or throwing scalding water on their crotches, both of which left me a little uncomfortable. Most of the girls had no greater wish than to see their feet again.

At one minute before midnight in New York City, I couldn't resist. I left my position of authority and joined them around the radio. They shouted "Ten, Nine, Eight . . ." all the way down to One and screamed "Happy New Year 1950." Then they sang "Auld Lang Syne" and hugged each other as best they could. It was one helluva lot more fun than any New Year's Eve I'd ever had, even without the Mogen David. Now I had to take charge. I stood at the door and used my loudest voice.

"Happy New Year and good night, girls," I shouted. "Time for bed."

There was a funny lump in my throat and my voice cracked. The words, "Time for bed," came out in a deeper tone. They all looked at me in surprise.

"His voice is changing," Eudora said. "Rene, you're becoming a man."

I was surprised enough that I didn't know whether to be embarrassed or not. Mom had never prepared me for a voice change, and I didn't know what to expect.

"Is that anything like getting your first period?" Shirley asked. They all laughed, and every girl in the room filed past and gave me a big kiss. Sarah even suggested that her bed would be more comfortable if I was in it. I was too startled to react, but it gave me something to think about.

By eleven twenty, everything was quiet and I sat behind the desk with nothing to do. My head started to droop when the doorbell snapped me to attention. Large flakes of snow swirled in the door, and I couldn't make out a thing. Then I saw the outline of a suitcase. A snow-covered girl held it. She looked surprised.

"I'm looking for Booth Memorial Hospital," she said. "I must have the wrong address."

"This is it," I said. Not knowing what to do next, I asked, "Do you have an appointment?"

"I'm looking for a Lieutenant Margit Olson," she said. "Is she here?"

"She's sick," I said. "Can you come back tomorrow?"

As the words passed my lips, I knew I'd made a dumb mistake. Her body began to tremble, and she started to cry.

"I can't," she sobbed. "I have nowhere to go, and I don't know where I am." I had a quick flash of the girl in the blue coat and thought, *I can't let that happen again.* I grabbed the suitcase, pulled her in, and brushed the snow off her coat.

"Lieutenant Margit has the flu and the rest of the staff won't be here until after midnight. Is she expecting you?"

"Yes, but I'm late," she said, still crying. "The roads are bad because of the storm so the bus had to just crawl."

She stamped the snow from her boots and took off her heavy overcoat. Even with a sweater, I saw the reason for her visit. Her skirt was tight and she appeared to be about three months gone.

"I really can't help you," I said as cautiously as I could. "I don't know if they even have room for you."

"Oh, they do," she said. "I talked to Lieutenant Olson this morning, and she said they had a sudden opening, and I should come right away."

Of course, I thought. *She'll take Mae's place.*

"I'm so cold," she said. "Is there anything warm to drink?"

The kitchen was closed, but Major Ellen always kept a pot of coffee on a hotplate in her office. "It may be a little strong," I said. "It's been here all evening."

She warmed her hands over the radiator. Aside from her stomach, she was trim, almost slim. She took off her knit cap, and blonde hair fell to the middle of her back. Her breasts weren't big, but they stuck out enough to catch my eye. She wasn't what I would call a glamour-girl but was still attractive in a natural way.

"I'm Rene," I said. "My mother's the head nurse here." I knew better than to ask her name because she probably hadn't picked one yet.

"You can call me Elise," she said finally. "Elise B."

So, she already knew about the names. I wondered if she was aware of the age rules.

"Are your parents with you?" I asked, trying not to sound like I was prying.

"No, they're not," she said sharply. "And to answer the question you haven't asked, I'm eighteen years old. Today is my birthday."

I was embarrassed how quickly she saw through me, but at least, I got my unasked question answered.

She jumped at the sound of gunshots and the wail of a World War II air raid siren. It was midnight, and the noise announced the arrival of 1950 in St. Paul, Minnesota.

"Happy New Year, Elise," I said. "I hope this'll be a good year for you."

"Happy New Year to you, Rene," she said. "It couldn't get much worse." She was about to give me a peck on the cheek, but Captain Karlsson interrupted the moment.

"What are you doing here, Rene?" she asked from the doorway. "Where is Lieutenant Margit, and who is this?"

I was startled, surprised and embarrassed all at once. Major Ellen came in, and I explained what happened and introduced Elise B.

"Ah, yes," she said. "At least you're here safely. Happy New Year, Elise."

131

"And Happy Birthday too," I said.

"Oh, good. We'll have a cake tomorrow," she said. "It's a tradition for New Year's babies."

Captain Karlsson walked into the Great Room, then turned and looked at me. "Looks like someone had a good time tonight," she said. "This room is a mess."

"But they're all in bed, Captain," I said, "and they asked me to wish you a Happy New Year." Her response was a frown.

"Thank you so much for helping out," Major Ellen said and then cocked her head. "Rene, what's happened to your voice?"

On the way back to the nurses' home, I tried out my new voice. It jumped back and forth, something I hoped would be temporary. I checked the driveway and looked up and down the street. Even though it was after midnight, the rented Chevy was nowhere in sight. I considered walking by the Happy Hollow Motel just to check and then felt ashamed for not trusting my mother. It was a nasty thought, but I didn't know how persuasive Carl was. After all, it was New Year's Eve.

~20~

For a Sunday morning, fewer people than usual were at church. Many of the men looked really tired, and some took a nap before the sermon started. It must have something to do with New Year's Eve because Mom was still asleep when I left for eleven o'clock Mass.

Father McGowan mounted the pulpit to kick off the New Year. I'm sure he had a theme or planned to expand on the Bible, but my mind was already off in another world. It was the only time in a week that twenty minutes were all mine. My thoughts drifted to Mom and the punishment she put herself through every New Year's Eve.

For as long as I can remember, she'd toast the arrival of the New Year with a glass of Mogen David and become very quiet. Then she would go to her room, close the door and cry. I knew why.

She relived New Year's Eve 1936, when my father moved out. He wanted more freedom and asked for a trial separation. That didn't come as a complete shock because Mom had heard gossip that he had cheated on her. She tried to ignore it and be a better wife, but an innate stubbornness made her more angry than hurt, an approach that didn't work well with Dad. He had interrupted her dream of becoming a nurse and offered to pay her tuition to re-enter training. A nursing degree would be insurance if the trial separation didn't work out. When he made that offer, Mom said she knew he wouldn't be back. He took a job several hundred miles away, and with Mom in nurse's training, they had the problem of what to do with me. When Dad's parents agreed to help out, the three of us packed our things. Mom said we all cried, the act she repeated every New Year's Eve. Now there was a new man in her life and I had misgivings. Hadn't he been married once before?

This Sunday I did my usual trick when Mom wasn't with me. After leaving the communion rail, instead of going back to my seat for the end of Mass I just kept on walking and headed home. This didn't work if nuns were at the door.

When I got to the house, the rental Chevy was nowhere in sight. I opened the back door quietly so not to wake Mom, but I heard a man's voice coming from the living room.

"I can make a man of him, Jo. He needs a father figure to show him the way," the man said. "You've done a good job, but the hardest part is coming. If you're not careful he could grow up to be a sissy."

Mom didn't say anything, which was her typical way of handling problems she couldn't solve right away.

"I don't expect an answer right now," he said, "but please think it over. My son will be there this summer. Rene can start a new life with a buddy."

I was afraid to even breathe. It sounded like a proposal. If Mom accepted, the little bit of normalcy we'd established here in St. Paul would be over. This time, not only would I have to move again, but I'd have to share my mother with a man I barely knew. I carefully back-stepped down the hall, went into my room and sat on the bed. When Mom came in, I pretended to be tuning the radio.

"What a night," Mom said. "We didn't get in until after three."

"I waited up for you," I said, using my most disappointed voice.

"I know, honey," she said. "I took your shoes off and covered you up."

"Where were you so long?" I asked, still pouting.

"We left the hotel about one o'clock," she said, "but when we got to the car, it wouldn't start. Carl had left the lights on, and the battery was dead. Of course, there were no gas stations open so we were stuck."

"What did you do?" I asked, now more interested. Apparently Carl wasn't perfect after all.

"He called the Avis rental place at the airport, and they told us to leave it there and take a cab home on them. Maybe they thought Carl had too much to drink, and they wanted to protect their car."

That explains why I hadn't seen the rental Chevy. If I had, maybe I wouldn't have been quiet coming in and wouldn't have overheard Carl's proposal.

"Did you have a good time?" I asked kind of hoping she hadn't.

"Oh, yes. It was wonderful," she said. "We had dinner, we danced, and I even had some wine that wasn't David Mogen. I haven't had an evening like that ever in my life."

She was excited enough that I hoped this was one New Year's Eve she didn't cry.

"Carl will be leaving soon," Mom said. "He'll take a cab to the airport so we won't be able to ride around town. Hope you're not too disappointed."

I wasn't sure if I was or not. Based on what I'd overheard, I had to start looking at Carl in a different way. He was no longer a guy who drove a new Buick and was just good friends with my mother. Now he was talking about making changes—changes in me. What was it he'd called me? A sissy?

"Jo, Rene. It's about to start," Carl yelled from the living room. "Come in or you'll miss the kickoff."

"Carl wants you to listen to the Rose Bowl game with him," Mom said. "Ohio State is playing California."

I made a "so what" face.

"I know you like Illinois," she said, "but he graduated from Ohio State, and he's very proud of his school."

"Well, at least it's in the Big Ten," I said, heading for the living room.

Carl was having little success finding the game on the radio.

"How old is this thing?" he asked. "I can't tune in the game."

"It's a 1929 Atwater-Kent Model Fifty Five," I said, "built in Philadelphia, Pennsylvania."

He looked up at me as if to say, "How the hell did you know that?" It was built to be a piece of furniture with a radio in it, but by 1950 it was just a terribly out-of-date cabinet on four spindly legs. When we moved in, they said it didn't work, which was probably why it was donated. Even though it was ugly, it was still a radio. One day, out of curiosity, I took the back off and found the power cord neatly coiled inside the cabinet. No wonder it didn't work. They couldn't find the plug.

"The signal's weak because it doesn't have an antenna," I said, hoping to impress the Ohio State graduate in some small way.

"Get me a coat hanger," he said without the bother of saying "please."

He flexed the hanger until it broke, hooked one end to the antenna connection on the chassis, and the game came in loud and clear. If we were playing a game, I would say he was ahead seven to six because he knew how to make an antenna.

I learned something else as I listened to the game with Carl. He was an intense man who sat on the edge of the couch during every play. If I tried to say something, I got a quick "shh." The only time he relaxed was during the commercials, and even then conversation wasn't easy unless it was about the game. I wanted to leave but didn't want to validate his sissy label by walking away from a contest that real men enjoyed. We finally made it to half time when he called a cab to take him to the airport. In less than fifteen minutes I'd be able to do what I wanted again.

I kept a close eye on Mom as she kissed Carl goodbye. It was a short kiss with no passionate groping, and there were no tears in her eyes, like in a parting scene from a Myrna Loy movie. I didn't know what to look for but would know it if I saw it. One thing she said caught my attention.

"I'll think it over and let you know." And then he was gone.

* * *

HOLIDAYS WERE NO FUN without family or close friends. Regular days were easier to take because there was some sort of routine, but on holidays I was on my own. I grabbed my skates and hockey stick and headed for the vacant lot, but no one was there. No one was at Eddie Henderson's house either because they went to his grandparents' across town. His dad still couldn't afford a car, which meant they had to take the streetcar. I imagined Eddie at one of those big holiday feasts like in Norman Rockwell illustrations on the cover of the *Saturday Evening Post,* and it made me envious. I messed around and chased the puck with my hockey stick, but it was boring without the guys. I did manage to get some practice in skating backward but still wasn't good enough to be out on center ice during a game.

A year ago who could imagine I'd be cruising around on ice skates in Minnesota? On New Year's Day 1949, I had been in Arizona and played football with a bunch of kids who lived in my trailer court. No gloves, no skates, no warm jackets, no wool hat—just us and a beat-up old football on a patch of desert. All we had to worry about was not falling into cactus. Was this what life was going to be? No control, no say, no security. What'd I have to look forward to? Mom had vague dreams of me becoming a doctor, but the thought of working in all that blood had no appeal for me. I knew I was expected to go to college, but no one had ever talked to me about it. I wasn't even taking college prep courses in high school. Was woodshop a requirement for college?

It was almost dark when I headed home. From the vacant lot I saw cars that would come and leave the hospital. Parents had visited their daughters, and girls were coming back from holidays.

New Year's Day had been the topic for discussion at yesterday's noon meal when Major Ellen reminded her staff that not all home visits were full of love and affection. Many parents still had anger over the social shame their girls had brought on them and to see them in their full pregnancy was a shocking reminder. Some didn't handle it too well.

"It's not unusual for residents to return with anger of their own," she had said, "and sometimes they take it out on us. Remember, it's not personal and it's our job to help them heal."

How do they heal, I wondered? After the girls delivered and gave their babies away, were they ever forgiven? Could their families trust them not to do it again? Would they go to church and, if so, how could they keep their heads up? I'd never know the answers to those questions because, once a girl left, she was rarely heard from again. It was one of the best reasons never to get too close to a resident of Booth Memorial.

"Ohio State won seventeen to fourteen," Mom said as we walked to the hospital for dinner. "They scored three points in the last inning."

Baseball was Mom's favorite sport, and she could never bring herself to understand the terminology of any other.

"Last quarter," I said. "There are four quarters in football."

"Yes," she said. "They got a touchdown for three points in the last quarter."

"Field goal, Mom," I said. "A field goal is three points. A touchdown is six."

"Well, Ohio State won," she said, "and if that makes Carl happy, then I'm happy."

Since Mom hadn't spoken with me about anything that had happened in the last few days I decided to push the issue.

"Mom, do you think you'll ever get married again?" I asked.

It was a question that had never come up before because, for years, I harbored the hope that Mom and Dad would get back together. That dream was scuttled when Dad remarried, and his new wife had a baby. Now I had to consider that my mother might marry another man, and I was uneasy with that thought.

"Well, I'd have to find someone I want to marry first," she said lightly. "The time might come, but I'm so busy with my work and raising you that it would have to be a pretty good offer."

"So you're not going to marry Carl?"

"Oh, honey, no." she said. "He's a real nice friend and lots of fun, but you're my man for a couple more years. I might think about it when you're out of college."

Suddenly I felt a lot better. The cold air seemed fresher, and I could feel my moodiness slipping away. I took a deep breath and coughed.

"Rene, are you sick?" Mom said. "Your voice sounds like you have a chest cold." Finally she noticed.

"I think it's changed," I said just as it reverted back.

"Rene, you're becoming a man," she said excitedly. "Who needs a husband when I've got my man right here?"

She grabbed my hand and squeezed it. I should have been elated, but her remark bothered me. Did she expect me to feel the same way about her?

Our shadows were projected on the snow by the headlights of a car pulling in the driveway. We stepped aside as a 1949 Cadillac four-door drove up to the side entrance. It carried Iowa plates, and I recognized it. We tried to walk past without looking because some parents were sensitive about being seen there, but a door opened and a girl called out. "Mrs. Dardenne. Mrs. Dardenne. It's Corrine. I might be having some problems, and I've got to talk to you."

Mom told me to wait and help with Corrine's suitcase and they both went inside. I recognized her father as the man I had given her suitcase to just a week ago. It felt awkward, but I asked him how Corrine felt.

"She's had a rough week what with the funeral and all," he said. "She's still trying to figure out what to do."

To me, that meant she hadn't decided whether to keep her baby or not. Before Christmas, there wasn't a question. Now she had to make the terrible decision that was never supposed to be part of her plan.

I dropped the suitcase off at the staircase in the anteroom. Some residents waited to use the phone outside the office. Jonna was in her usual spot waiting for it to ring, and she got impatient if anyone talked too long. She complained that her boyfriend had a Sunday night performance, and if he couldn't get through she'd have to wait till next week. This happened once or twice before, and she wasn't happy.

"Hi, handsome," she said. "Didn't we have a good time last night? We're going to suggest you run things on Saturday nights from now on."

I felt my face flush.

"Oh, look. You've embarrassed him," someone said. "Maybe he wanted something else to happen. What'd you have in mind, Rene?"

I had to stop the teasing because I knew they wouldn't quit. I saw Elise B. standing in the corner.

"Elise, did you find your bed okay last night?" I asked.

"Oh, isn't he a mover," Cassie said. "He already knows the new girl's name."

"If they couldn't find a bed for her," Sarah B. said, "I'm sure he could've."

They all broke out in laughter except Elise. I tried to get out of there gracefully, but as I turned to leave, I tripped over the suitcase. As I walked down the hall, all I could hear was laughter. At least, I thought, they're not crying.

~21~

ON TUESDAY, THE THIRD OF JANUARY, I was on the streetcar on my way to school. This was the day most kids hated because it was the end of Christmas, end of New Year's, and end of vacation. To get up early on a cold morning in Minnesota and trudge through snow to school wasn't something they looked forward to. Until we moved to St. Paul, I couldn't wait for this day because it was the day I was born. In Arizona, the teacher would always point me out, and the class would sing "Happy Birthday." Sometimes I even got cards and presents. That wouldn't happen today.

Murray High was a big, impersonal school and the only reason anyone knew my name was that it was called out every morning in homeroom. I made a mental note not to mention my birthday because no one else ever mentioned theirs. It was fun to be back though. I never realized how many new people I'd met since the transfer here, and because the semester wasn't over, we were still in the same classes. That meant I'd still sit next to Carolyn in English.

Since our date had ended kind of flat, I'd hoped to interest her in another movie. *Twelve O'clock High* was playing at the Como, but it was a war movie about airplanes and she might not be interested. Next week was *Little Women,* and I wasn't interested. Wasn't that from a book that girls read? Maybe the best bet would be *My Friend Irma.* I liked the radio show, and the movie would be at the Como in two weeks. This time I'd stay clear of any girls from the hospital.

Carolyn was already in her seat. She must've gotten a new sweater for Christmas because it wasn't nearly as tight as the one I remembered.

When I sat down, she just nodded and opened her book. I was expecting a smile, but all I got was the nod.

"How was your Christmas?" I asked.

"Nice." she said and looked back in her book.

"What did you do during vacation?" I asked.

"I was very, very busy," she said, without looking up.

This wasn't going well. Since my only experience was with girls who were pregnant, I didn't know what to expect from one who was not. I decided to go for broke.

"*My Friend Irma* is coming to the Como week after next. Want to go see it with me?"

"I'm going to be busy then," she said, once again not looking up.

I decided to sacrifice my preferences. "*Little Women* is going to be showing next week," I said. "Would you like to see that?"

"I'm busy then too," she said, still studying her book.

"When will you not be busy?" I said, trying to get around this problem. She finally looked up.

"I'm going to be busy for a very, very long time, so I suggest you find someone else to take to the movies," she said. "And just a piece of advice: don't take her anywhere near that filthy place."

Her remark irritated me because I knew it wasn't true, but I wasn't in a very good position to challenge it.

"I told my mother all about it." she said, "She thinks you know too much, and so do I."

Just then the bell rang and the teacher said, "Today we start our review of *Tale of Two Cities*. Open your books to Chapter One."

I went through the rest of the day in a fog. I was accused of knowing too much when the truth was I didn't know much at all. Some guys could have turned that into something positive, maybe even catch the attention of the girl who wore the pointy-pointy brassiere. It didn't work for me. Instead of being known as a sexy guy with a knowing smile, I had the reputation of a nasty mind and a dirty leer. The only ones who could appreciate that would be Johnny Boy and his buddies. I'd see them in gym.

I hurried from my last class into the locker room, and headed for the corner to change into my gym clothes. Johnny Boy came in just as I pulled up my shorts. Apparently I had been in his thoughts over the holidays because he had a name for me.

"Hey, Baldy," he shouted. "Anything new with your crotch?"

This got a big laugh from the guys because they suspected there wasn't. Some might have even sympathized but no one wanted to step into Johnny Boy Bittolini's line of fire. I dreaded the end of class because I knew I'd have to go through this again unless I wore my gym shorts home. No, that wouldn't work. It was January. But luck was on my side today. Johnny Boy elbowed someone in a basketball game and the PE instructor made him stay and sweep the gym floor for poor sportsmanship. God was on my side on my birthday.

When I got home I discovered a small present on the table in our anteroom. The card read, "Love from Mom and Dad." As little as a year ago this would have given me hope that they would get back together but the new baby took care of that. Most of all, I knew it was really a gift from Mom, but Dad had chipped in. On the positive side that meant it must be something expensive, maybe as much as fifteen dollars, but I'd have to wait until Mom was off work.

I checked to make sure no one was in the house before I dug the beginner's book out of the piano bench. I was embarassed. Here I was, a fifteen-year-old whose voice had changed, trying to play something called "Fluffy Kittens." I didn't do too badly except for hitting some wrong keys. I was almost encouraged until I heard, "You've got the Jack's and Jill's beginner's piano book," Cassie shouted from the hallway. "God, I hated that. I was five years old, and they made me start with 'Pop, Pop, Pop, Goes the Popcorn!' Have you gotten there yet?"

I had forgotten to check the basement. Cassie went down there to get the cleaning equipment.

"I found some beginning piano books in the bench," I said, trying to sound nonchalant. "I'm not sure they're right for me."

"Yeah, 'Fluffy Kittens' is a little advanced," she said, "But don't worry. I won't tell anyone. You just keep pounding away, and someday you'll be playing like Chopin."

That was a name I knew. For my tenth birthday Mom took me to see the movie *A Song to Remember*. It had been five years since then, but it had made such an impression that she still hadn't forgiven Merle Oberon for the way she treated the composer.

"If you're not going to play, make yourself useful," Cassie said. "Dust the keys."

She threw a wadded up pair of women's well-worn cotton panties at me. I made a face.

"This isn't the last time you're going to have your hands in a pair of those," she said. "Might as well learn to enjoy it—until you get some girl knocked up that is."

"Is that what happened to you?" I asked.

"You betcha," she said. "He swore he loved me but all he really wanted was to poke his pecker in my pussy."

"You let some guy do that to you?" I asked.

"Let him? I helped him," she laughed. "I was in love."

"What'd he say when you told him you were knocked up?"

"I told him we had to get married," she said. "He just laughed and said he'd get a couple of his buddies to say they'd balled me too."

"What'd you do then?" I asked.

"I told my brothers," she said. "They took him out for a little walk in the woods. He won't be poking his pecker anywhere for a long, long time."

With that sobering thought, I finished dusting the keys and took the books to my room to study them in quiet, and away from Cassie.

Mom came home before dinner to watch me open my cards and birthday present. I admit that I moved the box around a little but didn't know what it was. Couldn't even tell by shaking.

"Open it," Mom said.

It was a velvet box, and inside was a wristwatch, my very first. A Longines-Wittnauer that not only glowed in the dark, just like the ones pilots wore, but sported an expandable band, the very latest thing. It even had the right time.

"I set it just before I wrapped it," Mom said.

She was as proud as I was pleased.

"Let's go to dinner so I can show it off," I said, checking the time to make sure it was still right.

Everything at Booth Memorial was back to normal. The Christmas tree was down and the ornaments back in the basement. The Great Room had the same gloomy look as before the holidays. The residents, in their faded dresses, looked even dowdier than before but the one who wore her street clothes stood out. It was Elise B.

Dinner was an event to remember. Somehow Captain Tucker prepared everything I liked—meatloaf made with oatmeal, mashed potatoes with melted butter, thick brown gravy, green beans boiled with bacon strips, and fresh-baked bread. The beans weren't fresh but who could expect that in the middle of winter? When it was time for dessert, two resident servers carried in a cake with lighted candles.

"We usually do this only for New Year's babies," Major Ellen said, "but you're close enough."

Captain Tucker turned the lights down. Everyone sang "Happy Birthday" and challenged me to blow out all fifteen candles. That wasn't a problem, but I dragged it out just to make the moment last a little longer. Before the lights came on, I looked down to check the time on my luminous dial watch. It was six forty-five; almost time for *The Great Gildersleeve* on the radio. I looked around the table at people who had been strangers to me four months ago. In that short time I'd come to know them as dedicated women, Protestants or not, doing their best to handle the problems of a group of troubled young girls. It was sad that anyone would think of this as a filthy place.

Back home, Mom reminded me that Wednesday was our night to use the tub in the upstairs bathroom. It was a school night, and I could go first. By now I'd gotten used to all the female underwear and paraphernalia hanging around the bathroom, but I still marveled at the load Captain McTavish's brassiere had to carry. Funny, it looked a lot more interesting hanging there than when she wore it. As I dried off, I caught a glimpse of something new. I moved close to the mirror and stared at my crotch. Glory be. From now on I could no longer be called Baldy. For my fifteenth birthday, God's gift was two curly pubic hairs.

~22~

A MINNESOTA WINTER WAS SOMETHING that couldn't have been explained to me beforehand. Weeks on end of overcast skies, freezing temperatures, bulky winter clothing, endless snow shoveling and constant nosebleeds from the dryness. The residents of Booth Memorial really disliked this time of year because they couldn't even get out for a walk, especially the ones who were eight months gone. This was when many of them learned to sew, knit and crochet while others played Monopoly in the rec room. Older girls played cards. Euchre and Hearts were the most popular. It was the season Captain Trudy dreaded because there wasn't much to keep them occupied. The more mature girls usually volunteered for something, mostly small jobs in the office. To stay on the good side of Mom after the beard incident, Jonna kept her promise of helping in the Nursery.

"She has absolutely no practical skills," Mom said. "She says her mother always wanted a better life for her and wouldn't let her do anything around the house or in the kitchen."

That certainly explained Jonna's dislike of her time in the laundry with Captain McTavish. It was all new to her, and she didn't like the experience one bit.

Eudora volunteered to work in the classroom on the second floor and helped out in the nursery. She told Mom it took her mind off her boyfriend, who was still searching for her. According to the talk around the dinner table, she was a natural in helping the teachers and good at handling the girls. They looked up to her because she'd had some college. Eudora's greatest passion was getting them to read books they'd never touched in high school. I needed to ask Eudora for a recommendation because reading an elective book was required for my English class, and I didn't know what to choose.

"I'll go over my list from high school and come up with something for you," she promised. She still had months to go, but my deadline was much shorter.

Passing by the counseling office I heard the voice of Brigadier Thomas reciting the familiar rules and regulations for a stay. This was different though. Her voice sounded more professional, not the consoling tone she normally used.

"We'll take care of her again," she said. "The cost hasn't changed, and we expect payment on the usual basis."

The scene was different too. Usually a small suitcase stood outside the door but this time there was only one shopping bag with shoes sticking out. Another thing unusual was there was no sniffing or crying from the girl. What I did hear sounded more like grunts and labored breathing. I quickly grabbed a copy of *War Cry* and plopped on the couch.

"We'll call you when she delivers," Brigadier Thomas said. "You can decide where the baby goes."

There was a scuffing of chairs, and a woman came out of the office. Dressed more like a professional than a mother, the woman wore an ugly hat, a dark suit, and old lady shoes. I wasn't prepared for the next person. Following her was a female who looked like a big dwarf. She had thick, black hair and a large, square face, and her body was stunted. One leg, shorter than the other, caused her to walk with a severe limp and she wheezed with each step.

"Thank you," she said with a deep, almost raspy voice.

"You're welcome, dear," Brigadier Thomas said. "We'll take good care of you again. In fact, your clothes are still here."

The professional lady from the State of Minnesota Mental Health Department signed a few papers, and they followed Brigadier Thomas up the stairway to the dorm. I was so stunned I forgot to pretend I was read-ing *War Cry*.

"We've seen her before," Lieutenant Margit said. "She's been stunted from birth and has the mind of a four-year-old. The last time she delivered a perfectly healthy baby boy at term. When she left here, she went back into state care. They don't know who gets her pregnant and neither does she."

I didn't notice Lieutenant Margit at the administration desk and was caught off guard by her comment. Did she see me eavesdropping?

"How old is she and why do they bring her here?" I asked.

"We think she's about sixteen," she said, "but no one really knows. The state has no place for her, so it pays us to take care of the pregnancy. We admit her as long as she can climb stairs, follow instruc-tions and do simple chores. She loves to polish silver."

I had never seen a deformed person up close. Usually they were in sideshows at cut-rate carnivals and performed in some way, but this one was barely able to walk let alone do tricks.

"How does she get pregnant?" I asked, not realizing the question sounded naive.

"The usual way I guess," Lieutenant Margit said and then, recog-nizing I might not know what the usual way is, changed her tone. "No one knows," she said. "They don't have the personnel to monitor all their inmates, and a lot happens in the dorms at night. It could even be a staff member. Makes you sick."

Even in my most unusual fantasies, I'd never had the idea of doing anything like that with someone deformed like her. Lieutenant Margit was right. It made me sick.

"How do the girls treat her?" I asked.

"Oh, it varies," she said. "Most don't want to be around her, so she spends a lot of time alone. Some tease her, and others just want to get rid of her. They send her on wild goose chases. By the time she gets there, she's forgotten what they sent her for."

"Sounds mean," I said.

"Well, yes," she said, "but that's how some girls are. You'll find out someday."

"What do they call her?" I asked.

"Her name is Dolores," she said, "but the last time everyone called her Dodo. Maybe it'll be different this time. Dodo sounds so cruel."

* * *

ON MY WAY BACK TO THE NURSES' HOME, I checked the vacant lot to see if any of the guys were out yet. Not a soul and not surprising. Neighborhood parents insisted their kids do homework and house chores before they got to play. Most of the families came from immigrant backgrounds and were convinced the only way out of the dirty factory jobs was to get a good college education. That's exactly how Mom and Dad felt when I was born and the mention of college would always launch her into her favorite story.

"It was the middle of the Depression," Mom would begin. "Your dad was laid off and had to go work in the coalmines. The day after you were born, he took out an insurance policy that will mature when you turn eighteen. 'That'll be to put him through college,' he said. 'I don't want him to ever have to go into the mines like me.' Your dad's paid for that policy all these years," she said. "Now it's my job to see that you get to college."

I guess that meant doing homework, but since she was always on duty, I had no pressure to study after a long day at school. Maybe I'd go home and look at my books. Then again, my hockey skates could use sharpening, and I'd rather do that instead. Still going over my choices, I walked into the normally quiet nurses' home and heard piano music coming from the living room. It couldn't be Cassie because she told me how much she hated her lessons, and this was way beyond "Pop Goes the Popcorn." It wasn't pop music but more like something I heard in the Chopin movie. I crept down the hall, not wanting to stop the sound but curious to see who was making this wonderful noise.

I peeked around the corner and saw Elise. Not only was she playing with no music in front of her, but also her eyes were closed. She looked up and screamed.

"You scared me," she said. "I was sent over to do cleaning, but I don't know where the mops and brooms are and no one was here to ask. Then I saw the piano."

"I don't think it's in very good shape," I said, like I knew what I was talking about.

"Do you ever use it?" she said.

"I would if I knew how," I said. "How'd you learn to play like that?"

"I started lessons when I was four," she said, "and I've been giving them since fourteen. It was going to be my college money, but now I have to use it to stay in this place."

I showed her the door where the cleaning materials were kept. "Some girls don't like this job because they're afraid of the basement," I said. "If you'd like, I'll go down and get the stuff for you."

"I'm not afraid of any basement," she said. "At home that's where I'd go to hide from my stepfather. I'll get them myself."

Her attitude confused me, but I didn't know her very well. Elise had a softness about her and then, all of a sudden, there'd be this hardness, like I'd stepped over a line I didn't see. She began dust mopping the entryway while I sat at the piano trying to make sense of the notes for "Fluffy Kittens."

"Why don't you know how to play?" she said. "Everybody starts in first grade."

"We didn't have a piano in our trailer," I said, trying to keep it on the light side. "Really, though, Mom didn't have the money. Nurses don't make that much."

"So what are you going to do about it?" she asked. It sounded like a challenge.

"Why don't you teach me?" I said.

She looked at me like I was some kind of dummy. "I can't do my work and teach you," she said. "I have to be back at four thirty to get ready for supper. When am I supposed to teach?"

"What if I help you?" I said. "I can do the mopping and dusting on this floor and take care of my room later."

She seemed interested but didn't say anything. "I'm only thinking it over because I hate housework," she said. "The reason I'm over here is to get away from those dumb girls. All they talk about is knitting and movie stars. I can't even get a fourth for bridge. They say it reminds them too much of school because you have to think."

"I'm a quick learner and do real good in typing," I said, hoping to sweeten the pot.

"Play something for me." she commanded more than asked.

I put the *Jacks and Jills* book on the piano bench and hit a few notes.

"Oh, that's Irene Roger's 'Fluffy Kittens,'" she said. "That's a good starter for five-year-olds, but we have to find something a little advanced for you. After all, you know how to type."

I was pleased she thought I could handle more advanced music, but the typing remark sounded sarcastic. So far I hadn't found any connection between the two.

"I know your first problem," she said. "You can't possibly learn to play with the book down on the bench. Put it up on the music rack where it belongs."

I had put it on the bench to hide that it was a beginner's book, but I should have known if she were a real piano teacher she'd recognize the music.

"There probably are other books at the hospital," she said. "I'll take a look and bring some when I come back."

"What can I do till then?" I asked.

"We can start by getting you ready to play," she said. "Sit tall. Now, lean a little bit forward. Elbows slightly higher than the keys. Knees under the keyboard. Feet flat on the floor, but the right foot can be slightly forward. Curve your fingers. Good! Now, practice that before you ever touch the keys."

I felt like a robot, but it did feel more professional.

"When can I start learning?" I asked.

"Today's Monday," she said. "We'll start Wednesday after we finish cleaning. Remember—don't tell anyone, especially your mother. The last thing they said to me was, 'No fraternizing.'"

I couldn't believe it. I was on my way. Suddenly I had a piano and a teacher, and all it was going to cost me was dusting furniture with somebody's old underwear. I imagined being up there playing music like Chopin in no time. It never crossed my mind that Elise might become my very own Merle Oberon.

* * *

ON WEDNESDAY I THOUGHT SCHOOL would never end. I jumped off the streetcar and went in the front door of the nurses' home to avoid being seen from the hospital. Elise was at the piano playing more classical music. She threw a pair of worn-out panties at me.

"Get busy dusting. We don't have a lot of time," she said. "And mop up your footprints. You tracked in snow."

We whizzed through the cleaning, and then she started me on keyboard exercises.

"I found this in a piano bench at the hospital," Elise said and handed me a book with a red cover. It was John Thompson's *Modern Course for the Piano. For Grades One, Two and Three.* I expected something more advanced and showed my disappointment.

"This is the best I could do," she said, "but give it a try. If you have any talent, you'll breeze right through it and then start a harder book. Remember, you already know how to type."

That remark made me want to show her. "What was that you were playing when I came in?"

"I was just warming up," she said. "It's called "Für Elise," and it was composed by Beethoven. Every parent wants their kid to play it because they think it's classical."

"Well, if it was composed by Beethoven, isn't it?" I asked.

"It's the simplest thing he ever wrote, and he was so unimpressed that he never had it published. He probably rolls over in his grave every time it's played."

"Is it hard?" I asked.

"Not really," she said, "Kids usually learn it around age twelve. After their recital most of them stop taking piano lessons. It's all a big waste."

"Will you teach me to play 'Für Elise'?" I asked.

She turned and stared at me with the hardest look I'd ever seen.

"The answer is 'no'," she said. "The only good thing about being in this place is not hearing 'Für Elise' played badly for the next six months. I'll teach you how to play the piano, but I will *not* teach you that. Frankly, I'm sick of it."

"If you don't like it, why did you choose that for your name?"

She thought for a moment. "Because I want it to be a constant reminder of a time in my life I don't ever intend to repeat. After I leave here, I'll have nothing to do with babies, kids, or piano lessons. Elise will be gone, and I'll never let a man touch me ever again."

I tried not to take that personally. I probably wasn't a man in her eyes anyway even though my voice had changed. *Does she really hate men?* I wondered but didn't ask. First of all, it was none of my business and second, she might change her mind about teaching me.

"I'd prefer you call me Ellie," she said. "That's what the girls do. They all took piano lessons and can't stand the name Elise either.

I did ask one question. "What about the B.? What's it stand for?"

"Beethoven," she said. "If I hadn't had him I couldn't have gotten through the last four years. He wrote such beautiful music that speaks to my soul. That may sound corny to you, but it's true, and it makes me mad some people think the only thing he wrote was 'Für Elise.'"

I wanted to know more but remembered the words of Captain Berthe Karlsson. "Don't get involved with a resident and her problems," she said. "It could break your heart."

Ellie looked at my new watch. "It's after four," she said. "I've gotta go. See you tomorrow."

I grabbed my skates and hockey stick and hustled over to the vacant lot to join the guys. They would be ticked off because I was late.

"Get your ass in gear, Rene," Eddie shouted. "We're ready, and we need you."

They went ahead and picked sides without me because no one wanted to be goalie. Someday I might be chosen to skate but right then was stuck in place.

"Where the hell've you been?" Leo shouted. "It's damned near dark. Let's go."

I didn't dare tell them I'd had my very first piano lesson because most of them had bailed out of lessons by age twelve. They'd convinced their parents there was a greater future in professional hockey than being some piano-playing fairy. All the guys wanted to be like Maurice Richard of the Toronto Maple Leafs. Of course, no one called him Maurice. His nickname was "the Rocket." I heard the guys as they raced toward me with the puck.

"Here comes the Rocket," they'd shout. "He stops, he spins, he flips the puck and he scores."

If I were lucky, I'd feel this solid piece of frozen rubber hit my baseball mitt, and it would sting. If I was unlucky and missed it, the puck would hit somewhere between my belt and my chin and it wouldn't just sting, it would really hurt. When I caught it, I'd skate out holding the puck high over my head but my moment of glory would be short.

"Get the hell back there," everybody would shout. "It's gettin' dark."

They had a point. Even though there was a streetlight, it was hard to see a black puck after dark, and trying to catch one was almost impossible. That's how I got a lot of body bruises. No matter, it was a fun game, and I really enjoyed being with the guys, but my mind wasn't with them that day. Inside my gloves, my frozen fingers were practicing the first notes of "Fuzzy Kittens."

~23~

I PASSED A CAB SITTING AT THE SIDE ENTRANCE of the hospital on my way to breakfast. It must've been someone checking in because there had been no recent births and no one was ready to leave. That would change about the end of February when the prom babies began delivery. There was a suitcase in the hallway outside the counseling office, but instead of being cheap cardboard, it was larger, well built and looked as if it had been on more than one trip. Strangely, there was no one in the office. No mother, no crying daughter, and no admissions officer. In the dining room I learned why.

"Rene, you're just in time," Major Ellen said. Captain Karlsson's mother is ill, and she has to go to Milwaukee. Would you please help with her bag?"

Captain Berthe must've been worried because she talked all the way down the hallway to the cab. I learned she was raised in Milwaukee and that her whole family was Salvation Army except her father. She was the only one who was an officer and the only one unmarried.

"Thank you for your help, Rene," she said. "I'll see you in a couple of days."

She told the driver, "Milwaukee Road Depot in Minneapolis, please."

It was hard to think that Captain Berthe Karlsson cared about anyone. She was always ultra serious and insistent on following the rules that I thought she was raised in an orphanage. I said that to Mom and she set me straight.

"Everyone has a story, Rene, and so does she."

They got to know each other while working on progress charts. Captain Karlsson made no bones about not liking her transfer to Booth Memorial almost two years before.

"She had absolutely no interest in pregnant young girls and no sympathy for their situation," Mom said. "She was told this assignment would give her experience as a supervisor. It was a perfect career move, but she had to agree to stay single."

"Did she ever want to be married?" I asked.

"She told me she was engaged at one time," Mom said. "It was to another Salvation Army officer, and they were to be married in January, 1942. Then the Japanese attacked Pearl Harbor. He was too old for the draft and volunteered for wartime duty with the Corps.

"What would a volunteer do?" I asked.

"The Salvation Army does lots of things except fight," she said. "They go in right after the troops and help them."

"How could they help if they don't fight?" I asked.

Mom reminded me of a letter from Dad when he was hospitalized during the Battle of the Bulge. He told how the Red Cross came through the field hospital offering to sell cigarettes, coffee, and donuts to the patients. The Salvation Army did the same thing only they didn't sell them; they gave theirs away and one didn't have to listen to a sermon either. They would also write letters for wounded soldiers. Dad said he would never forget that kindness.

"What about Captain Karlsson's boyfriend?" I asked.

"He was behind the lines," Mom said, "and caught a flu that turned into pneumonia. He died on a ship to the U.S. He had no family, so his things were sent to her. You can't tell, but she wears a cross on a chain under her uniform. It was his."

"Has she tried to find someone else?" I asked.

"It's not that easy to replace someone you loved enough to marry," she said. "It depressed her so much she doesn't want to take a chance again."

It helped me understand why Captain Karlsson was always negative, but in her absence things could relax around here for a few days. At least, I wouldn't have to worry about her finding out about the piano lessons.

The breakfast talk was about how to share Captain Karlsson's duties. No one liked admittance, but Brigadier Thomas volunteered. Captain Karlsson's story brought up a question on my mind ever since we got here. Today I decided to find out.

"Why is everyone who works here not married?" I asked. "Aren't you allowed?"

"Rene," Mom gasped. "It's none of your business. You apologize right now."

"No, it's a fair question," Major Ellen said. "He deserves an answer."

Now I wished I'd kept my mouth shut because I was going to get it when we got home.

"What we call 'Women's Social' was formed decades ago to help young women get through their pregnancy," she said. "Hardly the place for a man to be in charge."

"Hardly the place for a married woman either," said Brigadier Thomas. "Babies don't know they're not supposed to come at night or on weekends. What does that do to a family's life? Can't be two places at once."

"There are some benefits in this division for single women who're making the Army a career," Major Ellen said, "although they are rather small."

Captain Trudy jumped on that.

"Where else but in a women's division could you make rank?" she said. "I know the war is over and we're in 1950, but it's still a man's world. Try and get a woman promoted who works at headquarters today."

"That's why I joined Women's Social when my husband was killed," old Colonel Thomas said. She startled all of us because we thought she was asleep.

"If I had stayed at a regional office, I'd still be a lieutenant today," she said. "It's those damn men."

"Mother, please don't swear in front of the boy," Brigadier Thomas said. "He'll be one himself someday, and you're giving him ideas."

Suddenly I learned more than I wanted to know and, because I was the only male, I felt like a target for some pent-up frustration.

There was a soft but insistent knock on the door. Jonna stuck her head in.

"Mrs. Dardenne, come quick," she said. "Corrine is hemorrhaging."

Mom jumped up and gave instructions to Lieutenant Margit.

"Call Dr. Hickman and tell him we have a possible long-term miscarriage," she said, "and let the hospital know we'll need an ambulance."

Poor Corrine I thought. First her boyfriend was killed and now she might lose her baby. What was God thinking?

As I headed for the streetcar, I walked through the entryway. It was filled with girls, some of them really emotional. I guessed they were afraid that something like this could happen to them. Mom told me most of the residents had never seen blood except during their periods and that didn't count.

"They really aren't prepared for any of this," Mom said. "Their mothers never told them what to expect when they grew up, and that's how they ended up here. My mother told me that babies came from under cabbage leaves, and I believed it until I was sixteen. I was embarrassed enough when someone told me how it really happened that I said, 'That'll never happen to a child of mine.'"

That explained a lot. Whenever I asked about babies, Mom described the process with great clinical detail but left out anything about feelings. I learned a lot about where they came from but very little about how they got there. Perhaps she thought by telling me the residents' stories, I could somehow piece things together. If so, it hasn't worked. There always seemed to be something missing and usually it was anything about the guy.

* * *

MOM HADN'T RETURNED FROM UNIVERSITY HOSPITAL by the time I got home from school. It reminded me of what happened to Mae and her twins, so it wasn't a good sign. Ellie played another one of those beautiful classical pieces she knew by heart, but this one was slow, drawn out and sad.

"What have you heard about Corrine?" I asked.

"Nothing yet," she said. "They never tell us anything over there except when to get up and when to eat and when to go to bed. I'm sick of it already."

For the first time, she wore one of those frumpy smocks. She didn't have much choice because she'd outgrown her street clothes. Her stomach was growing bigger, and so were her tits. When she'd lean over I'd sneak a peek.

"How do you like my new outfit?" she said. "It's the very latest, and I just couldn't resist it."

Not wanting to get caught in her sarcasm trap, I said something like, "You'll just be one of the girls now." She made a face at my remark, but it was the best I could do.

We did the dusting routine and then sat at the piano. When we were side by side, I couldn't help but notice how soft she was and how she always smelled clean, even without perfume. Even the ugly smock didn't hide her features. We made a plan of what to do if Mom came home unexpectedly. She gave me a lesson assignment at the piano and then stood by the front window looking for an ambulance or Doctor Hickman's Oldsmobile. I was doing fairly well on the Thompson book and was up to third grade level, but it was getting tougher. Ellie made me play the same song over and over.

"Because you're a beginner, you're stiff," she said. "When you learn to relax, you'll find even this simple stuff has passion in it."

161

I tried hard to follow the notes but would occasionally look down at the keys.

"Don't look at the keyboard. Look at the notes. You're not in typing class now."

"Just play it once for me," I said. "Then I'll get it."

"I'm not here to entertain you," she said, raising her voice. "Play it again, this time try a little feeling."

It was hard to overlook her smartass remarks even though it was for my own good I told myself. During the lesson I'd sneak looks at the guys passing by the front window with skates and hockey sticks over their shoulders. No wonder they gave up piano at thirteen. This was hard work and not much fun.

"What are you staring at?" Elise demanded. "Keep your eyes on the notes. You'll never learn to play looking out the window."

"Forty -Seven Olds just went by," I said. "Mom's home. You've gotta go."

Ellie went out the front as Mom came in the back door. I picked up my skates and hockey stick and went to the kitchen. Mom made coffee while Doctor Hickman, who looked whipped, sat at the kitchen table. It was almost a repeat of the Mae situation.

"How's Corrine?" I asked.

"She'll be okay," Doctor Hickman said, "but trauma to the fetus resulted in hemorrhaging. We went into surgery, but there was no way to save it."

"How does that happen?" I asked.

"Usually in a car accident or a fall," Mom said. "The fetus was so severely damaged, it couldn't survive. Corrine's lucky because she was in her sixth month. Sometimes it takes the mother as well."

"But she's okay?" I asked.

"Corrine's damage will be more emotional than physical," said Doctor Hickman. "That'll take longer to heal."

"We talked with her after the operation," Mom said.

Her voice was soft, like she had some bad news.

"Corrine induced her own trauma," she said. "The death of her boyfriend was upsetting enough, but then she had to attend his funeral. Yesterday she went to the top of the third floor stairs and threw herself down."

"Was she trying to kill herself?" I asked.

"I don't think she really knew or cared," Mom said. "She told us her whole world caved in. Her boyfriend was dead, and she was having his baby. Her choice was to keep it, and she knew she couldn't, or give it away and she knew she shouldn't. It was their baby, and she didn't want anyone else to have it. She did the only thing that made sense to her. It didn't matter to her if she died in the process."

"Do her parents know?" I asked.

"No, not yet," Mom said. "Her mother did tell me she was depressed and asked me to keep an eye on her. I've been watching Corrine closely since she came back."

I'd been holding my skates and hockey stick all this time, ready to go out and play. Now a hockey game seemed really unimportant.

"Jo, I promised you a dinner," Doctor Hickman said. "How soon can you be ready? Rene, you're welcome to come with us."

"No thanks, Doctor," I said. "I really don't have an appetite any more."

When they left it dawned on me that Mom must be going out on a date. They called it a dinner, but wasn't that the same as a date? It seemed like a good idea to pay closer attention to Doctor Hickman from now on. In the living room I rummaged through the music in the piano bench. It was still there, *Sixty Progressive Piano Pieces You Like to Play,* and on page ninety was what I was looking for . . . a piece composed by Ludwig Van Beethoven. It was titled, "Für Elise."

~24~

FOR THE PAST WEEK, EVERYTHING had been going great. I was finally allowed to skate in a hockey game because my buddy Eddie convinced the guys if I wasn't given a chance, I might stop showing up. Although I didn't score, it was great to be out there chasing the puck instead of dodging it. At the end of the game, the jury was still out on me.

Ellie was pleased with my piano progress and moved me into a more advanced book. The way she taught had changed a bit. She spent more time behind me with her stomach against my back. When I made a mistake she slapped my fingers or hit them with a pencil. It reminded me of the way nuns sneaked up in class and slapped my hands with a ruler. I could never figure out how they moved silently with those flowing robes and a big, clunky cross that was tied to their waists. I admit I was never hit for something I didn't do, but it still was spooky.

Sometimes Ellie said things that had nothing to do with piano.

"Corrine came back this morning," she said. "She doesn't have a big stomach anymore, but she looked so sad. Frankly, I think she's lucky."

I didn't know if Ellie was aware that Corrine fell on purpose, and I kept my mouth shut. Then she threw out another line for me to nibble on.

"Some of the other girls are thinking about doing the same thing," she said, "but they're afraid of all the blood. They realize she could have died, so it's not worth the chance."

I didn't say anything.

"Her parents are coming tomorrow to take her home, wherever that is. We'll certainly never know."

I knew her parents' car carried Iowa plates, but I still kept my lips closed.

"What time is it?" she asked.

I held up my new watch so the dial would catch the light.

"Four thirty three," I said with great authority.

"I've gotta go. Practice on that piece till you get it right."

When she left, I pulled out my copy of *Sixty Progressive Piano Pieces You Like to Play* and turned to page ninety. As I played the first notes of "Für Elise," a thought flashed across my mind. Mom never did say anything about her dinner with Dr. Hickman. Maybe that was because it was more like a business meeting?

Talk around the dinner table that night was that the kitchen staff, which knew Delores from her previous pregnancy, told the residents her nickname. It didn't take long for everyone to begin calling her Dodo, or in worst cases, Dumdum. It didn't matter to Delores because she was used to Dodo and it probably made her feel at home.

After dinner Mom and I went home to listen to the radio. Friday nights were great starting with *My Favorite Husband* with Lucille Ball, followed by *The Jimmy Durante Show* and then *The Life of Riley*. We had just gotten into *Jimmy Durante* when the phone rang.

"It's Eudora," Mom said. "Something terrible has happened, and they want me at the hospital right now. Come with me in case they need help."

Girls were bunched around the stairs leading to the basement. Some were hugging each other, and most were crying.

"She's in the laundry," Cassie said. "They're downstairs with her now. She might be dead."

Mom hurried down the stairs while I asked Cassie what happened.

"It's Corrine's last night, and we were just sitting around talking with her," she said. "She was upset about the miscarriage, depressed about her boyfriend and sad to leave because of the friends she'd made. There were tears in her eyes when she got the key to the lockup and went downstairs to get her suitcase."

"She was gone a long time," said June A. "Dodo kept pestering us to read her a story so we sent her to the basement to find Corrine."

"A little bit later she came running up the stairs, all out of breath," Joanne B. said. "Her eyes were a big as saucers. She pointed down the stairs and said something like, 'Corrine hurt. Help Corrine.'"

"Since Corrine was just out of surgery, we thought something went wrong," Eudora said. "We got Lieutenant Margit and followed Dodo back to the basement. She led us down the hallway and into the sheet folding room. It was all dark and spooky. Dodo pointed and way over in the corner there was a shape hanging from a water pipe. It was Corrine."

Eudora started to cry.

"Lieutenant Margit and I tried to untie her but couldn't reach her neck," she said. "I bumped into something and stood on that. It was a suitcase."

By now Eudora was sobbing.

"Lieutenant Margit sent me to alert Major Ellen and get Lieutenant Corliss to come help," she said. "Major Ellen called the ambulance and I called your mother."

Still in her bathrobe, Major Ellen came out of her office and sent me to have Max unlock the basement door for the ambulance crew. When I reached the bottom of the stairs, I looked over and saw Lieutenant Corliss kneeling over Corrine and pumping her chest. Mom had her mouth down to Corrine's ear shouting, "Hang on, Corrine. They're coming. Don't give up now."

I ran to Max's room and knocked. No answer, so I banged on it hard this time. It barely opened, and I saw Max's eyes staring at me. They looked really wild, like he was afraid of something.

"Max, unlock the basement door for the ambulance," I shouted. "One of the girls hung herself."

He came charging out of his room pulling up his pants. He'd been asleep and my banging on the door woke him up. He unlocked the door and slid open the deadbolt. The ambulance pulled up, and the crew came running with a stretcher.

An ambulance technician relieved Lieutenant Corliss, who was exhausted from her effort to push life back into Corrine. Another put an oxygen mask over Corrine's face, and they lifted her onto the stretcher. As they wheeled her by, her face was kind of blue and her arms limp. I remembered when Mae went out on a stretcher only, this time, there was no smile. Mom got in the ambulance alongside Corrine, and they were gone into the night.

We were all left together in the basement. Major Ellen asked for Delores to come downstairs and, very gently, asked her what happened. Poor little Dodo didn't know what to say because she didn't understand the importance of what she'd seen. In her four-year-old mind, it might have been a game.

"Delores, please tell me what you saw in the basement?" Major Ellen asked.

In her childish way, Delores described searching the basement for Corrine. She was afraid of the dark but saw something in the corner. She moved closer and saw Corrine's body hanging from the water pipe.

"I say, 'Corrine, Corrine'. It's Dodo. She don't talk to me."

"Did you see or hear anything else?" Major Ellen asked.

"Yes, I hear something," she said. "Man yelling. He goes, 'Uuhh, Uuhh, No, No.'"

She made a noise like someone in pain or being tortured.

"Scared me," she said. "I runned upstairs."

"Tell me," Major Ellen said, "Where did this noise come from?"

Dodo looked around the basement, stopping at the southwest corner.

"Over there," she said and pointed. Everyone turned to follow her finger. It was pointed directly at the opened door to Max's room. There was a long, uncomfortable silence. Captain McTavish, who had been

167

standing in the shadows, came up to Major Ellen and whispered, "Major, I think you'd better call the police."

* * *

IT WAS WELL AFTER MIDNIGHT when Doctor Hickman brought Mom home. He had been on duty at the hospital when the emergency call came in from Booth Memorial. Expecting to deliver a baby, he was surprised when Corrine was wheeled into the Emergency Room instead. One look told him that it was too late to save her.

"It was obvious to me that she died of strangulation," he said. "There may have been a faint pulse when you found her," he said to Mom," but there was no way she could have survived. What did she jump from?"

"A table where they fold sheets," I said. "She climbed on her suit-case to get up there."

"There are police cars at the hospital," Mom said. "What's going on?"

I told her about how Dodo heard something that scared her and how she pointed to Max's door. The police came and talked with all of us who were in the basement. When they got the call that Corrine was dead, it was decided to take Max in for further questioning.

"The officer in charge told us, 'Well, he's a foreigner, and we can't be sure he'll be here tomorrow,'" I said, "so they put him in the back seat and took him to the station."

"Max? They took Max?" Mom almost screamed. "He wouldn't hurt a fly. Why did they take him?"

"They wanted to talk with him some more," I said. "Max looked really scared and was almost crying."

All this time, Doctor Hickman sat at the kitchen table and just shook his head.

"I wish I hadn't told her," he said quietly. "Maybe it was too soon."

"Tell who what?" Mom asked.

"After the surgery, Corrine asked me what I'd done and I told her there was no way to repair the damage. I had to perform a hysterectomy.

168

'That means I'll never have babies again?' she asked, and I said, 'Yes.' She told me she wanted the truth, but maybe I should have waited."

"It's not your fault, Garson," Mom said. "You did what you felt was right."

I was startled to hear her call him by his first name. I'd never thought about doctors having first names. Same with priests. What kind of a name was Garson?

The phone rang early Saturday morning. Mom was already up and dressed for work. She listened carefully and took some notes.

"I'm wanted at the downtown police station right away," she said. "They started to question Max, and he requested a translator. Since I'm the only one he knows who speaks Lithuanian, he asked for me. Lieutenant Margit will drive me."

Even though I didn't have much of an appetite, I went to breakfast. All the talk around the table was about last night. Major Ellen had the unhappy duty of calling Corrine's parents to tell them of her death. I hadn't seen her look that sad since the suicide of the girl in the blue coat. Since Major Ellen didn't know when Max would be released, she asked me to be available to do small handyman things. I didn't even think of piano practice and hockey before I said, "Yes" and was proud of that.

"And be available today," she said. "A detective is coming to investigate and might want to speak with you."

On my way out, the anteroom and hallways were quiet—very unusual for a Saturday. The rest of the day I practiced lessons on the piano and even squeezed in some time for "Für Elise," but my heart wasn't really in it. Corrine's blue face and Doctor Hickman's fear that he had triggered her suicide was just too much to forget. To have to grow up didn't look very attractive that day.

After lunch, I saw a black, 1947 Plymouth parked at the side door of the hospital. Even unmarked anyone could spot it as a police car a mile away. Must be the whip antenna. I never got a call.

It was just after five o'clock when Mom came in the back door. She'd taken the streetcar home from downtown and had that glazed look, like she'd had a really hard day. When she got to the police station, she said, they took her in to meet with Max.

"He was so happy to see me," she said, "even though he doesn't know me all that well. His English is pretty good, but when the police began to question him, I repeated the questions in Lithuanian."

"Did you do okay?" I asked.

"At first he was kind of amused," she said. "I learned Lithuanian from Grandpa and Baba, who immigrated in nineteen hundred, and to him it was like I was speaking an antique language. Like saying 'Thee' and 'Thou.' I haven't spoken more than a couple of sentences in Lithuanian in the past five years so my brain is really tired."

"What about Max?" I asked.

"They asked him a lot of questions about why he was screaming that night," she said. "This was all news to me because I left before Delores pointed to his room."

Mom said the police were very patient as Max told the story about his days in a Nazi death camp for Jews when he and two other prisoners escaped and spent months avoiding the Germans. He told them bloodhounds were on their trail, and they hid out during the day and traveled by night trying to reach the Allied lines. The two other men were caught and executed while Max watched from a hideout. When he finally reached the Allies, he was sent to a Displaced Persons camp where he learned that the Nazis had exterminated his family. With nowhere to go, he was sponsored by family friends in Milwaukee and came to the U.S. They got him this job.

"But what about the moaning in the basement?" I asked.

"Max says that ever since, he's had nightmares about being captured and executed," Mom said. "He's afraid to go to sleep because of the dreams, and when he wakes up he is usually in a sweat."

"Mom, I didn't tell the police," I said, "but when Max came to the door, his eyes looked almost wild, like he was really scared. I didn't want to get him in more trouble."

"It looks like a terrible coincidence," Mom said. "Max must have been having a nightmare just when Delores found Corrine."

"Last night Captain McTavish told the police that some of the girls have complained at the way he looks at them," I said. "They wrote it down."

"Max told me that he feels so badly for the girls," Mom said. "They're the same age his daughter would have been if she hadn't been gassed. I'm sure he looks at them and compares. They don't understand that, but Captain McTavish should."

Mom said Max thanked her over and over again for being there for him. The police were keeping him in custody until the results of the autopsy told them if Corrine committed suicide or was murdered.

"Unfortunately, Dodo was no help to Max," Mom said. "It's all so tragic."

* * *

COMPARED TO THE ELEVEN O'CLOCK MASS, the one at 7:00 a.m. was almost deserted—just a few nuns, some people going to work, mothers with their small kids and me. I woke up early because I couldn't get that look of fear on Max's face out of my mind, especially after Mom told me what he'd been through in the war. Church seemed the only place to pray for Corrine's soul and for Max's release from jail, even though he was a Jew. I was taught that Jews were responsible for the crucifixion of Jesus, but I never knew one. Max was a real person to me, a friendly, kind man who probably wouldn't have harmed Jesus if he had been there. I also felt sure he hadn't hung Corrine, but it was only a gut feeling with no real proof.

I was just as sure about my prayers for Corrine. As I understood it, no one had the right to take a life, even their own. That brought up the question of her unborn baby and whether a fetus was a living soul before it was born. I gave it a try but it was a problem I couldn't solve in just one Mass. I went ahead and prayed for her anyway but very carefully.

As I came out of church, I still felt good even though I had prayed for a Protestant and a Jew, one who might have taken her own life and the other who might have murdered her. This was certainly nothing I wanted to discuss with Father McGowan.

At the hospital, the dining room was filled with officers having breakfast before going to their church. All the talk was about Corrine and poor Max. After the service they planned to visit him in jail as a show of support.

"The detective who was here yesterday might come back later today," Major Ellen said to me. "Captain McTavish and Lieutenant Corliss will be on duty but would you be available in case he needs something?"

I felt flattered she thought me important enough to be called on but really who else was there to ask?

"We plan to be back by then," she said. "Just a precaution."

Mom was either still in bed or on her way to Mass, while I stayed in the hospital anteroom—just in case. The girls were quieter than usual, but they still hung around the phone waiting for a call that never came. Jonna was waiting for her boyfriend to call. If someone stayed in the phone booth too long, she glared at them. Most weren't strong enough to take a Jonna glare for very long.

After lunch, the office phone rang and Captain McTavish answered.

"The detective is on his way, Rene," she said. "He didn't say what he wanted so just be available. The others will be back soon."

I didn't know what a detective was supposed to look like, but the guy who walked in didn't fit my image at all. I'd listened to all the crime shows on radio and knew what to expect. He wasn't it.

Detective Olafson was short but still taller than I was. Instead of a uniform, he wore civilian clothes: a black, rumpled suit, a wrinkled white shirt, and a green striped tie. Strangely, his shoes were highly polished, like he was ready for a military inspection.

"I'd like to see the crime scene again," he said to Captain McTavish.

It sounded real official. "Crime scene." Just like on radio. I showed him the way to the laundry room. Corrine's suitcase was still on the floor because we were told not to touch or move anything.

"Do you think Max did it?" I asked, even though he probably wouldn't tell me if he knew.

"Can't tell," he said. "No sign of a struggle. No scratch marks on him or bruises on her. Funny thing. She smelled like stale cigarettes, but we were told she didn't smoke."

He stood on her suitcase like he was testing to see if it could hold his weight.

"Usually women leave a note," he said, "but nobody found one." Then he looked at me with accusing eyes. "Did you?"

Suddenly I felt guilty even though I wasn't. Quickly I shook my head, "No."

He lifted the suitcase by the edges instead of the handle and put it on the table. *Doesn't want to smudge any fingerprints*, I thought. He opened the suitcase slowly and used his fingertips to pick up something. It was a note. He read it slowly, put it up to his nose and thought for a moment. It was written in the Palmer Method that was popular in Midwest schools.

"I remember, there's a room where the girls go to smoke," Detective Olafson said. "Where is it?"

He was talking about "the Den," just down the hall. We walked in and he took a deep breath.

"That's the smell," he said. "Her body smelled like this room."

He saw a writing tablet on the table, put it up to his nose and then laid it next to the note from the suitcase. "Same paper, same smell," he said. "She could have written it here and went next door to hang herself." I leaned over his shoulder and read the note.

Dear Mom & Dad,

I'm so sorry to leave you without saying goodbye but I don't see a future for me on earth. I don't want to live without Rick and didn't want anyone to have our baby. I was told I'd never have children again so I don't see any use in going on. If only I had died in the fall as well. Please don't blame anyone here for what I'm going to do. They've treated me well, and I'm sorry to leave. Remember I love you both and always will. It just didn't work out the way we planned. Please forgive me.

Joanne (Corrine) xoxo

"Who is she? Joanne or Corrine?" he asked.

"Joanne is her real name," I said. "All the girls who live here have other names."

"And you live here," he said. It wasn't exactly a question but more like a questioning statement.

Just then Major Ellen and some other officers came down stairs. I asked them how Max was doing.

"Oh, that poor man," Major Ellen said. "He's frightened that he'll be accused of murder. We joined hands and prayed for him and he was a lot calmer when we left."

"Well, he doesn't have to worry anymore," Detective Olafson said, holding up the paper. "We found a note in her handwriting that lets him off the hook," he said. "When I get back to the station I'll start the paperwork. He should be released soon."

The screams and "thank yous" of the grateful officers melded into the background as I processed what had taken place. I had just witnessed a real, live detective solve a case at the scene of the crime and an innocent man was saved. Bulldog Drummond couldn't have done it any better on the radio.

~25~

FOR THE SECOND TIME IN THREE WEEKS, I was at a Protestant memorial service to, as Major Ellen phrased it, "celebrate the life of one of our sisters who has been called home to be with the Lord." I'd only been to a few Catholic funeral masses but never heard death described that way. Maybe it was because our services were in Latin. There was no mention of purgatory or the possibility Corrine might be sent to hell for taking her own life and that of her baby. Major Ellen made it sound like she had a straight shot to God but it was possible she was going easy on her not to upset the other residents. Corrine had been a popular girl, and for many of them it was like they'd lost a sister. Max came in and sat in the back row. He usually didn't attend these services, but of course this one had meaning for him.

After his ordeal, Max had asked for a few days off to visit his friends in Milwaukee. He was concerned they'd discontinue their sponsorship if they knew about jail, and he wanted to set things straight. Major Ellen agreed he needed some time away because he'd worked seven days a week for three years, taking time off only to go to synagogue on Saturdays. He'd more than earned it.

"Rene will cover for you," Major Ellen said, this time without even asking. She probably knew I wanted some adult responsibility to go along with my new voice. When I promised to help with household chores, I didn't realize the amount of work involved. On Sunday I was constantly being paged to replace light bulbs and to check radiators that weren't giving heat. The routine never varied. I started at the bottom of the stairs and yelled, "Man on second" or "Man on third" as I climbed higher. Each time a resident solemnly led me to the job to be done. On the way, invariably, a resident ran out of a room in her panties and brassiere, looked at me, squealed and ran back. Another came out of the bathroom wrapped in a towel and ducked back in, screaming. One even dropped her towel and gave me a look at her buns. The first couple of times, I enjoyed the household problems but it didn't take too many trips to realize that the light bulbs weren't burned out, only unscrewed. Same with the cold radiators. The valves had been shut off. I was about to mention it to Lieutenant Margit when another light bulb call came in.

"We seem to be having a rash of problems with light bulbs today," she said. "I'm afraid we're going to run out." I kept my mouth shut.

When I reached the second floor, a group of girls led me to the problem. This time the bulb wasn't just loose, it was missing. I reached in my pocket, fixed the problem and headed toward the stairs.

"Rene, we've got a game that needs four to play," Sarah B. said. "It'll just take a minute."

"I'm not supposed to stay up here," I said.

"Oh, come on," Cassie said. "It's so boring on Sundays. This'll be fun."

I looked up and down the halls and said, "Okay but just for a minute."

We all got on our knees in a circle.

"We're going to play Horserace," Shirley T. said. "I'm the first horse, and my name's What's Happening. Sarah, you be Something Stinky."

"My name is Hoof Hearted," Cassie said. "Rene, your name is Hi Diddit."

"Now, everybody bend down and beat your hands on the floor like hoof beats," Shirley said. "The object of the game is to pass the horse in front of you."

When they all bent over none of them wore brassieres. Their tits and nipples were plainly visible and jiggled when they beat their hands on the floor. I'd never seen a girl's nipples before, and now I was seeing six.

"Okay, post time," Cassie shouted.

Round and round we went. Shirley said, "What's Happening," followed by Sarah's, "Something Stinky." Cassie yelled, "Hoof Hearted," and I said, "Hi Diddit." The faster we went the more their tits jiggled and I couldn't take my eyes off them. Suddenly I realized they had set a trap. It was about the time they all fell over laughing. My face turned several shades of red and that made them laugh all the more. I stood up with what dignity I could manage and headed toward the stairs.

"Oh, come on, Rene," they said, still laughing. "Be a sport."

"Next time you want something screwed in," I said, over my shoulder, "you know where you can stick it."

"Oh, you naughty boy," Cassie said. "Just wait till we tell your mother."

I wished I had come up with a snappier remark, but it was the best I could do on short notice. On the way downstairs, I wondered if I had to tell Father McGowan about those jiggling nipples and tits.

* * *

"I HEAR YOU'RE QUITE the horse racer," Ellie said, keeping time with her pencil. "And you have a problem with natural gas." Her stomach started to shake, and she broke out in a big laugh.

"Rene, you've got a lot to learn about women," she said. "Those three girls would eat your lunch if you let them."

I lost my concentration and hit a couple of wrong keys.

"Come on, pay attention to the notes," she said, as she slapped my hand. "You're doing better, but you've got to practice."

Who had time for practice? Between going to school, helping at the hospital, playing hockey and taking piano lessons, there wasn't even time for homework, and it was beginning to show. Mom understood about being in a new school during the first semester, but now I'd run out of excuses.

"I don't have time on my hands like you," I said. "I go to school everyday."

"Well, so do I," Elise said. "I go to classes in the hospital, and by the time I have this baby I should have my high school equivalent certificate. I really don't care about either one."

"Who's your teacher?" I asked.

"It's a girl from the university who's working on her Masters, but I'm learning the most from Eudora. She really knows about books."

That reminded me I'd never spoken to Eudora about my book assignment. Another thing I had fallen behind in.

"Oh, guess who's back," she said. "I saw Captain Berthe Karlsson in the hallway today. She came up and said how glad she was to see me again. What a surprise. Usually she just looks at me and frowns."

Well, it's back on alert I thought. I'd never seen Captain Karlsson do anything but frown, usually at something I'd done. Ellie must be mistaken.

"Play it again and do it right this time," she said. "I've gotta leave in a few minutes." It was hard to believe I'd volunteered for this.

Captain Karlsson was at dinner that evening and told us about her mother's painful death. I didn't know much about cancer, but it seemed everyone at the table had a personal story to tell. Whatever it was, it didn't sound good.

"I'm truly glad to be back," she said. "I have a better understanding of what God has in mind for me now." Everyone around the table nodded and smiled.

That kind of talk always made me uncomfortable, but I guess that's how nuns and priests speak to each other as well. There was never anything about the weather or what President Truman was doing or things like that—just talk about God. I'd never given a thought to what God had in mind for me. So far, I just did what I was told.

That evening Mom and I were sitting in the kitchen listening to *Edgar Bergen and Charlie McCarthy*, another favorite radio show. She ironed her nurse's caps, and I polished her shoes. I knew no babies had been delivered because there was no blood to remove. These were the days I liked.

"Captain Karlsson seems different," I said, without mentioning Ellie's observation. "She even smiled, gave me a kiss and asked me to call her Captain Bertie. What's going on?"

Mom kept ironing her cap while she tried to come up with the right answer. Even with my voice change, pubic hair growing and all, I think Mom was still uncomfortable telling me the truth about life. I hadn't told her about the pubic hair so it wasn't all her fault.

"What I'm going to say is for your ears and your ears only," she said. "I'm telling you because it'll give you a better understanding of why she's changed."

Her tone was more serious than ever. Maybe she had noticed I'd changed too.

"Captain Berthe and I are friends, and she spoke with me for a long time. She told me something she learned after her mother's death."

I almost wished I hadn't brought it up because Mom's stories could go on well into the next radio program.

"After the funeral she was driving home with her aunt who said, 'Now that your Mother's gone, there's something you should know. When she was a young girl she had to go to a place like where you work.'"

That her mother had a baby out of wedlock was a shock to Captain Berthe, but how it happened was even worse. While her mother's mother was away, her alcoholic father ordered her to fix supper for him and his brother. After a long evening of heavy drinking, they both raped her.

"Rene, you understand what rape is, don't you?" Mom asked. "It's when a man forces himself on a woman. She can get pregnant from it."

Wait a minute. The rape part I understood, but her father and uncle doing it to her! How could that happen? Weren't there laws against that?

"The baby was born deformed and with mental problems. They placed her in a state home where she died when she was sixteen."

"Is that what happened to Dodo?" I asked.

"It's hard to say because I don't know Delores's history. In her case, it could be other things."

"What happened to Captain Berthe's grandfather and uncle?" I asked.

"They were arrested and sentenced to prison for life where they finally died. Captain Berthe's mother married, and she had three children. Because of her experience, she joined the Salvation Army and that's how Captain Berthe was raised."

"Why didn't Captain Berthe know about this until now?" I asked.

"The family was so ashamed no one ever talked about it," Mom said. "Her mother always planned to tell her, but she never got the courage."

Mom began to cry over her ironing.

"Captain Berthe told me, 'If only I had known. I could have done much more to ease her pain. There was no way I could blame my mother for what she had been through, and now it's too late.' We were both crying by then," Mom said.

I was starting to swallow hard myself but tried not to show it.

"We agreed that she has been sent to Booth Memorial for a reason, and she understands it only now," Mom said. "Captain Berthe told me, 'I have not been a very nice person to these girls, and I am going to change that starting now.'"

Mom's tears dripped on the cap she was ironing, and I could hear the sizzle from the iron, a sound I had heard before.

"Rene, I know you don't care for Captain Berthe but I'm asking you to give her a chance. 'I understand my purpose now,' she told me. God put me here for me as much for as for them.'"

~26~

A T SUPPER THE NIGHT BEFORE, Major Ellen reminded her staff the next day was Valentine's Day. It was nice of her to mention it, but she had another reason.

"Next to Christmas, Valentine's Day is the worst time for depression among residents," she said. "Few of them, if any, will receive cards from friends or relatives because no one knows where they are. Many times even their own parents don't send a card because they're still angry. Keep an eye out for the signs and just be there for them."

I'm sure it didn't help that the sun rarely shone in February, and it was too cold or icy to walk to the drug store. Even if they could, the girls didn't have money for cards, so their grumpy moods were easy to understand.

"Well, I'm ready for it this year," Captain Trudy said. "Bring it on."

Captain Trudy actually looked forward to this day as a challenge. In her position as creative and spiritual leader, she was responsible for seeing that residents didn't fall into the depression trap. For weeks she had them in the Arts and Crafts room making Valentine hearts with lace and coming up with sayings for them. On my way to breakfast, I saw a large heart pasted on the side door. "GOD LOVES YOU," it said in big letters. Down the hall was another that announced, "GOD LOVES YOU AND YOURS," which I took to be a reminder that they were going to have a baby. At the end of the hall was a bigger heart with the message, "GOD LOVES YOU. LOVE HIM BACK." They reminded me of Burma Shave signs on the highway. I went into the dining room early and put my card on

181

Mom's plate. I couldn't afford a gift, but I bought the biggest card I could find. She loved it, of course.

Valentine's Day was not as big a deal at Murray High as at my last school. The girls did wear a lot of red and white and some had heart pins on their blouses, but otherwise it was business as usual. I'm glad it wasn't special because there was no one to give cards to anyway. Carolyn had spread my undeserved reputation among the girls and hardly any of them would speak to me. Somehow, I was still the envy of some of the guys, also undeserved.

During our cleaning of the nurses' home I sneaked a card onto the piano keys. When Ellie and I sat down for the lesson, it would be there as a surprise.

"Oh, how sweet of you," she said, using a tone of voice I'd never heard from her before. "I've always gotten Valentine's cards from my students, but frankly I didn't expect anything this year. Thank you, Rene."

She gave me a kiss on the cheek. I'd gotten kisses on the cheek before, but this one was different. I didn't know why. It took all my effort to remember Captain Karlsson's caution.

"When you play with hot coals," she said, "sooner or later you're going to get burned. Don't get involved, Rene."

When I got to the hospital for supper, the mail still hadn't been delivered.

"It's one of the busiest days in the year for the post office," Lieutenant Margit said, "except income tax day on March fifteenth. Of course, the weather doesn't help."

There were more girls than usual milling around the administration desk. If they didn't get mail, they were hoping for a phone call. The phone booth was empty. There was a small pile of mail for me, none of it postmarked. Thanks to Captain Trudy, the residents made their own Valentine's cards and exchanged them. Mine were homemade too and all built around a horse racing theme.

"Giddyup, Rene. You're always first with me," was one of them.

Another read, "Roses are red, violets are blue. So you lost at our game. Well Boo Hoo to you."

The last card got right to the point.

"Tits and Nipples, Nipples and Tits. Keep your eyes to yourself or we'll cut you to bits." It was signed, "Love, Cassie D."

I decided not to show any of them to Mom because I'd never shared the horse race story with her. Why ask for trouble?

Jonna opened a card from her "on the road" boyfriend. She no longer announced his location, and the girls snickered that she didn't know where he was. She was in her regular chair staring at the phone, daring it to ring. It hadn't yet.

One of the girls complained that her prom night date hadn't sent a card. If she hadn't gone with him that night, she wouldn't be here now, she complained. Jonna was in a bitchy mood.

"I'm from Carolina hill country, and I've heard that line before," she said. "You want us to believe that the first and only time you did it was on prom night? I think most of you did it on prom night and, after that, it was prom, prom, prom all summer long. We'll see if you all have your babies in March."

It wasn't hard to tell the prom night girls from the others. Since they were in their ninth month, they had the biggest stomachs. The ones closest to delivery began pairing up and went everywhere together: mealtimes, pelvic exams, walks outdoors, even the bathroom. Not knowing what to expect, they didn't want to be alone when it happened.

The doorbell rang and a Western Union messenger came in with a bunch of roses, a box and a big Valentine's card.

"I'm looking for a Josephine Dardenne," he said. "Is that any of you?"

His eyes opened wide as they moved around the room. He had probably never seen that many pregnant girls in one place. Lieutenant

Margit came out from behind the counter. "I'll take them for her," she said.

By now the messenger was staring.

"What the matter?" Cassie asked. "Haven't you ever seen a Salvation Army officer before?" The girls broke out laughing and the messenger, clearly embarrassed, backed away and tripped over the step on his way out. This time they laughed so hard that one girl peed her pants. Everyone thought her water broke.

"He didn't get a tip," Jonna said, "but he'll have one helluva story for the office."

The phone rang, and Jonna was in the booth like a shot even though she had trouble getting the door closed. Those closer to nine months had to stand outside the booth.

The girls called Mom down to open her card and gift. She didn't want the attention but knew the girls lived through her experiences. In fact, they'd already put the dozen roses in a vase on the desk.

"Unaccustomed as I am," Mom said, opening the envelope, "but I could get used to it." She pulled out a satiny card with a big heart in the center. It had a goopy message inside that she read out loud. Everybody said, "Aahh." She left off the "Love, Carl," part because it was personal.

"What's in the package?" somebody shouted.

Mom unwrapped the box carefully, as she always did. Drove me crazy because it took forever. It was a box of Whitman's Sampler chocolates.

"I'd love to share it with you," Mom said, "but chocolate isn't good for your babies now." I didn't know if that was true or not but they all bought it.

The bell rang and the girls filed down the stairs for supper.

"Mrs. Dardenne. Here's another one for you," Lieutenant Margit said.

It was a small envelope but I recognized the handwriting. It was from Doctor Hickman.

Supper was a real treat. Captain Tucker loved to cook for special occasions, and Valentine's Day was a good excuse. On the menu were swedish meatballs, mashed potatoes, red cabbage and those same old boiled green beans with bacon bits. Dessert was ice cream, devil's food cake, and heart-shaped cookies.

I had just put the first bite in my mouth when Mom said, "Rene's learning to play the piano."

I choked on my meatball. How did she know? Did Ellie spill the beans or did I talk in my sleep?

"I know he wanted to surprise me," Mom said, "but I saw the beginner's books on the piano and put two and two together. We can't afford lessons so he's teaching himself."

My face was still in my napkin. *She doesn't know the whole story. Now I'll only have to lie about part of it.*

"I'm so proud of him," she said.

The women around the table oohed and aahed, sharing Mom's pride in my initiative. Captain Trudy even applauded.

"I'm so glad that ugly old piano is finally getting some use after all these years," Major Ellen said. "We were about to give it away, but now that you're using it, it stays."

Still swallowing my meatball, I managed a weak smile and tried to consider the positives. Now I could practice in the evenings but it meant that I would have to live a lie. How much of that must be confessed to Father McGowan I didn't know. My biggest concern was could I learn to play before Ellie delivered?

* * *

THE PROM NIGHT GIRLS were delivering on a regular basis and that meant Mom and I spent a lot of evenings in the kitchen listening to the radio and waiting for the phone to ring. Tonight was *Fibber McGee and Molly*, our favorite, followed by *I Love a Mystery*. Every baby delivery meant shoes for me to clean and caps for Mom to iron. By now I had decided that all dried blood looked the same, even if I know whom it came from. How Mom got blood on her cap puzzled me but I was not going to ask. Birthing must be a messy process.

The first girl I'd met here had a baby boy about a week before. Mom said June A. was staying in the Mother's ward and took care of him herself.

"She's very good in the nursery," Mom said. "She knitted booties, caps, and even a little jacket and spends her time changing his clothes. June really wants to breast feed him. Of course, we can't allow that."

"Why not?" I asked. She said it so matter-of-factly that I felt dumb not to know.

"We don't want the baby to get used to his mother's milk," she said, "because, in a few days, she'll be giving him away. He has to have the same formula."

"Of course," I said, now feeling even dumber.

The next day was Tuesday, and by then I knew better than to use the front door on my way to the streetcar. I could picture June as she sat on the steps, crying her heart out, after her baby had been taken away. I didn't think I'd ever get used to it.

On Wednesday morning, a black '46 Ford sedan was sitting at the side door. It was a farmer's car because it had snow tires and mud almost up to the windows. The driver wore a red plaid hunting cap and was reading a newspaper. As I walked by, he slid the paper up to keep his face hidden, the same thing he had done last September. June and her mother stood in the hallway saying goodbyes. Her makeup was stained, as if she'd been crying. She gave me a kiss on the cheek.

"Good luck, Rene," she said. "Thanks for being my friend."

I mumbled something about being nice to know her and to take care of herself, but Captain Berthe Karlsson's warning was on my mind.

"Believe me, for the sake of the girl, don't get involved."

She didn't mention to watch out for my own feelings. I just said goodbye to someone I would never see again, and that meant something, so I returned her kiss. Her mother just looked away. I felt sorry for June and for what she was going back to. Last September, her father wouldn't even say goodbye, which meant it wasn't going to be a fun ride back to Wisconsin.

I'd just put June's suitcase in the car trunk when Doctor Hickman pulled up. He'd been at Booth on a regular basis for the past month and, as usual, brought an intern. The interns liked it because it was a practical way to get experience in the delivery process. The girls liked it even more and put on fresh makeup and brushed their hair when the interns were around. When he didn't bring an intern, Doctor Hickman usually took Mom to dinner. I told myself they were just professional friends.

The Minnesota winter continued to surprise me. Here it was almost the middle of March and there still was snow on the ground and hard ice on the vacant lot. The natives claimed it was unusual but that sounded like a Chamber of Commerce thing to me. What really got me was that basketball was almost over, and we were still playing hockey. The Minneapolis Lakers had had a great season and would be in the play-offs. They could take the NBA championship but not everyone was impressed. After all, the NBA was only four years old and didn't have the same status as the National Football League.

The guys agreed to let me skate in some games though it meant they'd have to take turns at goalie. I'd learned all sorts of great moves, like skating backward, body checking, high sticking and puck flipping. We practice hard because we got boxed into a game with Johnny Boy and his buddies from across the tracks. It started with an argument in the gym locker room, and the coach suggested we settle it this way. Johnny Boy jumped on it right away. It bothered me a little because I heard they played dirty. I was still trying to learn how to do that.

187

It was well after dark when I got home. Mom was back from dinner with Doctor Hickman, but he wasn't around. He usually came in for coffee, and he and Mom would discuss things not always medical.

"How was your dinner?" I asked. She turned to me with tears in her eyes.

"He's married," she said.

Until then I never thought about whether Doctor Hickman was married or not. He was on staff at University Hospital but always available when Booth Memorial needed him. Because he asked Mom out to dinner, I just assumed he was single. How could he go out with my mother if he was married?

"He told me the whole story tonight," she said. "They married while he was still in medical school. She helped put him through, doing secretarial work. He was commissioned in the Marines at the start of the war and spent his time in the Pacific treating soldiers near the battle lines."

She stopped to blow her nose and dry her eyes.

"When he got home he noticed something was wrong. His wife would forget simple things and had trouble putting a meal together. He took her in for tests which showed she was suffering from senility in its early stages."

"I don't know what that is, Mom," I said.

"It's a problem with memory but usually doesn't show up until a person is really old. Seventies or maybe eighties. They forget small things at first and finally don't remember names of their husbands or wives or even their children. Eventually they have to go into a home and that's where she is now."

"How old is Doctor Hickman's wife?" I asked.

"She's only forty-five," she said. "That's not that much older than me."

"He's a doctor," I said. "Can't he do something for her?"

"He's done a lot of research," Mom said. "There's a doctor in Europe who has studied this same condition. His name is Alzheimer. He says there's no known cure, and because it is a disease of the brain, the person will eventually die of it."

I didn't know what to say. I'd never heard of a disease with no cure except the cancer thing they talked about. "What's he going to do?" I asked.

"It's his wife," Mom said. "What else can he do but stay with her to the end?"

The phone rang. "It's Shirley T.," Mom said. "She's having problems with labor. I'll be gone a while."

~27~

EUDORA HAD A PIECE OF PAPER in her hand when we met in the anteroom.

"Here's the list of recommended reading you asked for," she said. I read most of these during my sophomore year so this should work for you in English class."

I glanced over the list quickly and recognized only one title out of the bunch.

"What's *A Connecticut Yankee in King Arthur's Court* doing on here?" I said. "I read that on my own in the seventh grade."

"Well, you might have," Eudora said, "but you're older now and will probably find a new meaning to the words. Mark Twain's books are like that."

That sounded strange to me. Words were words and I'd already read those once. How could they change just because I was older? A couple of residents looked over my shoulder and made suggestions.

"Oh, Rene, read *Gone with the Wind*," Joanne said. "It's so romantic."

I had gone to the movie even though the rumor was there was a swear word in it. There was and I went to confession right after.

"Try *A Tree Grows in Brooklyn*," Cassie said. "I haven't read it, but I hear there's some juicy parts. You might learn something, Rene."

Knowing Cassie, I'd better check with the Catholic Legion of Decency before I brought one of her recommendations home. It told you what films not to see so they must have something for books too. *Mutiny on the Bounty* sounded interesting but I finally chose *The Sun Also Rises* because I'd heard of the author, Ernest Hemingway.

"That's perfect," Jonna said. "I won't spoil it for you, but what happened to the hero should happen to every man."

I didn't know what she was talking about but figured I would soon enough. When I checked it out, the librarian smiled and said, "I hope you're ready for this."

The teacher okayed my selection, and I decided not to check with the church. Someday I was going to have to make my own decisions so why not start now. I told Ellie about my decision.

"Does your church always make up your mind for you?" she asked. I could tell right away she wasn't raised Catholic.

"What does your church say about the Salvation Army and the women you eat with every day?"

"Well, they call them Protestants," I said. "I'm not supposed to hang around with Protestants."

"And what does your church have to say about Booth Memorial and all of us who live here? Her voice was rising and it made me uncomfortable.

"Because you've done it with a man and you're not married, they think you're all sinners," I said, quietly. I was out on a limb because I'd never discussed this with Father McGowan.

"What does the Catholic Church know about me or any of us for that matter? Every girl here has a different story. Some just fell in love, some were lied to and some were raped. There might be sinners here, but no one deserves to be called that without knowing their story."

Her questioning made me uneasy. I'd been raised in a black-or-white world with nothing in between. Ellie had dragged me into gray.

"What about me. Do you think I'm a sinner?" she said. "Do you think I was in the back seat of some guy's car every night until I got knocked up?"

I stared at the piano keys and wished I were somewhere else.

"No, I don't think that, Ellie," I said, "but I don't know what to think. I mean, you're pregnant aren't you."

"Yes I'm pregnant, and it's because I was raped and raped and raped. I know it sounds like Jonna's little joke but that's exactly what happened to me."

Her anger turned to pain as she told me the story. Her father was a Navy doctor stationed at fleet headquarters in Hawaii. On December 7th, 1941, the Japanese attacked Pearl Harbor and a call went out for all available doctors. He was on his way to the hospital at Schofield Barracks when a Jap plane strafed his car.

She and her mother were evacuated and returned to their hometown. Her mother couldn't cope with the loss and began going to a local bar. She met a guy who had money to spend and regularly bought rounds of drinks. Her glass was never empty.

"Why wasn't he in the Army?" I asked. "Was he too old?"

"He was 4-F," she said. "His father was a liquor distributor and the rumor was he bribed members of the local draft board with booze to keep his son out. He spotted my Mom right away and, before long, he was driving her home in his new Ford convertible."

"Where were you all this time?" I asked.

"On those nights, I stayed at Grandma's and, before long, I was there every night. One morning Mom told me I was going to have a new daddy, and things would be just like they used to be. She didn't mention a new baby would be part of it."

There was a hurry-up wedding but then her mom, after too much to drink, fell down some stairs and aborted the fetus. One problem remained—her mother was an alcoholic. Her stepfather was the one who gave Ellie her nightly bath and tucked her into bed. Then he'd lie next to her and read a bedtime story until she was asleep.

"I liked it," she said. "I never really knew my father and, since Mom was drunk every evening, it was the only attention I got. Even after my breasts began to develop and I got pubic hair, he kept up the routine. The bedtime stories got longer and more mature. Then, when he thought I was asleep, he began putting his hands where they didn't belong."

"Why didn't you tell your mother?" I asked.

"She was passed out and when she was awake she didn't want to hear about it. All she wanted was the next drink. I began to pretend that it didn't happen, but he wouldn't go away."

"You said he raped you," I said.

"At first he would lie on top of me and just move his thing back and forth and that satisfied him. Then, one night, he pushed it in. It hurt so much I cried. The next morning there was blood on my sheets."

"Where'd it come from?" I asked.

"Well, that's normal for the first time, Rene," she said, like I was supposed to know. "I began staying up late to avoid him but he came in after I fell asleep. I cried every time."

"Why didn't you go to your grandmother," I asked.

"Grandma died when I was thirteen," she said. "I think it was from a broken heart after watching her daughter become a drunk. She was the one who warned me about getting my period and taught me what to do. After she died, there was nowhere to go."

Ellie threw herself into giving piano lessons, trying to save enough money to move out. Her dream was to go to college but this pregnancy was taking most of her savings.

"Does your mother know where you are?" I asked.

"When I told her my stepfather made me pregnant, she swore at me, called me a lying whore and told me to get out. That's when I called Booth Memorial."

"What did your stepfather say when you told him?"

"He was drunk again, and all he could do was mumble 'Sorry,'" she said. "I couldn't wait to get on that bus, snowstorm and all. That was New Year's Eve."

"And I almost turned you away," I said. "It was so stupid."

"So, that's my story," she said. "I'm having this baby because I can't get an abortion, but that'd be a sin too, wouldn't it? What would your nuns and priests have to say about that?"

I just sat there and didn't know what to say. This never came up in Catechism class.

"What you can tell them is that it won't happen again. I will never let a man touch me like that again—ever. Am I still a sinner in your eyes, Rene?"

~28~

I T WAS THE FIRST DAY OF SPRING but who could tell? The snow would melt a little in the daytime, and then freeze again at night, which made the morning walk to the hospital an icy exercise. Following Doctor Hickman's advice, I kept my hands out of my pockets.

The last of the Prom Night girls had delivered, and they spent a final week at Booth Memorial to get to know their babies. If they chose, they learned to bathe them, changed diapers and gave them a bottle. It was their last chance to decide. Since I had been here, not one girl had kept her baby even though some wanted to. They all spent time with a counselor, who explained the options and problems of raising a baby without a father in today's society. It turned out the options were next to none and the problems were huge, so they placed their babies for adoption. This was always followed by tears on the stairs.

Earlier this month Captain Trudy was given an almost impossible assignment. Because of the extended winter, Major Ellen decided she wanted an Easter celebration this year. She brought it up at supper.

"The older residents are getting antsy and new ones are coming in," she said. "We need something to keep them busy until the snow melts. Trudy, will you come up with something?"

Captain Trudy was always up for a challenge but had already lost some of her good choral voices. Since my voice had changed she'd stopped asking me to join.

"Well, I don't know, Major," she said. "I can't guarantee anything."

"I'm sure you and Jonna will come up with something wonderful," Major Ellen said. "Just make it a priority, and God will provide."

195

Jonna was still a ball of fire even though she could no longer fit into the phone booth to talk with her boyfriend. I think she wanted to go out with a bang and, looking at the size of her stomach, her fuse was getting short. She was not beyond wheedling and begging the new girls to get what she wanted.

Jonna had been helping Mom with record keeping in the nursery, but after being asked to do the Easter program, she said she'd be too busy to continue.

"'Mrs. Dardenne, music and dance is what I love to do and I don't know anything else,'" Mom said, as she mimicked Jonna's mountain twang. It sounded funny.

"Jonna's mother told her, 'If you learn to cook you'll always be some man's slave and you'll be stuck in the kitchen or on your back in the bedroom, just like me.'"

According to Mom, Jonna's mother always wanted to get away from their small mountain town and do something with her life, particularly in show business. Instead she got married young.

"Jonna told me she found their wedding license and discovered she was born early, way early," Mom said. "She said something about her parent's attendants being named Smith and Wesson. Now, why would she tell me that?"

I almost laughed out loud. Apparently Mom never went to western movies or she would know that Smith and Wesson made shotguns.

"Her father turned out to be a 'no good,'" Mom said. "Jonna says her relationship with him was prickly at best. After he died, her mother worked as a cleaning lady to pay for Jonna's singing, dancing, and ballet and acting lessons. Her graduation present from high school was a Greyhound ticket to New York. No wonder she can't fold a diaper. All she knows how to do is be cute."

I couldn't disagree with Mom, but right then cute really appealed to me. Of course Jonna's stomach was a distraction, and her dumpy clothes didn't help.

"I asked her what she was going to do after the baby comes," Mom said. "She didn't miss a beat. 'Oh, I'm going right back on stage. I can't give up everything I've invested in my career just because I have a baby,' she said."

Her answer really set Mom off. When she asked Jonna what would happen to the baby, she said her mother would raise it, and they would come visit it between Broadway shows. There were plenty of relatives around to make sure it would be raised with family instead of in a New York apartment. Besides, her mother would love raising a show business baby.

"Jonna told me that's what the star of *South Pacific* did with her baby boy," Mom said. "When I made a face she said, 'If it's good enough for her, it's good enough for me.' It is so selfish that it disgusts me. She might as well give it up for adoption. I'm so disappointed in Jonna."

All of a sudden Jonna didn't seem so cute. I'd always overlooked her attitude because she was talented and full of charm but to ignore her baby was another matter. Even the key in her brassiere didn't seem as sexy anymore.

At supper, Captain Trudy made her presentation for the Easter program.

"We're going to do something modern and traditional," she said. "The first part of our program will be about what Easter is today and the closing part about why we celebrate it."

"What's the music?" Major Ellen asked. "It's not all from *South Pacific* is it?

"Oh, no Major," Captain Trudy said. "We're still selecting, but you're going to love it."

"Okay, but no surprises like last time," she said. "I'm still explaining that the site of the manger in Bethlehem was not a Booth Hospital."

It was Jonna's idea to do an Easter parade, just like on Fifth Avenue in New York City. At first Captain Trudy was cool to it because it wasn't religious, but when Jonna said the parade would end at a church and there would be hymns she gave in.

The hallways began to hum again. Girls in the Arts and Crafts room were busy cutting out patterns for costumes while others made sketches of Easter hats. The choir robes from the Christmas program were still in a closet. Jonna had a tougher job because her trained Prom Night singers were gone, but New Year's Eve girls had come in. After she'd signed her papers and put her suitcase away, every new resident was asked, "What's your name, when are you due, where are you from, and can you sing?" The last question took them by surprise but Jonna didn't have time to make nice.

Ellie was drafted as the accompanist, which disrupted my piano lessons. She did give me pieces to practice on my own, but I had my own schedule problems. The neighborhood guys were serious about the hockey game with Johnny Boy and his buddies, and they upped the practices. The game was scheduled for the Saturday after Easter, so that gave us time to work on strategy during Easter vacation. Was I nervous about my first real hockey game? You bet, but I was more concerned about what I could do against the guy who wouldn't stop calling me "Baldy."

* * *

EVERY AFTERNOON, THE HALLWAYS of Booth Memorial were filled with sounds of music coming from the Great Room. With new girls coming in, Jonna was able to put together a good-sized choral group. Rehearsals bounced from modern music to traditional Easter hymns to make sure the girls wouldn't get bored. Major Ellen's plan to keep the residents busy during the gloomy winter days seemed to be working.

"It certainly is taking their minds off their own problems," she said at supper. "Trudy, I hope you're keeping a close eye on Jonna. You never know."

Major Ellen was careful not to say it, but I was aware the daily letters from Jonna's boyfriend hadn't been daily lately. Ellie said Jonna just tosses off something like, "It's near the end of the tour, and he's very busy," but they've seen her cry afterward. Maybe that's why she had put all her energy into this program.

Every time I saw Jonna in the hallway, I put my guard up. She hadn't said a thing to me about being part of the Easter pageant, but I had my suspicions. Jonna wasn't the type to leave anything overlooked or unused when she did a production. I was especially wary when I saw girls working on a large bunny costume.

With Easter coming, Mom suggested we shop for a new suit at Montgomery Ward's and that made sense. Along with my voice change and a few pubic hairs, since we moved here I'd added several inches to my frame. I had one good dress up outfit when we got here but the last time I wore the jacket, the shoulders were tight, the front barely buttoned, and my wrists stuck several inches out of the sleeves. Even I knew it was time. Mom wanted me to look good on Easter Sunday, so we hopped on the Snelling Avenue streetcar and headed for "Monkey Wards." I looked forward to the trip because, to get there, we'd have to ride the new street-cars on University Avenue. After a lot of trying on, Mom decided I looked best in a dark-blue suit instead of the light gray one I liked. The final touch was a blue tie with a silver pattern. I thought it made me look ready for a funeral, but Mom convinced me that it was classy. The only remaining problem . . . I didn't know how to tie a tie, and they didn't sell clip-ons. The salesman gave me a quick lesson on tie tying, and I practiced on the streetcar all the way home.

The Easter program was scheduled for Saturday evening with a dress rehearsal on Friday night. When the girls came in for rehearsal, Max and I had just finished putting up risers and a low runway that Jonna had charmed him into building.

"Let's all hear it for Max and Rene," Jonna said. "We couldn't do this without them." There was a round of applause, and Max and I took a bow.

The rehearsal was going fine. The choir sounded beautiful and the mix of modern and traditional music worked really well. The fashion part of the show called for the girls to walk down the runway and show off their original clothing designs and Easter hats, but the first two girls tripped stepping on the runway.

"Oh, damn," Jonna said. Captain Trudy put her finger to her lips. "They can't see the step because of their stomachs. I didn't think about that."

The rehearsal ground to a halt while Jonna thought up a solution. All too soon, to my way of thinking, she had one.

"We need someone to help them on and off," she said, like it was a bright idea. "Rene, don't you have a new blue suit and tie?"

"Yeah, I do," I said. "How'd you know?"

All of a sudden it dawned on me. I had walked into another trap that Jonna and Mom worked out days ago. No wonder she was eager to buy me something I didn't really want. This made about the fifth time I'd been taken in by girls who wanted something, but this time it included my own mother.

"I can't because I don't know what to do," I stammered.

"Well, darlin', that's why we have rehearsals," Jonna said. "Come on, I'll show you how."

That's how I found myself walking down the runway over and over again, each time with a pregnant girl on my arm. Eudora was the emcee and announced each girl and her costume. One had an Easter bonnet made of starched napkins and piles of ribbons. Another hat was a ring of colored poster board with a feather duster sticking straight up. Some girls sewed old sheets into costumes including one that was dyed and sewn in the shape of an Easter egg. The girl didn't need padding to fill it out. As we walked back and forth, the chorus sang all the verses of "Easter Parade," twice. I felt pretty good about my part. No girl tripped, and I didn't step on the hem of one single costume.

Cassie bounded out in the rabbit costume and did a takeoff on Bugs Bunny in a Looney Tunes cartoon. She sang, "I Am a Yegg" and carried an Easter basket filled with colored eggs. As she danced she'd toss an egg into the audience.

"One of these isn't hard boiled," she said, "but I can't remember which." Good thing Captain McTavish ran the laundry because she ended up with a big yellow stain on her white uniform. No one doubted Cassie knew for sure which egg was raw but figured she was so far along that she couldn't draw laundry duty.

As she promised, Jonna smoothly switched the chorus into traditional Easter music and did a medley ending with "Christ the Lord Is Risen Today." It was a hymn I'd never heard in the Catholic Church and it was beautiful. When I saw tears on Major Ellen's cheeks, I knew the program was a hit.

As we expected, Jonna saved the last number for herself. She ducked around a corner and when she reappeared, she was wearing some old draperies made into a gown. Eudora announced her costume as inspired by Scarlet O'Hara, the lead character in *Gone with the Wind*. Even though she was close to delivery, Jonna still looked beautiful to me. When she began, it was like hearing an angel sing.

"Morning has broken, like the first dawning," were the first words. The melody was familiar but the words weren't. Then I realized it was the Catholic hymn, "This Day God Gives Me" but I had only heard it sung before by sixth-grade girls. Jonna's voice was still clear and powerful, and it gave me goose bumps. When she finished, the audience sat silent for a moment, like they didn't want it to end. Then there was loud applause from everyone including the choir. The ovation wouldn't stop, so Captain Trudy shouted, "Encore, Encore," and the crowd picked it up. Jonna smiled modestly, bowed a couple of times and generally milked it for all it was worth. She looked to Ellie at the piano, nodded and turned back to the audience. As Ellie played the first bars, Jonna's smile suddenly disappeared, she bowed her head and her jaw dropped. Ellie did a repeat. Then Jonna got a sparkle in her eyes and began to sing the same tune but with different words.

"My water has broken. The baby is coming. I can't go on singing. Now what do I do?"

* * *

THE AUDIENCE WAS STUNNED. Some even laughed at her little joke until we looked down and saw a puddle of water slowly spreading out from under her dress. Mom jumped from her seat, took Jonna by the hand and headed for the stairs. It was hard to believe the coincidence and there were those who swore Jonna had this all planned.

* * *

THE SUN WAS SHINING ON EASTER MORNING but it was one of those weak winter suns where everything outside the window still looked cold. The door to Mom's room was open, and the bed hadn't been slept in, which meant she spent the night at Booth Memorial. On my way to Easter Mass, I stopped by to see if Jonna had delivered. Mom was having toast and coffee in the dining room and looked really bleary-eyed.

"She started her labor late last night," she said, "but she's having trouble moving the baby. It looks like a breech to me, so I've called Doctor Hickman to come in."

A loud scream came through the dining room ceiling.

"She's in a lot of pain," Mom said. "We don't want to give her too much medication or she won't be able to help us. She insists she doesn't want a Cesarean unless it's absolutely necessary."

The smells of breakfast were almost too much to bear, so I left for Mass. Since neither food nor water are allowed to pass your lips before communion, I didn't want to mess up today of all days. Taking communion was already a chancy thing because I missed confession due to the Easter production. I wasn't sure how I would have confessed participation in a Protestant program celebrating the ascension of Christ anyway. I only hoped God would understand because I'm sure Father McGowan wouldn't. All through the sermon I prayed hard for Jonna and a safe delivery. The memories of Mae and Corrine were still fresh, and I didn't want to attend another memorial service.

At Communion, I knelt at the altar rail with a creepy feeling. Father Farelly placed the host in my unforgiven mouth. Nothing happened. My tongue didn't shrivel up, my lips didn't turn to stone, and I was able to get up and walk away. Was I concerned about nothing all these years? It was another thing to put on the list of questions I had about Catholicism.

When I got back, Doctor Hickman's Oldsmobile was in the driveway. Lunch was soup and sandwiches because the staff was at their church for the Easter services. It never occurred to me to ask how others worshipped in their churches. Did they have priests or deacons or elders to guide them? Did they have confession and communion? Was their God the same as ours? It was a bit much for me to understand.

A loud scream brought me back to reality. Jonna was still in labor.

"That's her all right," Lieutenant Margit said. "She has a great set of lungs because I can even hear her in the office."

Old Colonel Thomas was the only other person at the table. Because of her age, she wouldn't go out in the winter anymore, and she passed on Easter services. I think she was eating only soup because her false teeth were on the table, something her daughter would never allow.

"He is risen," she said loudly. I didn't know how to respond so I said, "He sure is."

"No, no, no," she said. "You're supposed to say, 'He is risen indeed.' Now, try it again. He is risen."

"He is risen indeed," I mumbled, feeling very uncomfortable saying religious things in English because I was used to Latin only.

I gobbled my sandwich before she found something else to say and asked to be excused. Several of the girls hung around the phone like they always did on Sunday. They'd all decided if Jonna's boyfriend called, Eudora would take it. I was as curious as they were and thumbed through the latest issue of *War Cry* to pass the time

Finally he called. Eudora told him about the Easter production last night and of the dramatic way Jonna went into labor. She ended the call ended with, "Okay, I'll tell her to look for it. Goodbye."

Mom came down the stairs and said, "Ladies, I have an announcement. Jonna has delivered a beautiful baby girl. She's seven pounds four ounces and eighteen inches long. The mother is doing fine but exhausted. We've sedated her so she'll probably sleep through the night. You can see her tomorrow."

Mom, Doctor Hickman, and I walked back to the nurses' home. Mom was so tired, she slipped on the ice a couple of times. Doctor Hickman offered to make the coffee.

"I'm used to doing this," he said, "since I don't have anyone to make it for me."

I remembered his wife couldn't recall his name let alone how to make coffee.

"How did it go?" I asked, trying to sound professional.

"It was tough," he said. "We'd turn the baby in the right direction and she would slip right back into breech. Jonna was weak enough that I almost called the ambulance to take her to University Hospital for a Cesarean. Your Mother said she didn't want it."

"We gave it one more try," Mom said, "and out she came, screaming all the way."

"Why didn't she want a Cesarean?" I asked.

"Something about a scar and her career," Doctor Hickman said. "What the hell does she do for a living that a scar like that would show up on the job?"

* * *

It was Monday morning, and there was the promise of a great week. School was out for Easter vacation, and there was no homework. The hockey team practiced every day, and Ellie was back on the housekeeping schedule. I hoped she wouldn't notice I didn't do all the lessons she laid out. After taking piano for three months, I realized I was a much better typist than a piano player. Ellie had been patient but why not? I did her housework. "Für Elise" came along, but I was no better in secret than I was in public. Frankly, I was a little discouraged. Mom went to the hospital early that morning, and I met her at breakfast.

"Jonna is holding her baby," she said. "After breakfast we'll move her into the Mother's nursery and start the breast-feeding program. She should be able to leave in about a week."

That news made me sad. Of course I was glad for Jonna, but I couldn't imagine Booth Memorial without her. To remember Captain Berthe Karlsson's cautionary words didn't help one bit. I was attached to Jonna, warts and all, and I'd really miss her.

As I left breakfast, a mailman was at the desk with a special delivery letter for Jonna. Lieutenant Margit was busy and asked me to take it to the nursery. I did my usual "Man on second" routine but this time there were no screams from girls in towels because I wasn't expected. I handed the letter to Mom and headed off for hockey practice.

It was a great day for me. The guys included me in more and more plays and taught me all the tricks I'd need to be a competitive skater. I was not very good in attempts to handle the puck, but they said that would come. We practiced into the afternoon until I realized I had a piano lesson with Ellie. I made an excuse to leave.

As I tromped in the front door, she was waiting and looked peeved.

"You're tracking in snow," she said. "Take your boots off and let's get busy."

We did our cleaning work quickly but without saying a word. Finally we were at the piano.

"The son of a bitch dumped her," she said.

I hadn't the least idea what she was talking about.

"Jonna's boyfriend sent her a letter. He's not going to marry her after all."

"What happened?" I asked. "Jonna had it all worked out."

"I don't know the details," she said. "All I know is she was holding the baby when she got the letter. She read it, shoved the baby at your mom and said, 'Take it away. I don't ever want to see it again. Get it out of here.' That's all I know," Ellie said.

I didn't know what to say. I felt hurt for Jonna and surprised that someone could be so cruel as to break her heart with a letter. It was not like she was just a girlfriend or something.

"I don't know any more details," Ellie said, "but that's what she gets for trusting a man. Maybe your mom can tell you more."

Supper that evening was quieter than usual. Major Ellen did include Jonna and her baby in the prayer, but nothing was mentioned after that.

"Why's it so quiet," old Colonel Thomas said in a loud voice. "Did somebody die?"

"No, Colonel Thomas," Major Ellen said. "It's just that we are all in a reflective mood tonight."

"Thank God," she said. "I thought my hearing aids stopped working."

After supper, we listened to *Arthur Godfrey's Talent Scouts* on the radio while I cleaned Jonna's blood off Mom's shoes and she ironed her caps. I didn't want to miss the program but couldn't stand not knowing.

"Mom, what happened to Jonna today?" I asked, but didn't tell her I knew part of the story.

The hiss from the iron as it hit her tears was quicker than usual. She didn't even bother to start with her usual "Well, it's like this."

"Jonna's boyfriend isn't going to marry her," she said. "He sent a Special Delivery letter breaking his promise and saying she could do what she wanted with the baby."

"Did he say why?" I asked. "I thought she had it all planned."

"So did she," Mom said, "but things changed after he left her here. She was so hurt and angry that she threw the letter at me and said, 'This is what you get when you depend on a man to keep his word.' Even though I've had differences with Jonna, it still makes me cry."

After making me promise never to repeat a word, Mom told me about the letter. "It started out, "Dearest Ruthie."

So, that's her real name. Nothing nearly as sexy as Jonna. In the letter he said his wife refused to give him a divorce, and if he insisted she would report him to the draft board. The Army had geared up because of problems in Korea, and he was afraid he'd be called up in no time.

Also, *South Pacific* was going to tour Europe, and his boss was promoted to producer. She chose him to be her assistant producer, which means he'll be busier than usual.

"Here's the cruel part," Mom said. "He told her the show has already been cast so there was no spot for Jonna—especially if she has a baby to take care of."

"But I thought her mother was going to take care of it," I said.

"That's only if they were married," Mom said. "She says her mother has spent twenty years living down Jonna's early birth. She was just made an elder in her church and can't take the shame of raising a bastard."

I must have reacted because Mom said, "I'm sorry, Honey, but that's what they're called; especially in mountain country."

"What's Jonna going to do?" I asked.

"She doesn't have much choice," Mom said. "He sent her a money order for a railroad ticket to New York with enough for a month's rent. As soon as she's recovered, she'll go on auditions looking for a job. He said he'll call her after the European tour."

"What about the baby?" I asked. "Does Jonna like it?"

"When she was holding that little girl, she looked so happy and pleased with herself, and then that damn letter came. She read it and almost threw the baby at me and said she never wanted to see it again. So far, she hasn't."

"Where is it now?" I asked.

"Moved to the adoption nursery," she said. "A couple of the girls are taking care of her. They named her Nellie (Forbish?)."

~29~

FINALLY SATURDAY ARRIVED, the day of the big game with Johnny Boy and his neighborhood buddies. It took the whole of last evening to sharpen my skates and put new tape on my hockey stick. I also oiled my baseball mitt because I was sure I'd see some duty as goalie. I had an uneasy feeling in the pit of my stomach, but Mom said I just had too many sausages at breakfast. I thought sausages gave you energy, not indigestion.

Lieutenant Margit asked me to help Max move Jonna's big trunk out to the driveway because a railway express truck would come for it. I remembered when we struggled to get that heavy thing inside the lockup six months ago. How fast the time had gone. Just as we reached the driveway, Jonna appeared at the top of the steps wearing the same outfit as the day we met. Since losing her stomach, she looked absolutely stunning, and she came down the stairs with the elegance of a dancer.

"Hold it a second, darlin'," she said. "I need to put something in."

She reached inside her blouse and removed the key that had given me so many sleepless nights for the past six months. Jonna opened the lid and put a baby's knit cap and some booties inside.

"Just something to remind me," she said. "Another one of life's lessons."

She locked the trunk and the key went back in her blouse, presumably nesting somewhere in her cleavage. Then she winked at me, just like the day we met. A cab pulled into the drive.

"I'm going to miss you, sweet thing," she said, "but not much else. Good luck in your hockey game."

I looked into her eyes for any indication of regret that she was leaving her baby behind, but they were sharp and focused. Jonna leaned in close to me.

"I'm going to give you some advice," she said. "No matter how good you are, no matter how hard you try, there'll always be someone wanting to knock you down. Just keep movin' and don't look back." She gave me a kiss, got in the cab, flashed a big professional smile and said, "Come see me when I'm famous but don't you dare tell anyone where we met. Remember, when it comes to the truth, just tell as much as you need to."

As the cab pulled away I felt an uncomfortable sensation but couldn't tell if it was the sausage or Jonna.

Johnny Boy and his buddies got off the Fort Snelling streetcar right in front of the nurses' home and headed for the vacant lot. They were friendly enough, but there was still a feel of tension. We were there to settle a score, but I'd forgotten what the original problem was. When they took the ice for practice, they looked taller than I remembered and their workouts were rougher than ours. Because no one thought ahead to get a referee, we agreed to play by street rules. Those turned out to be flexible.

I was on the ice for the face off. The puck shot toward me and suddenly it was gone, heading in the other direction. I chased it but was constantly tripped up by Johnny Boy's hockey stick poking the rear of my blades. As I made a move toward the puck, somebody jammed his stick between my legs, and I slid across the ice on my face. I got up and was immediately flattened with a body check as the puck sailed by. By now I sensed I was a team liability. Not only could I not get a stick on the puck, I couldn't even see it. My teammates no longer encouraged me, but accepted the fact that it was like they had a man in the penalty box. I'd been taught some aggressive tricks but each time I tried one, I ended up with an elbow in my ribs or my face. One time I was buried in a snow bank and they stopped the game to pull me out.

Finally we called a time out, and it was decided I should move to goalie—permanently. Even that was no safe haven. Johnny Boy came hurtling toward me and at the last second turned his skates sideways, showering me with ice. Then he flipped the puck as high as he could. In self-defense I raised the mitt to my face and caught the puck in mid-air. I couldn't believe it. Johnny gave me the finger as he skated by.

"You lucky shit," he sneered. "I'll get you next time."

I spent the rest of the game on my knees or flat on my back as they hit me at full speed or hacked at my hands as I tried to grab the puck. I did get a couple of saves but there wasn't time to celebrate because they'd be right back at me. By now my buddies were ticked off at how I was being kicked around and started using more aggressive tactics. Without a referee the game had turned into a brawl, and we had gotten the worst of it.

Out of the corner of my eye I saw figures on the sidewalk. They were Booth girls coming back from the drugstore. They stopped to watch and started to chant.

"Come on, Rene," they shouted. "Stop that puck. Stop that puck."

Johnny Boy and his team were so startled they stopped to look.

"Look at those bitches," he shouted. "Are they cheering for you, Baldy?" He turned to the girls. "Hey, you whores, let me show you something big and round with lots of hair around it."

"Are you talking about your mouth or your ass," Cassie shouted back.

"Shut up, you bitch, or I'll shove this stick up your cunt," he said.

"You try it and we'll cut off your balls and stick them in your mouth," she laughed.

By now I was mad. "Don't talk to them like that," I shouted.

Johnny Boy turned to me and said, "Are you kissin' up to those whores, you little queer? Maybe that's where you came from. Your old lady ain't married is she? You're just a little fairy bastard with a girl's name."

I charged Johnny Boy, knocked him down on the ice, and then hit him in the face with my fist. All of a sudden I felt the sting of hockey sticks that hit me in the head, on my back and across my legs. Johnny Boy got up and kicked me with the blades of his skates.

"You little asshole," he whispered. "When I'm done with you you're gonna wish you had some dope cause you're gonna hurt real bad."

By now both teams hit and clawed each other while the girls cheered us on. Suddenly I heard a dog's bark and a man's voice shout,

"Okay, cut it out, boys. Break it up. Hey, you bullies, quit picking on the smaller guys."

I looked up and saw Father McGowan tossing guys around like they were toothpicks. His poodle tried to bite our heels but slipped on the ice and fell on its butt.

"Where'd you guys learn to play dirty like that? And you, bully," he said, pointing to Johnny Boy, "What makes you think you can talk to anyone using that kind of language—especially a girl! It's punks like you that got them in trouble in the first place. You were raised in a good Catholic family, Johnny, and I'm telling your parents everything you called them." He pulled Johnny Boy and me off to the side.

"I want you to apologize to this guy for the vile things you said about his mother," he said to Johnny. "I'm surprised at your attitude, especially after what happened to your sister."

He looked around at the rest of the guys in disgust.

"Is this how you're going to settle things when you're adults?" he said. "You'd better grow up in a hurry or you're going to end up going to hell. I'll make sure you do."

The girls were gone. We just stood around and didn't know what to do.

"I want you boys to shake hands right now," Father McGowan said, "and I expect to see all of you at confession tonight. Then we'll see who's so tough."

"I'm Lutheran," Eddie said and a couple of others held up their hands.

"Well, all I can do is pray for your souls," he said, "but when you have your own confession, don't skip over this. Remember, God is watching you, and so am I. Now, get out of here before I get mad."

I limped my way home and opened the kitchen door. Mom had made coffee and, when she saw me, she let out a scream.

"What happened to you? Were you hit crossing the street?"

"No, Mom," I said. "We just finished the game. We lost."

"You mean this happened in a game," she said at the same volume. "I'm going to call the police. You've been beaten up."

"Just talk to Father McGowan," I said. "He was there and can tell you everything. Right now I just want to lie down."

I headed for my room with Mom right behind me. She stopped only to dampen a washcloth to wipe my face. That was the last thing I remembered. I woke up to the sound of men's voices. I managed to lift myself out of bed and limped to the kitchen. Doctor Hickman was having a cup of coffee with a younger man, probably an intern.

"Hey, here's our warrior right now," he said. "We were at the hospital and your mom called to say you might need a little attention. Now, was this hockey or a grudge match?"

He and the intern laughed at his joke, but I could barely move my jaw. He checked me over carefully, all the while explaining to the intern what he was doing.

"See here, he's got a bad cut over the eye," he said. "Probably from a skate blade or he fell on something sharp. It's going to take a stitch or two. His hands are badly cut, most likely from a hockey stick or a blade."

He pulled my sweatshirt off and pointed to marks on my back.

"See these welts?" he said. "Looks like multiple contusions from a hockey stick or sticks. How many guys were there?" he said to me.

213

"Here's a cut on the ear lobe. My guess is that's from a skate blade, which means he must have spent some time on the ice."

So far he was dead right about every place that hurt.

"How're your ribs?" he asked. "Usually guys will elbow you in the ribs, and it knocks you in the snow."

My ribs hurt so much I could barely talk. I just pointed and nodded.

"Well, let's get him fixed up," he said to the intern. "Get my bag out of the car and I'll show you how to do field repairs."

For the next hour, he and the intern treated every painful place. They sewed two stitches above my right eye, wrapped an elastic bandage around my waist, put alcohol on the welts, applied Merthiolate to the open cuts on my hands and bandaged my fingers. I could barely move but did feel a little better.

"Well, did you win?" the intern asked.

"Take a look at his condition," Doctor Hickman said. "What do you think?"

Mom was assigned to boil water for hot towels to go on my legs. She still made noises about calling the police on those "hooligans," a word I hadn't heard in a long time.

"Didn't you have brothers, Jo?" asked Doctor Hickman.

"No, just three sisters," she said.

"Well, I had three brothers," he said, "and this is just SOP for boys. He'll be able to defend himself when he learns to skate better. You don't want him to be a sissy."

It was the second time I'd heard that sissy thing, only this was from a different man. I looked at the kitchen clock. It was almost seven.

"I've gotta get to confession," I said.

"You're not going anywhere tonight, young man," Mom said. "Not in that condition."

"Father McGowan said, because of the game, I'd fry in hell if I didn't get to confession tonight," I said.

"I was in a Field Hospital on Iwo Jima," Doctor Hickman said. "You can tell your priest, I've already been to hell, and they weren't using hockey sticks there."

What he said didn't make me feel better. It just gave me something else to think about. Doctor Hickman must have had second thoughts about his smart-ass remark because he said, "We're going by the church, Jo. "We'll drop him off."

* * *

I COULD BARELY GET OUT OF BED Sunday morning. My legs, my arms, my fingers, everything ached, and the cut over my eye throbbed. On my way back from confession last night, I felt pretty good. I confessed to being in a fight but slanted it toward self-defense. Not wanting to overload Father McGowan, I didn't confess about taking part in a Protestant Easter program. I'd slip that in sometime when things calmed down. Whoever said, "Confession is good for the soul," knew what they were talking about, but they didn't have to do a long penance on sore knees.

Mom had gotten over her concern but now she was mad at me for being in a fight. She thought Mass could fix anything, and out the door we went. Father McGowan's sermon subject was on Tolerance, Understanding, Justice, and Peace. It wasn't aimed at me, but I was surprised he came up with a sermon overnight that hit so close. Mom listened too and nudged me in the ribs several times. It hurt, but I kept quiet. Johnny Boy and his parents were across the aisle. When he turned and slipped me the finger, I saw he had a big shiner, so at least one of my punches landed. His dad hit him on the head with a Holy Missal, which I took to be an example of Justice.

At Booth Memorial, the lunch conversation was about everything but what happened yesterday. No one mentioned the bandage on my head and the Band-aids on my hands even though I caught them as they sneaked peeks. Finally, old Colonel Thomas spoke up. "What happened to the boy?" she said in a loud voice. All the chatter stopped.

215

"Was he in that fight all the girls are talking about?"

"Rene defended some of our residents," Major Ellen said. "Some boys were saying nasty things to them, and he spoke up."

"That's always been a problem," Colonel Thomas said. "I hope you knocked the hell out of them."

"Mother, please," Brigadier Thomas said. "Try not to swear in front of the boy."

"I imagine he heard worse yesterday," she said. "Damned hoodlums."

"The girls shouldn't have egged them on," Major Ellen said, "but thank you for sticking up for them, Rene. We are impressed."

That evening Mom wanted to hear me play the piano but my fingers hurt too much. Instead we settled for the radio. Sunday night was the best. There was *Our Miss Brooks* with Eve Arden followed by *Jack Benny* and then *Edgar Bergen with Charlie McCarthy*.

As much as I liked the programs, my mind slipped back to all the names Johnny Boy called me yesterday. "Queer" and "fairy" were the two that bothered me most. The guys all said dirty things about girls and made jokes about sex. I laughed along but never told any jokes myself, and they noticed. They thought I had access to a place they could only dream about, and yet I didn't share sexy inside information. The fact that I stood up for the girls when they called them bitches and whores didn't help. Because I didn't join in, it was easy for them to say, "He's a fairy," or "He's gotta be a queer." The guys all joked about the girlish behavior of a couple of boys in school but they didn't do it in fun. I didn't want them to start to pick on me.

"You look tired," Mom said. "There's school tomorrow. Why don't you go to bed?"

In my room, my thoughts ran deeper. I didn't know how I should feel about girls. There were these boners every night and again in the morning. No one said it was a sin to do something about them, but it sure

216

seemed to be a confession item to me. The rumor going around was, if you used your hands they'd shrivel up and then all you could do was fan the hard-on to make it go away.

Jonna was my fantasy for the past six months and, even though she was gone, she was still on my mind every night. How did I confess my thoughts about her?

Then, there were the nasty thoughts about doing it with a girl. Why would I want to? I didn't love anyone and weren't you supposed to love the girl you did it with? Maybe not. Just look at all the girls at the hospital. No one was loving them.

What if I did it and got a girl pregnant, and she had to come live here? Then I'd really roast in hell or, at least, spend some time in purgatory.

What did priests do? They must have a secret. Maybe I should become a priest and then I'd know. It was hard to believe that every guy went through this. If they did, why hadn't I heard about it by now? I wished I had a dad to talk to or at least a guy who cared enough to listen to me.

I was almost asleep by the time my head hit the pillow, but I had to wipe some tears from my face. Dammit, I didn't want to cry. That was for sissies.

~30~

When Ellie saw my cuts and bruises, she said she'd do today's dusting.

"Just sit there," she said. "The girls told me about the fight but didn't say you were this beat up. What'd they say at school today?"

Some guys had made fun of me for taking a licking, but others said they'd always wanted to take a poke at Johnny Boy Bittolini but were afraid. I was glad I did it, but they were smart to think it over. One guy pounded me on the back in congratulations. I knew he meant well, but it hurt like hell.

"Try practicing something if you can," Ellie said. "I haven't heard you in a week."

I pulled out *Sixty Progressive Piano Pieces You Like to Play* and turned to page ninety. With stiff fingers, I played a few measures. Ellie straightened up like she'd been goosed.

"How did you learn to play 'Für Elise'?" she said.

"I did it myself," I said. "That's my surprise for you."

"That took a lot of work and you did it for me?" She sat next to me and kissed my cheek. Her thigh, against mine, felt good.

"I don't know how long these lessons can go on," she said.

Her voice was softer than usual and a little sad. "They change our jobs every two weeks, and I've been trading with girls who don't like working here," she said. "Captain McTavish has been asking questions. You know what a snoop she is."

That caught me off guard because Ellie and her piano lessons were what got me through the week. She saw the disappointment in my eyes.

"It's not the end of the world, Rene," she said. "You have a good start, and you've just shown me you can learn on your own."

"But I don't want that," I said. "I don't want you to leave." I couldn't hold my feelings any longer and told her everything I'd held inside. The guilt I felt in being with Protestants, lying in confession, girls who thought I knew too much, being called a queer and a sissy, my confusion with sex.

"What good is sex?" I asked. "It does nothing but get people in trouble." I was too embarrassed to tell her about jacking off.

"I'm thinking about becoming a priest," I said.

She smiled and said I couldn't be that confused.

"Rene, I know how you feel, and I'm telling you to forget it," she said. "You're just feeling sorry for yourself because you've had no one to talk to."

Ellie told me that girls had questions about sex too. When they finally did it with a boy, it was mostly out of curiosity, but many just wanted someone to love them.

"When it happened to me, there was no love involved," she said. "For a while, I even thought it might be my fault. Just like you, I had no one to talk to."

I stared at the music for "Für Elise." The notes turned blurry.

"Sex isn't a mystery," she said. "It's nothing but physical unless you have feelings for the other person. I care about you, Rene. I care enough to want to help."

I felt tears welling up and thought, I CAN'T DO THIS. I CAN'T CRY IN FRONT OF A GIRL. Ellie sensed my discomfort and pointed to my watch.

"It's getting late," she said. "I have to leave but need help with the basement stairs."

Ordinarily Ellie refused any help but since last week she could no longer see her feet and was afraid she'd trip. I held her hand and backed down the stairs to the bottom. On the last step, she tripped on the mop, dropped the bucket, lurched forward, and I caught her. We stood with arms around each other for a few moments, her bloated stomach up against my groin. I'd never been this close to a girl before and nature made itself known almost immediately. Ellie pushed back slowly, and I saw tears in her eyes. She led me to the couch, stepped out of her panties and lay down. A quick look answered any question about her having pubic hair, but I was still surprised. The hair on her head was blonde but there it was dark. And what happened to her belly button? It was stretched out to about twice its size and was almost flat.

All I could think was, she was seven months pregnant and there was a baby in there. What if I hurt her? What if I hurt the baby? No amount of confessions would make up for that, and God would punish me forever. My hands trembled, my legs quivered, and my breath shortened. I wanted to back away, but she took my hand.

"Just calm down," she said softly. "This probably won't take long."

She laid back and guided me. "Lucky you, Rene," she said. "You can't get in any trouble. I'm already pregnant. Now, let's answer that question about becoming a priest."

My knees and arms ached as I tried to keep my weight off her extruded stomach, almost like balancing on a balloon while trying not to break it. My reward was a sensation I'd never before experienced.

"You're having your first," she said. "I hope you enjoy it more than I did mine."

My fingers and knees pained but I concentrated on Ellie's face, and looked for any physical or emotional hurt. Instead she had a slight smile, and then she opened her mouth like she was in pain but not really. Her breaths were deep at first, and then turned into steady pants as they brushed past my ear. I felt an extended rush of excitement that I hoped would last forever, followed by sudden exhaustion and limpness—a wonderful sensation that left as fast as it came. There was barely a chance to enjoy it.

We heard the back door close, followed by footsteps on the hard-wood floor that creaked as they passed over us. Ellie pulled her panties on, grabbed the mop and calmly walked up the stairs while I retreated to a far corner of the basement.

"Where've you been?" Captain McTavish demanded of her.

"I just finished and was putting things in the basement," she said. "I'm on my way back."

"Where's Rene?" she asked. "I see his books on the table."

"Don't know," Ellie said. "Maybe he's in the bathroom."

"Get going," the captain said, "or you'll be late for the supper bell."

When I went upstairs, Captain McTavish waited in the kitchen.

"What were you doing down there?"

Her tone was more than suspicious.

I held up two cans of V-8 juice.

"Mom asked me to bring these up," I said. "The one in the refrig-erator tastes like the can. Would you like a glass?"

~31~

I HAD ALL WEEK TO THINK ABOUT the importance of what happened in the basement. There was terrible guilt about doing that with a girl who was pregnant, even though she said it wouldn't do any harm. It was over so fast, I reviewed it moment by moment, almost like looking at a film frame by frame. Memories of the climax made it difficult to fall asleep at night, especially on my stomach.

At school I looked at girls differently, even visualized some of them in place of Ellie on the couch. I wasn't sure doing it with her made my life less complicated, but it did answer a couple questions about having sex.

Ellie's concern about the end of piano lessons turned out to be real. A new girl showed up the other day during piano practice. She was in street clothes and introduced herself as Marlene D., only she pronounced it "Marlaynuh." Like all the other girls, I had to show her where the supplies were kept in the basement. The office told her Ellie was assigned to another job because she was too far along to do housework.

I pulled out my *Piano Pieces You Like to Play* lesson book and turned to page ninety. "Für Elise" didn't have the same passion for me now. All I could think of was the surprised look on Ellie's face when I first played it for her. I had run that image over and over in my mind too.

"Oh, that's pretty," Marlene said. "Wish I could learn to play like that."

That was encouraging. My first audience liked my playing, which meant it hadn't been a waste of time after all.

Each day I tried to come up with the right thing to say in Saturday confession. I didn't want to make it so vague that a priest wouldn't understand but I didn't want to come right out and say I did it with a girl either. There must be a right way; I just hadn't found it yet.

It almost made me wish I were like Jake Barnes in *The Sun Also Rises*. Because he was impotent, he never had to confess about women, but he had other problems that cost him. There was a line in the book that I couldn't forget. "You paid, someway, for anything that was any good."

I wouldn't give back that moment with Ellie for anything, but what would it cost me? Not only that, the pile of sins I hadn't confessed had grown. I might never get off my knees.

At confession, I expected to play Roman roulette, but only one confessional was in use. Hopefully it'd be Father Farelly. I waited in the silent darkness, hoping the priest was bored enough by now that he wouldn't even listen. I started my ritual chant.

"Bless me Father for I have sinned. It has been one week since my last confession."

No recognition. I started off with the little stuff and finally mumbled that I'd touched a girl "down there." My hope was the vague reference would zip right by him, but this priest was experienced in boy's confessions.

"Wait a minute, son," he said. "Are you telling me that you were intimate with a girl?" Bad luck! It was Father McGowan.

"Yes, Father."

"Do you know this girl well?"

"Yes, Father."

"How far did you go?" he asked.

"All the way, Father,"

"This is a serious matter. Do you realize it could lead to an event that could change your lives forever?"

"Yes, Father," I said. Now I wished I'd passed on confession and carried the guilt instead.

"You must promise you'll never do this again," he said. "God trusted you to remain pure until marriage. You've already violated that, but it can be regained through penance and self-denial. Do you promise to practice abstinence?"

"Yes, Father," I said, though I wasn't sure what abstinence meant and made a mental note to look it up when I got out.

"One final thing," he said. "Promise you will never again associate with this girl. Her loose moral character has pierced your innocence and drawn you into sins of the flesh."

That made me mad. He judged Ellie without knowing her painful past and the risk she took to help me. She had nothing to gain from it. I should have defended her but didn't have the guts.

"I promise, Father," I said. With those words, I betrayed Ellie.

As I left the confessional, I felt worse than when I went in. Whoever said confession was good for the soul was full of crap.

For the next thirty minutes, I was on my knees in front of the statue of Saint Joseph where Father McGowan specified I do my penance. It wasn't any comfort that some other guys my age were there with me. I saw girls doing their penance in front of the statue of the Virgin Mary. It made me wonder what they had done.

After five minutes, the priest's confessional door opened. Father McGowan stuck his head out and looked in our direction, like it was a head check. I'd always heard that confession was private and the priest was bound by an oath not to repeat what he'd heard. It never occurred to me that he might want to know who confessed what. Even if he did, what would he do with the information? Still, I had an uneasy feeling as I walked home.

The next morning, Mom and I went to eleven o'clock Mass. Father McGowan usually delivered the sermon because it was the best attended Mass. Today it was Father Farelly, and as usual, I tuned out the minute he mounted the pulpit. I was glad it wasn't Father McGowan because after my confession I had a feeling that he would preach a sermon right at me.

As we left church, he stood at the door to shake hands. When he spotted Mom and me, he came right over.

"Hello, Rene," he said. "How are your battle wounds healing?"

Before I could even answer, he turned to Mom and asked if he could speak to her in private. She looked at me as if to say, "What have you done now," and told me to go on. She'd see me at lunch at the hospital.

The conversation around the table was all chitchat about the sermon at the Salvation Army church. Since they didn't have priests, it was hard to figure out who did the preaching. I got the idea they passed it around. That would mean they were all priests and that made absolutely no sense to me. I'd learned not to ask too many questions because they'd invite me to their church again. They didn't seem to understand that it was a sin for me to do that.

Mom came in late and just sat there sipping her coffee. Didn't talk, didn't even nibble at her food. That's not like her because Mom was always a good eater. I had to reassure myself that priests weren't allowed to tell what they heard in confession, but I was still a little nervous. When Mom was that quiet, something was wrong.

We walked slowly on the way to the nurses' home. Since the snow on the driveway had melted, it was slipperier than usual. I tried to sound nonchalant, but my heart pounded when I asked, "What'd Father McGowan want?"

"Oh, he just wanted to talk with me about his concerns for you," she said. "He thinks you should be in a Catholic high school. You might be falling in with the wrong crowd, and your beating might be the start of something worse." So far, so good. Nothing about girls or sex. "I told him the Catholic high school is on the other side of town," Mom said, "and we can't afford the tuition anyway." Father McGowan wouldn't give up. He got personal and asked Mom if there was any chance she and Dad could get back together. When she said Dad was remarried with a new baby, he just shook his head.

"He told me, 'That boy needs a man in his life, but you can't do anything about it and still have God's blessing.' It made me mad," Mom said.

She was usually careful what she said to me about the church, but mom also had a temper—especially about unfairness.

"Do you remember back when our priest used to visit every home in the parish on Sunday nights?" she asked. "He started that when I was a little girl living with Grandma and Grandpa."

I did remember because when Mom and I went to live with her parents, we had to open up the front room, turn on the porch light and wait for him. My job was to look down the street to see whose porch light was off to estimate when he'd get to our house. We always hoped he wouldn't show up until Jack Benny's radio show was over.

"He'd come in and sit in my father's favorite chair," Mom said. "He'd make small talk for about ten minutes and then go to the next home."

During Mom's time the priest was highly respected and probably the only one in the parish who had been past the sixth grade. His flock included immigrant men who stopped at a tavern every morning to get their nerve up before going to work in the coalmines. They stopped again after work to thank God for having gotten out alive. My memory was having to go to the tavern to fetch my grandfather for supper. After a few drinks, some of his buddies got pretty rough and settled their arguments out back in the alley. By the time they got home they weren't in the mood to take any crap.

"It wasn't until after I was in nurses' training that I understood the real purpose of the priest's home visits," Mom said. "He was looking for bruises, and if he found any, he would have that miner on his knees on the front porch for all the neighbors to see. 'If you don't stop beating your wife and kids,' he'd say, 'I will see to it personally that you will fry in hell.' Hearing those words from God's representative was enough to melt any tough old miner," she said, "and that would protect the family for a week or two." Mom shook her head. "I guess it was the only way the priest could handle an uneducated man who put his life on the line every day. Scare him to death."

"Yeah but all that's changed now," I said. "The mines are closed and you all graduated from high school."

"That's what caught me by surprise," Mom said. "I grew up, finished high school and graduated from nurses' training, but the priests still acted like I hadn't gone past the sixth grade. 'Rules are rules,' they'd say. 'You married for life, and it's up to you to make it work.' Now is that fair?" Mom said. "It's not my fault I'm divorced, but the church acts like it is. I go to a priest for counsel, and all I get is blame. I think the Catholic Church is out of touch, and I'm tired of it."

Mom's rant hit me pretty hard. Beside her, the one thing I felt I could count on in life was my religion and the priests who ran it. While I wasn't always happy with them, it never occurred to me to question the Catholic Church itself.

We reached the house, and Mom went to her room to lie down and think a few things over. She asked me to play something on the piano, and I pulled out *Sixty Progressive Piano Pieces* and turned to page ninety. I was shaky on some of the parts because my mind was distracted by anything else the priest had said. It didn't matter. Mom loved "Für Elise" even though she had no idea who I learned it for. She dozed off before I reached the end of the page.

On our way to supper, Mom said she'd come to a decision about our future.

"Several times, Carl has asked me to marry him," she said.

I held my breath.

"I've decided to say, yes."

"Is that because you love him?" I asked.

"He's a fine man and should be a good husband and a good step-father for you," she said. "Besides, I always wanted to be a June bride."

Her decision to marry, after her conversation with Father Mc-Gowan, seemed too sudden and, for some reason, I didn't believe that June bride stuff.

Mom announced her marriage at supper, and it created quite a buzz. The officers were happy for her because they'd met and liked Carl. They were sad, however, about the loss of a nurse who worked so well with the residents. The residents, on the other hand, were amazed that an older woman could find someone to marry so late in life. For Major Ellen, it meant starting the tiresome process of searching for a replacement.

If she was upset, Major Ellen didn't show it. At supper she asked Mom what plans she'd made for the wedding ceremony. Mom looked surprised.

"I hadn't even given it a thought," Mom said. "I'd better get to work on that."

"I'd like to make a suggestion," Major Ellen said. "We would be honored if you would repeat your vows in our Great Room. Colonel Payton will be here to make his recommendations on the future of this building. I hear he does a beautiful wedding, and he'd be flattered to be asked."

Mom thought it over. "I'll do it, only if you stand beside me as my maid of honor," she said.

That knocked me out. Father McGowan had really made Mom mad, and now she planned something no Catholic could do . . . be married outside the church by a Protestant to a Protestant. No priest in his right mind would perform that ceremony.

Major Ellen was surprised and delighted to be asked. She probably saw a hidden advantage to a wedding at Booth Memorial. Preparation for a big event was just the thing she needed to keep residents busy into June. Then she could turn her full attention to finding a replacement for Mom.

~32~

H OW QUICKLY MY LIFE HAD CHANGED. I no longer had a reason to rush home from school. Ice on the vacant lot had melted, it was too early for baseball, piano lessons were over but, most importantly, no one was waiting. I went to my room, lay on the bed and stared at the ceiling. My thoughts were about Ellie and our moment in the basement. The past week was full of firsts. I learned about sex, experienced feelings for a girl, confessed an adult sin, did heavy-duty penance, proved I wasn't queer and gave up any idea of being a priest. If that was the right way to grow up, I wasn't sure I much cared for it.

The biggest change was still to come. Mom decided to remarry, and perhaps it was my fault. Did Father McGowan tell her what I did or just suggest it strongly enough that she had to do something? Now I could lose my mother to another guy. How the hell did I screw up so badly?

What about Ellie? Did she expect me to marry her when the baby was born? I was only fifteen and didn't want to be married. What would I do if she asked? Was she in love with me? I hoped not, but I didn't want to hurt her feelings. Mom would kill me if she knew any of this. How did I get into this mess?

There were too many questions with no answers, at least, not right now. I headed for the piano. Maybe something would come to me if I played "Für Elise."

I opened the piano bench and saw an envelope with my name on it. On a piece of lined paper, Ellie had written, "Monday, 3:30 p.m., Snelling Avenue Bridge."

That was today! I looked at my watch. Three thirty one. She was there now. I grabbed my jacket and ran to the corner. With no streetcar in sight I ran at full speed through Eddie's neighborhood and took short-cuts across vacant lots still patched with ice and snow. When I reached Snelling Avenue, the bridge was two blocks away. I strained to look for Ellie in the distance and made out a figure in a red coat on the bridge, looking over the railing at the train tracks below. A streetcar approached from the other end, and the figure walked toward the stop to board. My leg muscles burned, and my lungs were ready to burst, but there was no way I could beat the streetcar. I skidded to a stop, took a deep breath and shouted, "Ellie. Ellie," over the traffic noise. Nothing. The figure started to board, turned, looked my way . . . and waved.

I half walked, half stumbled the rest of the way and tried to catch my breath to look calm and assured. Except for the sweat running down my face, I almost pulled it off, but then I collapsed against the bridge railing.

"Oh, my poor Rene," she said as she wiped my face with her handkerchief. "I was afraid you'd failed my test."

"What test?" I said, still panting.

"You promised you'd practice even though I wasn't there," she said. "The envelope has been in the bench since Saturday, so you haven't kept your word. Bad boy."

I stammered some weak excuse.

"No matter, you're here now," she said. "I saw a bench at the end of the bridge. Let's go sit down, and you can catch your breath."

The bench perched on the edge of a ravine that harbored a railroad-switching yard. It was like a toy train layout, only this was full size with real sound effects. We sat for a few moments and stared at the busy rail yard without saying a word. I leaned toward her and tried to kiss her on the lips, but she turned her cheek.

"I'm sorry everything ended so quickly last week," she said. "There was so much I wanted to say."

"I missed you," I said. "There's a new girl cleaning."

"They changed my assignment. I won't be coming back. Now you have to practice without me."

"It's not the same without you there to slap my fingers," I said.

The steady hum of traffic noise was broken by the sound of quacks. A flock of ducks circled overhead looking for the nearest lake.

"The first sign of spring," she said. "June will be here before you know it."

"You like Como Park a lot," I said. "Why did you want to meet here?"

She stood up and looked toward the bridge.

"When I first got to Booth, one of the older girls told me that a girl jumped from this bridge. She said you knew all about it."

I couldn't figure out why she asked, and I was careful with my answer. "It happened on the day Mom and I arrived," I said. She wasn't a Booth girl yet because they couldn't take her that day. They gave her money to stay overnight at the Happy Hollow Motel, but she came to the bridge instead—and she jumped."

Ellie didn't say a word, just stared ahead.

"She'd been tossed over by the guy and turned away by her family," I said. "She had nowhere else to go." Without realizing it, I'd left myself open.

"Sounds familiar," she said. "Didn't you almost do that to me?"

I started to protest, but she cut me off.

"Frankly, if I'd known about this bridge that night, I would have done that too."

Here I was again, not knowing what to say.

"'Well, at least her troubles are past," she said. "Up and over. Simple."

She sat beside me.

"I heard about your Mom," she said. "Did you expect it? The better question is, do you want it?"

Her questions triggered a flood. I told her about confession, how Father McGowan collared Mom after church, how quiet she was at lunch, and how she never answered my question about loving Carl. Did I expect it? Well, sort of. Did I want it? Not really, but what could I do? Mom always made those decisions.

"Is it punishment for what we did?" I asked.

"Please, don't be so Catholic," she said, shifting on the bench. "The baby's kicking. I need to stand up."

As I helped her to her feet, I tried to kiss her. Again, she turned away.

"I'm not in love with you, Rene," she said.

I was stunned. Everything I worried about an hour ago was suddenly gone. She said she didn't love me—but now I wondered why.

"But you and I did it," I said.

"I didn't plan that, but you were confused enough that I had to do something to take your mind off those awful thoughts."

"You did that just to help me?" I asked.

"Yes, but I now know it helped me too. How bitter I was. I never wanted to be touched by a man again because feelings were never involved."

She told me every time he raped her, she cried—at first because it hurt and then because she couldn't stop him. She felt helpless. I looked down and saw her hands were shaking but I couldn't tell if it was from the memories or the cold. I held them in mine.

"Did you notice, with you I didn't cry?" she said. "I was all ready to suffer again, but for the very first time I loved it. I didn't know that feelings for another person could make such a difference."

I'd only heard talk like that in the movies and never understood the real meaning. Now it was clear because my feelings for her were real too.

"We didn't do anything dirty," she said, "It was special love, just between you and me. Couldn't you tell?"

My mind was mixed up and I couldn't tell anything. Did I love what we did? Yes. Did I love her? I didn't think so.

"I don't love you," she said, "but I care for you deeply, and that's what makes it right. I won't ask but I hope you feel the same way about me."

The sun was low in the sky. Newly assembled trains left the rail yard, and Ellie had to get back to Booth Memorial. It was cold, so we held hands as we walked through neighborhoods I'd become really familiar with. I told her how I'd relived every moment over and over and would never forget her, but we both knew it would never happen again.

"I want to talk about your future," she said. "When I leave Booth Memorial, I don't expect to see or hear from you again. After you meet other girls, you'll forget about me, but I want a promise."

Here it comes, I thought. She wants something. Then again, I didn't have anything to give so what could it be?

"What kind of promise?" I asked.

"From today and until you marry," she said, "When you have sex, pull out before your climax. If you do that, it won't ruin the girl's life, and you won't be forced to marry someone you don't love. Promise me, Rene."

I'd never given serious thought to having sex with anyone else but Ellie, so this was out of the blue, but one look at her swollen belly told me her request was for my own good. She wanted me to make an adult commitment.

"I promise, Ellie."

She wasn't finished with me.

"One last thing," she said. "All boys brag, and I don't want to be just another of your trophy stories. Be the gentleman who remembers but never tells. Promise me that."

I did.

On the walk back, we talked about her future after the baby was born.

"The strangest thing," she said. "Captain Berthe reviewed my file and assigned me to work with Eudora in the classroom. She's offered to help me work toward my high school equivalent certification. Now I can help the other girls and learn at the same time. Captain Berthe used to be really difficult. I'm really surprised."

I wasn't. I knew her story but didn't have the right to share it with Ellie. I think God finally found the right spot for Captain Berthe Karlsson—just in time.

* * *

THE NOISES IN THE HALLWAY took me back to Christmas and Easter when everyone was busy in preparation for the big day. This big day was for Mom, and the girls were given assignments. In the Arts and Crafts room, they ripped up and sewed old sheets into garlands and ribbons to be hung in the Great Room. Spring flowers were in full bloom all around the hospital, and the university sent someone to teach flower arranging. Every day there'd be a new floral display on the dining table as the girls polished their new techniques.

Since no one with Jonna's directing ability had come in, Captain Trudy had taken over the choir. She must have taken notes because, from a distance, she sounded just like Jonna as she chewed them out and then offered encouragement. I hope she didn't try to do the solo work though. The comparison would stop there.

Mom asked me to give her away. It caught me off guard because I'd never wondered who did that in regular weddings. I guess it should have been the father of the bride, but that wouldn't work. He'd died in 1943.

"Sure," I said. "It'll give me an excuse to wear my blue suit again."

She said that Carl had chosen his son, Carl Junior, to be his best man. He was only twelve years old, but I guessed there was no law against that. She called him Carlie. Mom told me that Carl bought a house and was having it remodeled so it'd be ready right after the wedding. The bad news was that I'd have to share a room with Carlie, but that wouldn't be a problem since he was there only for the summer, and I spent most of my summers with my dad.

Mom planned to go downtown to shop for her wedding dress and asked me to go with her but not because I was good at that sort of thing. Eudora offered to help Mom choose something, and I'd be needed to help her on and off the streetcar. She was about eight months gone and hadn't seen her feet in months. I was concerned that people might think I was the father, but Mom said she looked more like my older sister. I decided to go with that.

We went to Dayton's Department Store and then to the Emporium and back to Dayton's. Watching Mom try on dresses held no interest for me, but it gave me a chance to hang around the television department. That was a real marvel. Radio with pictures. Programs didn't start till 3:00 p.m., but all the TV sets were tuned in to a test pattern. A salesman explained about signal sharpness and the importance of black and white contrast. There were only three screen sizes. The seven-inch screen seemed too small, but I didn't think we needed the giant ten-inch. If we had the dough, I would have spent it on the eight-and-one-half-inch model. It was one hundred twenty five dollars with a payment plan. I felt real important about making those decisions and only hoped the salesman didn't know that I had no money.

Back in the Women's department, Mom stood on a platform trying on a light blue-dress made of shantung, but it looked like silk to me. She found a pair of linen shoes to go with it, and together they looked great. Mom was a good-looking woman, but I was always embarrassed when I thought about her that way. Everything went with us on the streetcar, and my hands were full what with helping Eudora to load the boxes. We walked into the hospital in time for supper.

Doctor Hickman's car was in the driveway, and he stood in the entryway when we came in.

"I hear congratulations are in order," he said. "When's the big day, Jo?"

"The third of June," Mom said. "It's a Saturday, so I hope you can come, Doctor."

"I'll try," he said, "but I've been spending a lot of time at the nursing home."

"How is your wife doing?" Mom asked.

"Not well," he said. "She's on medication and has early symptoms of pneumonia. I'm recommending that she be hospitalized. Thank you for asking."

Doctor Hickman looked like a man who had been beaten down. Concern for his wife would be worry enough, but I had the feeling news of Mom's wedding was like a second punch to the gut.

"Why are you here, Doctor?" Mom asked.

"One of the girls tripped over a desk leg in the classroom and fell," he said. She's about eight months and complained of pain in the groin. Thought I'd better check."

"Who is it?" Mom asked.

"The girl that played piano in the Easter program," he said. "I think its Elise B."

When I heard her name, my heart leaped to my throat.

"Is she okay?" I blurted without a second thought. "I mean, is the baby all right?"

"Yeah, I think so," he said. "I did a pelvic and didn't see anything unusual, but my recommendation is that she spend the next couple of days in bed. She's a little early to deliver but you can't be too careful this far along."

My first thought was I had caused some damage to the baby when Ellie and I had sex on the couch. Did I put too much pressure on her stomach? Maybe I poked the baby by going in too deep! Was that possible? I'd have to look it up in my science book because I sure couldn't ask Doctor Hickman—especially with Mom there.

"Rene, what's the matter?" Mom asked. "You look pale."

I was trying to think of a good excuse for my pale look when Cassie came to my rescue.

"Oh, Mrs. Dardenne, after supper show us your dress," she yelled on her way downstairs. "Maybe it'll fit me in a month. Then all I'll need is someone to marry."

~33~

ACH MAY THE SALVATION ARMY Booth Home administrators from all over the U.S. met to share experiences, discuss common problems and plan for the coming year.

"Not much happens at those national meetings," Captain Berthe said at breakfast. "They drink coffee, compare notes and talk a lot, but in the end there's not much they can tell us about pregnant girls that we don't already know."

"Major Ellen is due back this afternoon, and we'll hear the same old stuff," said Lieutenant Margit. "But this time she wants a staff meeting as soon as she gets here."

That evening I showed up for supper, but the dining room was empty even though the bell had rung. I sat alone at my place and wondered what was going on. I heard voices from the Great Room, and just as I was about to eavesdrop, the door swung open and the staff filed in.

"What's the matter with kids today?" Captain Trudy asked loudly. "You'd think that tobacco, alcohol, and sex would be enough."

"Just when you think you've got it figured out, they change the rules," answered Lieutenant Corliss. "Are we supposed to be policemen now?"

I hoped that Major Ellen's "no shoptalk" rule would be suspended tonight because it sounded like the talk would be about something besides babies and religion. There was no way to guess I would become the focus of their continued conversation. After the server girls left the room, Major Ellen turned to me.

"Rene, I've been attending a national meeting in Chicago and a serious problem came up for discussion."

I couldn't imagine why Major Ellen told me this.

"It seems that Booth Homes in New York and Chicago are experiencing problems beyond the usual reasons girls come to us for help," she said. "Several new residents have shown up with evidence of addiction to drugs."

I nodded my head as if I understood, but so far I hadn't a clue.

"After questioning, they admitted they got the drugs in high school, and that it's more common than we suspect," she said, still not coming to the point. "The national council is concerned because this drug thing might spread, but none of us has been trained to recognize or treat it. In fact, the only drugs I know about are those we give to residents in labor to ease the pain, but we get those legally."

"Where do high school students get drugs?" asked Brigadier Thomas. "Isn't everything supposed to be done by prescription?"

By now it was clear they had zeroed in on me. Every time high school was mentioned, they all swiveled their heads in my direction, even Mom.

"We were told that this drug thing all started in New York with a group called the Mafia," said Major Ellen. "They use older students to give it to the younger ones for free. When they become hooked . . ." She stopped to explain she'd learned that word yesterday and apologized for using what she called, "street vernacular." I made a mental note to look up the word vernacular.

"Once they're hooked, they begin charging for the drugs. The boys then turn to stealing and, in the case of girls, to prostitution to feed their habit. It doesn't take a genius to figure out where we come in."

"But at least they're off drugs after they get here," said Lieutenant Margit.

"Maybe off drugs but not off the craving," said Major Ellen. "They continue to lie, steal and do whatever necessary to get them or risk a painful withdrawal."

"What are we supposed to do about it?" asked Captain Trudy. "I wouldn't know a drug addict if I saw one."

"A national committee was formed to come up with a training program for Booth Homes to recognize drug users, and we'll all go through it," said Major Ellen. "Until they do, we must be on the lookout for obvious signs. Mrs. Dardenne, would you go through them."

I was surprised she called on Mom because, to my knowledge, she'd never had experience with drugs except those given in labor.

"It all starts during the admittance process," she said. "Look for inattentiveness, bleary eyes, runny nose, and sloppy dress. A good tipoff is if she's not crying. When she gets to me, I'll look for the obvious like needle marks in her arm and any signs of jaundice. Continually asking for water is another sign."

I saw another Mom. We'd never talked about drugs, but I could tell that she'd used me as a practice dummy to sharpen her observation skills.

"As you all know," Mom said, "we keep a supply of pain reliever drugs in a locked cabinet in my office. The key is in my desk, but as a precaution, it will now be kept in Major Ellen's office in a locked drawer. Let me know if you see or hear anyone hanging around in the delivery area or going through desk drawers."

Major Ellen thanked Mom and then got right to the point.

"Rene, have you ever been approached with an offer for free drugs in your high school?"

After this conversation started I figured that this drug thing would somehow work its way to me, and I had a ready answer.

"No, Major Ellen," I said truthfully. "I've never been offered free drugs at Murray High."

"Oh, thank God," she said with obvious relief. "Hopefully that horrid Mafia hasn't reached the Twin Cities yet, so we still may have time."

240

After I left the dining room I realized that I'd followed Jonna's advice. Her last words to me were, "Tell only as much of the truth as you have to." When I told Major Ellen I'd never been offered free drugs at Murray High, it was the truth. What I didn't tell her was a guy in the locker room once said, "Hey, Baldy, if you ever wanna buy some dope and get blitzed, see Johnny Bittolini's brother. Their dad has contacts."

This really set up a moral dilemma for me. Was I right to give Major Ellen a false sense of hope about lack of drugs in the Twin Cities by shading the truth? On the other hand, I really didn't know anyone who was on dope, and all talk about Johnny Boy's dad might be guys just talking shit. Either way, I was almost through the school year, and the last thing I wanted was to give Johnny Boy a reason to single me out. I decided to keep my mouth shut.

* * *

BEFORE THE STREETCAR CAME TO A STOP, I saw a patrol car from the St. Paul Police Department in the driveway. I flashed back to the day we arrived, when the police came in with a blue coat and a cardboard suitcase. Ever since, a police car in the driveway meant trouble.

I went to check our mail and heard a man's voice in Major Ellen's office. Since I hadn't read the latest issue of *War Cry*, I plopped down on the couch and turned the pages quietly. There was a scraping of chairs and shuffling of feet. A policeman walked out followed by a woman who fit the exact image of a social worker. She wore a funny swirled black hat, a dark business suit and laced-up Enna Jettick shoes. It wasn't a uniform, but might as well have been. The next person was a surprise. It was Ellie, dressed in a pink robe and wearing scuffies. She looked like she'd just gotten out of bed.

"Let us know where you settle after you leave here," the woman said. "We'll get together with the lawyer and work out details. Good luck with your baby."

Ellie wiggled her fingers at me and went back into the office. She looked like she'd been crying. I'd have to wait until supper for details.

At home I tried to practice piano but couldn't manage any enthusiasm. Even working on "Für Elise" didn't help although I had improved. I wondered if the day would ever come when I could play it all the way through without stopping. Imagine the look on Ellie's face then. Damn it, there she was in my mind again.

What happened today? Why the police? To pass the time, I tuned in to the Mutual Network to get the day's time trials results from the Indianapolis 500. Mauri Rose was my favorite driver and had the best time so far.

Supper hadn't provided the flood of information I hoped for. Instead, it was mostly small talk and Captain Trudy's nightly report of preparations for the wedding. The girls made enough garlands out of old sheets to cover the Great Room, and they enjoyed it so much they didn't want to stop. We were at the dessert course and I'd almost given up on learning anything.

"There were police here today," old Colonel Thomas said, loudly. "Is somebody in trouble?"

"No, there are no problems, Esther," Major Ellen said. "One of the residents had a death in the family, and no one knew where to find her. The police were called in to help."

"How's the girl?" the old lady asked.

"She took it fairly well considering it was her mother," Major Ellen said. "A few tears, but she's rather stoic about it. She keeps her thoughts to herself."

For once it seemed that I knew more than the rest of the table. I knew the hell Ellie went through at home, so it was no surprise that she wasn't emotional. Because of the alcohol, she hadn't known her mother for years. I couldn't imagine what it would be like to lose a parent, even though Dad hadn't been much of an influence in my life for thirteen years. I might lose a part of Mom when she married, but maybe that would prepare me to go away to college.

Mom and I listened to the radio as the St. Paul Saints played the Indianapolis Indians. It was only AAA minor league ball, but at least, after such a long winter, it was baseball.

"How did Ellie's mother die?" I asked.

"Oh, it's very sad, Rene. Ellie told me about it after the police left. Her mother died from cirrhosis of the liver a few weeks ago. She has no relatives now, except for a no-good stepfather who's alcoholic too. The police found a phone number in Ellie's room at home and traced it here."

"Is she upset?" I asked.

"It's hard to tell with Ellie," she said. "She's learned to mask her feelings. Maybe that's what happens when you've been abused as a child. I do know that she doesn't want the baby. The good part about that is she won't be upset at giving it away."

"What's she going to do after that?" I asked.

"She told me she wants to go to college," Mom said. "I think there was some insurance money or a college fund from her father. She's a bright girl and should go on to school, especially since she's going to have to take care of herself."

If the news about the money was true, then I felt much better about Ellie's future. Maybe now she'd get the break in life she deserved.

The phone rang, never good news in the evening.

"Okay. I'm on my way. Get everything ready," Mom said. "It's Ellie. She's started labor even though it's early. Don't wait up."

That was easy for Mom to say, but I did wait up, at least until midnight. I'd heard stories of men who paced the floor in waiting rooms, smoked packs of cigarettes and read magazines until the doctor came out to announce whether it was a girl or boy. I didn't smoke yet so that wasn't available, but I did pace from the kitchen to the living room. To listen to the ballgame didn't help since I didn't know the players. I thumbed through a baseball magazine but couldn't keep my mind on it. I couldn't hang around the hospital because everyone might guess our secret. I didn't have any feelings for the baby, but Ellie had to come through okay. I didn't remember when I went to bed, but in the morning I woke up in the same clothes. Mom's bed hadn't been touched.

Most of the staff was at the table when I slipped in for breakfast. Mom had that tired look that came from a long night's duty. There was a cot in her office but she said trying to nap through labor pains was a guarantee of a restless night.

"How's Ellie?" I asked.

"She had a bad night," Mom said. "We have her under medication, but she's getting very tired. We're considering a Cesarean, but I'm going to wait a little longer."

Just then there was a piercing scream followed by a groan.

Old Colonel Thomas looked up and scowled.

"Damn committee of men," she said.

That was what she had said the first time I heard labor in the dining room, and after eight months I still wasn't used to it during meals. Today was worse since it was the pain of someone I cared about. I was about to ask Mom to do something else for Ellie when she said, "I think that's it. Shouldn't be long now." She excused herself to go upstairs.

How did she know, I wondered. Before we came here I'd never had a chance to see Mom at work, and now I was really proud of her.

Time had gotten away from me, and I had to run across the lawn for the streetcar. I had given up hiding my tie-in with the hospital long ago, and my schoolmates were tired of teasing me about it. School would soon be over anyway. There were a couple of finals left, but today I turned in my book report on *The Sun Also Rises*. I felt like Brett and Jake in the book. They had feelings for each other that weren't going to go anywhere either, but at least I'd proved I didn't have his problem with impotence.

At noon, I was in line behind Carolyn Lautner in the cafeteria. She nodded and looked away. Man, if she and her mother thought I knew too much months ago, what would they say about this wait for the birth of a baby by a girl I had sex with during her pregnancy. My guess was they'd call me a pervert. Frankly, I felt pretty good about it.

The ride home on the streetcar was one of the longest in memory. When I jumped off and looked across the lawn, my heart almost stopped. An ambulance, its rear door open, was in the driveway, and the crew was lowering a stretcher down the stairs. It was Ellie. Something was wrong. I broke out in a run, jumped the hedge and headed for the ambulance. Lieutenant Corliss walked next to the stretcher and blocked Ellie's face. I moved around for a better look and saw a girl I didn't recognize.

"She's new," Lieutenant Corliss said. "Came in today complaining of stomach pains. She's losing blood and is probably aborting. We're taking her to university just in case."

I tried my best to act nonchalant, but I was out of breath from the run. "I thought it might be Ellie," I said between heavy pants.

"Oh, no," she said. "Ellie delivered this morning. It's a beautiful baby boy. He came a little early so he's small, but he has a great set of lungs."

I felt a sudden relief but hoped it didn't show. Maybe that's what it was like to be a father. Back in the nurses' home I celebrated the only way I knew how. I opened *Sixty Progressive Piano Pieces* to page ninety.

~34~

Friday, May 26th, was the last day of school—also the last time I would take the Toonerville Trolley to Murray High. A rider held up the morning edition of the *St. Paul Plain Dealer*. "TWIN CITIES GANG DRUG BUST" read the headline, news that would either bring joy or sorrow to Major Ellen because it meant that drugs were already here.

The ride gave me a chance to review this crazy year. Last May I rode my bike to school through the desert, trying to avoid cactus and coyotes. For the last nine months I'd ridden a streetcar and, during the winter, got more comfortable on hockey skates than I ever had been on a bike. I was with kids I didn't know when school started, and today they were my friends. The sad part was, after one week, I'd never see them again. Then it was back to being the new kid who had to learn whatever sport was popular in Indiana. I thought it was basketball, and I wasn't good at that either. Wonder if they had a drug problem there?

Grades were handed out at the end of each class that day, and I hadn't done badly. A couple of B's and a few C+'s, but I was most proud of the A I got on *The Sun Also Rises* book report. That helped me get an overall A- in the class. The last class of the day was PE, and the instructor insisted we do laps around the track.

"This might be the last exercise you're gonna get for a while," he shouted. "Most of you'll probably sit on your asses all summer, so let's move out."

Back in the locker room, I put my underwear on, this time without facing the wall. By now I had a fairly nice patch of pubic hair, and the first to spot it was Johnny Boy.

246

"Well, look at Baldy," he said as he pointed at my crotch. "Can't call you that anymore." He thought for a moment, and said, "From now on, your name's Fuzzy."

That got a big laugh from Johnny's buddies and they chanted, "fuzzy, fuzzy, fuzzy." But Johnny Boy wasn't through with me.

"I'll bet a little bit of liniment might make that patch grow faster," he said with a smile that I'd call evil. "Get the First Aid Kit down guys. We're gonna give him a goin' away party he won't forget."

The school intercom cut through the din. "Angelo Bittolini, please report to the principal's office. Angelo Bittolini to the principal's office immediately."

Johnny Boy's face dropped when he heard his brother's name. "I gotta get outa here," he said and headed for the door. Saved again for the last time. I hoped this was something I wouldn't have to face at my new school. By then, my crotch should be right up to standards, liniment or no.

My final memory of Murray High was serendipitous. As I stopped by the principal's office, two policemen were standing on either side of Johnny Boy's older brother, Angelo, who was handcuffed to a radiator pipe. The intercom squawked ominously, "Johnny Bittolini, please report to the principal's office immediately. Johnny Bittolini, on the double."

As I walked away from Murray High for the last time, I looked over my shoulder and thought, "I guess there is a God after all."

Ellie's baby was two days old when I asked Mom how they were doing.

"Oh, it's a real surprise," she said. "Ellie is up first thing in the morning, changes the baby and gives him a bottle. Then she fusses around with him all day long."

"Is she thinking of keeping him?" I asked.

"I don't see how she can," Mom said. "She'll have to get a job, and there's no one to take care of him. Also, society isn't kind to young girls without a husband, even though it wasn't her fault. I can't say they're a lot nicer to divorced women either."

"Can I come see her?" I asked.

"Well, I guess so," Mom said. "Why do you want to do that?"

"She loaned me some beginning piano books and gave me some pointers," I said, as I shaded the truth a bit. "I want to return them and thank her before she leaves."

"Let me check with Major Ellen tomorrow," she said. "I don't think they've ever allowed a visitor in the nursery ward."

"Man on second. Man on second," I yelled as I climbed the stairs to the nursery ward carrying the books. I wasn't sure if anyone heard me because I was shouting through a gauze mask.

"Only three minutes, Rene," Lieutenant Margit said. "And be sure to wear the mask so you don't contaminate the baby."

Ellie was trimmer than the night we met and looked much different without that huge hump on her stomach. She led me to the Placement Ward, which meant she'd decided not to keep him. We looked through the window at a tiny thing dressed in booties and a knit cap.

"He's wearing the things Jonna made for her baby," she said. "She gave them to me because I didn't bother to knit anything. Isn't he beautiful? He looks just like my father, so I've named him Norman after my dad."

I didn't know what to say because the baby was still red, shriveled up and didn't look very cute to me. Ellie reached for my hand.

"Rene, this may be a lot to ask but I want him to be our baby," she said. "I can't stand the idea of my stepfather being even a small part of his life. I want somebody honest and kind to be his father, even for just a few days. Will you do that for me?"

This was really from nowhere because I thought Ellie would ignore the baby and give it up without a second thought. I never believed she would take any interest in it, especially to go as far as to pretend we were mommy and daddy. I didn't know what to say and time was running out so I squeezed her hand and nodded. The intercom interrupted the moment.

"Rene Dardenne. Time's up. Please report to the office."

"I'll see you at the wedding," Ellie said. "I promised your mom I'd play."

On Sunday I attended my last Mass at Our Lady of the Lake Catholic Church. Father Farelly delivered the sermon while Father McGowan worked the door after church. He motioned me over.

"Your mother told me the news," he said. "We're going to miss you both. It's a shame she's marrying a Protestant, but that's what happens when the devil gets his foot in the door. On the positive side, I am so pleased that you'll be leaving that evil environment."

For the first time I seriously questioned whether a priest knew what he was talking about. If so, this one would know that Booth Memorial Salvation Army women dedicated themselves to helping girls in need and they did it without being judgmental, just as priests and nuns were supposed to do.

He stuck his hand out and said, "Good luck, Rene. See you in church."

I walked away feeling strangely liberated. He didn't specify which church.

* * *

MEMORIAL DAY WAS SPENT GLUED to the radio listening to the Indianapolis 500. I'd been following the time trials and my favorite, Mauri Rose, had the third fastest time and started on the front row. The official pace car was a 1950 Mercury convertible driven by Clark Gable, who got them off to a good start. Unfortunately, the race was plagued by rain and was stopped after 138 laps instead of the usual 200. Johnnie Parsons was the winner, and Rose finished where he started—third. There was always next year.

Captain Tucker called before breakfast and asked me to bring a case of V-8 juice to the basement kitchen. Usually she asked for just a couple of cans, but I guessed they were stocking up before I left. Mom insisted that V-8 juice got me through the winter, but frankly I didn't care if I never saw another can of it.

At breakfast, no one cared about the Indy 500 except old Colonel Thomas.

"I was at the Booth Hospital in Detroit in 1911 when they ran the first one," she said. "I was putting a flag on my husband's grave when somebody told me there was a 500-mile race in Indianapolis. You never heard such complaining. 'Who the hell does Indianapolis think it is?' people were saying. 'We're the automobile capital of the United States.'"

"Mother, please don't swear in front of the boy," Brigadier Thomas said.

Old Colonel Thomas swept her hand like she just brushed off a fly.

"It was just a bunch of Detroiters bellyaching because they were jealous," she said. "They said it'd never last and how old is it now?"

"Thirty-nine years," I said.

"Serves 'em right," she said.

I always remembered the date of the first race because it was just two weeks after Mom was born. Her birthday always kicked off the Indy 500 season for me.

"Rene, could you move a step ladder into the Great Room for me?" Captain Trudy asked. "The girls want to hang something."

I walked into the hallway and heard the sound I had been dreading. Ellie was sitting on the stairway where so many girls had been before only this time it was her turn to sob. The Social Services lady was there, and Ellie had just given up little Norman for placement. Months ago Major Ellen warned me about interfering, but I headed for the stairway. Captain Berthe Karlsson came out of the office, wagged her finger, and went to be with Ellie. I was almost relieved, even though it was someone I cared for, I still didn't know what I would have said.

As I walked down the driveway there was a black, 1948 Plymouth with state license plates. A man and woman sat in the front seat as she filled out papers. In the back seat, inside a small baby bed, was tiny Norman wearing the clothes Jonna had knitted for her baby. He would start his life again, but this time with someone other than his birth mother. I walked in the back door of the nurses' home and headed right for the basement. I lay on the couch where Ellie and I had had sex, and tried to dope out the things in life I didn't understand.

What kind of God lets bad things happen to good people?

Wasn't rape by her stepfather punishment enough for Ellie?

Why was she punished again by having to give up her baby?

Why was Mom punished for a divorce she didn't want?

Am I being punished for sinning with Ellie?

Is God taking my mother from me because of that?

Will she marry someone she doesn't love just to put a man in my life?

Why was there only fear and punishment from the God I'd come to know?

Where was the loving God I learned about in Catechism?

I sat there for a long time and couldn't come up with one single answer. I even prayed, something I'd never done outside of church. When my mind wandered, the same images came back—Little Norman in the back seat of a '47 Plymouth and Ellie in tears on the stairway. I swallowed, blinked my eyes and even bit my tongue but nothing worked. In the end the emotion was too much. I sat on the couch, put my head between my knees and cried.

~35~

OM'S WISH TO BE A JUNE BRIDE was about to become a reality. It was Saturday the third, and Minnesota had given her a beautiful blue-sky day. Carl and his son, Carlie, had arrived the previous day and checked in at the Happy Hollow Motel. We all went out to eat at what was called a bridal dinner. Carl told us all about the newly remodeled house, but something else he said stuck in my mind.

"I'm going to teach you to drive," he said. "Then we'll get your learner's permit. By January you'll be a licensed driver."

That was seven months away I thought. Seemed like forever, but then I'd be behind the wheel of that Buick. I could hardly wait.

I packed my suitcase and put it by the door because we'd leave right after the ceremony. My very first room looked just as stark and sterile as the day I moved in. To put anything on the wall was never allowed. No pictures, no pennants. In a day or two, no one would even remember I'd been here. I put on my new blue suit and looked in the mirror to tie my tie. Mom was right. I looked pretty sharp.

She looked beautiful in her shantung dress and matching shoes. Carl was a pretty lucky guy, I thought. We walked to the hospital where people were already gathered in the Great Room. Ellie was at the piano and played the kind of music people would recognize but didn't really hear when in a crowd. Mom introduced Carl to Colonel Payton, who would perform the marriage ceremony. He took them into Major Ellen's office for a last-minute conversation.

The decorations in the Great Room were beautiful. Every place one could hang a garland the girls had hung one. A large table was covered with a white linen tablecloth and in the center was a two-tiered wedding cake with a bride and groom on the top. For this special occasion, Major Ellen brought out the very best crystal punch bowl and cups with no chips. I had never seen anything more elegant, and I thought Mom deserved this.

I sat next to Ellie on the piano bench. She smiled and played "Für Elise" with a flair I could never hope to achieve.

"I have some news," she whispered. "I'll tell you later."

Doctor Hickman was with an intern he introduced as Jack Howard. "Jack's a new intern but an old soul," he told Carlie and me. "He was a medic in the war so he's seen the deadly side of doctoring. He's never seen a birth though, and we're hoping we'll get lucky soon." Jack smiled but looked over our shoulders toward the dining room. "Like most interns, he doesn't make much money," Doctor Hickman joked, "so I promised him a good mid-western meal if he'd come with me today. The truth is I promised your mom I'd be here," he said. We'll make Saturday rounds after the ceremony."

I had to admit, given a choice I would have picked Doctor Hickman to be the one Mom would marry, but his wife was still alive and who knew when that would change. I wished Mom could have waited but it could take years.

Major Ellen joined the conversation.

"Doctor Hickman, I'm very sorry for your loss," she said. "We just heard this morning."

"Thank you, Major," he said. "The funeral will be on Monday so I won't be here for regular exams."

"Of course," she said, "and you'll be in our prayers. At least her suffering is over and now she's with the Lord."

"I would like to believe that," he said. "Thank you for your thoughts."

I was stunned and tried to keep my face frozen in a sad look but my mind raced ahead. Did I hear right? His wife died? I wondered if Mom knew. She was in there with Carl and Colonel Payton so how could she. Was it too late for her to change her mind? Did she and Doctor Hickman ever talk about the future? Probably not because Mom wasn't that kind of person. Did she know if he even cared about her that way? Too many questions and no answers. It was lousy timing because if this had happened a little bit sooner things might've been different. Why did God do these things?

The answers would have to wait because the dining room door opened and Captain Tucker rang her little dinner bell. As we filed in, I saw this was a special meal. Extra leaves had been added to the table to handle the two large floral displays of freshly picked spring flowers created by the residents in Arts and Crafts. The silverware absolutely sparkled, courtesy of Dodo, who still loved to polish. Mom and Carl were seated at the head of the table with Carlie and me on either side. The rest of the table was filled with Salvation Army officers. Doctor Hickman and Jack Howard sat at the opposite end. Colonel Payton prayed one of those lengthy Protestant blessings that included best wishes for a long and happy marriage. With the "Amen," the parade of food started.

From the kitchen, residents floated through the swinging door, each responsible for a portion of our feast. Cassie carried a glazed ham that was almost as big as her stomach. It had pineapple slices on top with cherries in the center. Next was a bowl of boiled green beans with strips of bacon floating in the water . . . still not my favorite. I was surprised to see Eudora with a serving dish. She was close to delivery but wanted to be a part of the wedding. She was about to set the mashed potatoes on the table, when Jack Howard suddenly jumped up from his chair.

"Allison," he shouted. "What are you doing here?"

We all looked around. There was no Allison at the table. Eudora looked at Jack, and her face turned white. She dropped the bowl of mashed potatoes right in front of Colonel Payton and fainted.

Jack ran over and knelt beside her.

"I know her," he said. "Her name is Allison, and I've been looking for her for months. We were supposed to get married."

So, this was the guy she'd been hiding from all this time. She told us he was a med student but must not have known he was an intern at University Hospital.

Mom and Doctor Hickman jumped right in. She poured some ice water on a napkin and put it on Eudora's forehead. Her eyes opened and she blinked a couple of times.

"Jack," she said, "how did you know I was here?"

"He didn't," Doctor Hickman said. "I brought him along today just to observe."

They helped her stand up and saw a large wet spot on the carpet. Her water had broken. Eudora was in labor.

After she was moved to the labor room, Jack stayed at her side. Colonel Payton used the time to remove most of the mashed potatoes from his uniform, and we all sat down to re-start the wedding luncheon. We were well into the dessert course, fresh blackberries over vanilla ice cream, when we heard familiar labor noises. They were several minutes apart at first but grew closer. Neither Carl nor Carlie had been through a labor meal before and looked at each other kinda funny. Captain Karlsson came in and asked Mom, Doctor Hickman, and Colonel Payton to come with her.

"Eudora and Jack want to be married before the baby comes," she said. "We already have a minister here, and they want you to be their witnesses. We'd better hurry."

The rest of us sat around the table making small talk as Eudora's screams punctuated the conversation.

"Damn committee of men," old Colonel Thomas said loudly.

Everyone at the table just looked away but Carl and Carlie were a fresh audience for her favorite subject. She continued to damn those men, but I knew the real truth. While moving suitcases in the trunk room,

I found a pamphlet printed for the dedication of "The New Salvation Army Rescue and Maternity Home of the Twin Cities." It was dated March 19th, 1913, and showed floor plans for this building. On the original layout, the officer's dining room was down the hall where the arts and crafts rooms were now. The present dining room was originally a workroom and not the result of poor planning by a "Committee of Men." The workroom was bigger than the dining room so they swapped, but with the extra space, they got the screams. I'd been waiting for the right moment to spring this information, but now wasn't the time. The women seemed to enjoy being able to complain about men's poor decisions—especially Colonel Thomas. I didn't want to spoil the old woman's fun.

Mom, Doctor Hickman and Colonel Payton finally returned from the impromptu wedding ceremony. I searched for some sign that Mom and Doctor Hickman might have an announcement, but we went back to our dessert almost as if nothing had happened. One thing was different though. We were no longer hearing labor screams of Eudora. Now they were the labor screams of Mrs. Jack Howard.

* * *

LIEUTENANT MARGIT OPENED THE DOORS to the Great Room to reveal a thirty-voice residents' choir dressed in white robes. Captain Trudy stepped up and cued Ellie, who began to play "Some Enchanted Evening" from *South Pacific*. It immediately brought back memories of Jonna. She would have loved this and, of course, she'd have a solo. The attendees were seated in chairs arranged in a semi-circle toward the fireplace. Seated in the back row was Max, who wore his best suit and tie and had even trimmed his beard for the occasion.

Mom and Major Ellen were in her office. The tradition was for the bride to come in from somewhere on the arm of somebody, and that would be my job. When everyone was seated, I went to get her. As I entered the outer office I heard Major Ellen's voice. "Do you really love him?"

"He's a very fine man, Major, and I'm sure we're going to be very happy together. That's really all I want for us."

"What are your feelings toward Doctor Hickman?" Major Ellen asked. "Things have suddenly changed for him."

"We've never even talked about that, Major," Mom said. "Besides, it's too late to think about it. In a few minutes I'm going to marry Carl."

I made a scuffling noise with my feet and knocked on the wall.

"They're ready to start," I said. "I just have to give the signal."

Mom took a deep breath. "Go ahead," she said. "Now or never."

I waved to Captain Trudy, and Ellie started to play Lohengrin's "Wedding March." Until last night's rehearsal, I always thought it was called, "Here Comes the Bride" so my music education wasn't complete yet.

"Girls, people notice when you slouch," Captain Trudy reminded the choir during rehearsal, "so tomorrow please remember your posture, stand erect and throw your shoulders back when you sing."

Captain Trudy had learned a lot from Jonna, but she still couldn't bring herself to say "knockers up."

Mom gripped my arm so tightly that I could feel her body shaking. We followed Major Ellen who walked behind Dodo, the flower girl. She took such care to distribute the flower petals evenly that we almost ran out of music. Ellie saw the problem, threw in a little something extra and we ended up in front of Colonel Payton just as the music ended.

The choir sang "Indian Love Call," Mom's favorite song since Nelson Eddy and Jeanette MacDonald sang it together in a movie. Carl looked sharp in a dark suit that looked even more serious than mine. Carlie wore a greenish, striped sport coat that stood out from all the Salvation Army uniforms in the room.

Colonel Peyton, with his beautiful speaking voice, started the ceremony.

"Dearly Beloved, we are gathered together here in the presence of God to unite this couple in the holy bonds of matrimony. Who is bringing Josephine to be joined to Carl?"

For a moment I drew a blank. Mom elbowed me.

"I am," I said in my most adult voice.

Just as I said the words, we heard a scream from the dining room. Eudora was still in labor and Captain Tucker hurried to close the door. I looked around the room at the strange ceremony I was a part of. Mom was about to be married to a Protestant by a man in a uniform. No robes, no vestments, no incense, no Latin. The guests were non-Catholic women who had dedicated their lives to God. The room was filled with pregnant girls whose morals had been compromised by sins of the flesh. It made me wonder if this marriage would be considered legal.

Colonel Peyton was at the place where, in most weddings, people freeze and are afraid to cough because everyone would look at them. In the movies, it was the part where someone stepped forward and said, "Yes, I have a reason . . ."

"If anyone has any good reason why these persons should not be married," he said, "speak now, or forever hold your peace."

The timing was incredible. We all heard what must have been the most piercing scream ever delivered at Booth Memorial. Mom looked up.

"That's it," she said. "Excuse me for a minute."

She motioned to Doctor Hickman and they left the room to go upstairs.

Poor Carl didn't know what to do. He hadn't exactly been left at the altar, but he certainly had some unexpected time on his hands. With nothing better to do, Carlie picked up a copy of *War Cry*, but in just a matter of seconds put it back in the magazine rack. Ellie flipped through her music and played "Some Enchanted Evening" again, and the chorus joined in without Captain Trudy conducting. They ran through "Indian

Love Call" twice and finally sang church hymns they knew by heart. Finally, Captain Trudy gave everyone a break while we waited for Eudora to deliver.

Ellie motioned to me to sit with her.

"I've got some news," she whispered. "Captain Berthe is working on a scholarship for me at the University of Wisconsin. She also found me a part-time job, and I can rent a room at her aunt's home in Madison. I'm thinking it over."

Mom and Doctor Hickman reappeared.

"It's a girl," he said. "Six pounds, twelve ounces and thirteen inches long. Mother and baby are doing fine and the father's recovering. He'd never seen a birth before. May change his mind about medicine."

I had to nudge Carl, who'd fallen asleep after the big lunch.

"About time," he said with a groggy voice.

He and Mom stood up again in front of Colonel Peyton. To save time, he picked up the ceremony at "If anyone has a good reason this couple should not . . ." I stood next to Doctor Hickman and half expected him to come up with a reason, but it was just wishful thinking. His eyes blinked faster, but he didn't say a word.

"I now pronounce you man and wife," said Colonel Peyton. "You may kiss the bride."

So, that was it. Despite delivering a baby in the middle of her wedding, Mom still looked fresh and lovely but when I looked down, her new blue linen shoes were spattered with Eudora's blood. My first thought was, I'd never get those clean in a million years.

The cake cutting ceremony was something you'd see on the cover of the *Saturday Evening Post*, only with an older bride and groom. Mom and Carl held the knife together and cut the first piece. In the movies, the bride took the piece of cake and shoved it in the groom's face. Since this wasn't the movies the first piece went to Major Ellen. It was a vanilla cake made from Pillsbury dough milled right down the street in Minneapolis. The fluffy white icing was the kind that stuck to your finger if you accidentally touched it, like I did. It also tasted great when you had to lick it off, like I did. Captain Tucker and her staff worked on it all night and now peeked from behind the dining room door to see how we liked it. When the party was over, Mom carefully put the bride and groom figure in a napkin as a keepsake of our time in St. Paul.

While Mom changed clothes, everyone gathered outside at the base of the steps and waited for her to toss the bridal bouquet to the eligible single women. Since this was a home for unwed pregnant girls operated by unmarried women, everybody was. The busy Arts and Crafts girls had painted "Just Married" across the rear window of the Buick. "Two kids already" was on the side windows with arrows that pointed to Carlie and me in the back seat. The traditional tin cans were tied to the rear bumper but these were #10 sizes that would make a helluva racket.

Mom stood on the stoop ready to toss the bridal bouquet, but someone stepped in and turned her around. According to tradition, it had to be thrown over the shoulder so she couldn't be accused of favoritism. Whoever caught it would be the next to be married. She pitched it high in the air, and it landed in the grasp of old Colonel Thomas, who had just raised her arm to shield her eyes from the sun.

She saw the bouquet in her hand and said, "I'll be damned."

"Mother, please don't swear," Brigadier Thomas said. "The residents can hear."

The old lady gave her a dirty look and chucked it back in the air. Almost as a reflex, Ellie reached up and snagged it. Since today was the day she would leave, they all took it as a good omen and cheered.

Mom and I stood at the top of the steps as everyone lined up to say goodbye. It turned out to be a review of the last nine months of my life.

Captain Tucker said she'd really miss me at mealtime because I ate everything she cooked and even asked for seconds. I wouldn't miss her boiled green beans with bacon floating in water but didn't say so.

Captain Trudy, who I never saw with a hair out of place, told me she was sorry I never sang with her choir.

"I would have loved a boy soprano in there," she said. I still cringed at the thought.

"Maybe you'll have a bathroom without women's unmentionables hanging around," Lieutenant Corliss said. "And, don't forget, I can still beat you in ping pong."

She was right. I had never won a game unless she let me.

Max gave me a firm handshake. "I can never thank you and your mother enough," he said in heavily accented English. "*Sudie, jaunuolis. Geros keliones.*"

My sketchy memory of Lithuanian translated that to be, "Good-bye, young fellow. Have a great trip."

"You're the little brother I always wanted," Lieutenant Margit said. "I'm gonna miss you, Reneé," she said, misprouncing my name on purpose. We both laughed, and I gave her a big hug.

Captain McTavish, of the cantaloupe bra, said, "Every time I see a can of V-8 juice, I'll think of you." What did she know about what happened in the basement, I wondered.

"You're not going to have *War Cry* to read anymore," Brigadier Thomas said. "We can arrange a subscription if you'd like." I thanked her for her thoughtfulness but said it just wouldn't be the same in Indiana —especially since there wouldn't be any eavesdropping to do.

Old Colonel Thomas was direct and to the point, as always. "Don't let anybody push you around or try to tell you what to do," she said. "Just listen to God and tell the rest of 'em to go to hell."

I thanked her for her words of wisdom.

"You've got your whole life ahead of you," Captain Berthe Karlsson said. "Make every minute count, Rene, and don't forget to count your blessings." Of all the officers I'd met in the past nine months she had changed the most—from authoritative and judgmental to almost kind and loving.

Major Ellen, usually reserved and proper, gave me a big hug and said how much she would miss my questions at the dining table.

"This is another new start for you, Rene," she said. "I hope your future goes well from now on. God bless you." I was less sensitive to someone saying "God bless you" now since I'd learned it often came from the heart and not just from the mouth—but you still had to consider the source.

I was about to choke up. These people had been strangers to me nine months ago, and now it was like I was about to leave my family. What would Father McGowan say about that?

With some effort, Cassie climbed the steps and tried to give me a hug. She was so close to delivery that we had to do it sidesaddle. I wondered what would happen to her once she delivered because she was no cuter now than the day she arrived.

"Remember, keep your eye on the puck and your pecker in your pants," she teased. Cassie laughed so hard at her own joke, I thought she'd go into labor on the steps. I hoped her personality would be enough to overcome what God hadn't given her in looks.

Eudora waved to us from the mother's nursery while Jack held the baby up like some sort of prize. She mouthed the words, "Thank you."

Ellie sat off to the side with her suitcase.

"I didn't want this day to come," she said. "I never thought I'd say that but I've never been alone before. Rene, I'm scared and not sure I can do it."

You'd think, after nine months, I'd have learned some words of reassurance, but I still couldn't come up with the right thing to say. I leaned over and gave her a kiss on the forehead.

"Everything's going to be okay," I said with not much conviction. "When you're feeling alone and scared, just hum a few measures of 'Für Elise' and think of me."

All I got was a sad smile, and then she slapped my hand.

"One final promise," she said. "I'm so fond of you but don't ever try to find out what happened to me. I want to end this part of my life with no strings, no attachments and no worries. Promise?"

For one last time, I did.

There was one hand left to shake before I left Booth Memorial. Dr. Hickman was off to the side talking with Carl while we said our good-byes. I didn't imagine they had a lot in common except Mom and me, and she was probably off limits. If it was me, I hoped the topic was not just how to keep me from becoming a sissy. As I looked at them together I saw two men successful in different ways. One a well-respected physician dedicated to saving the lives of his patients. The other a well-respected businessman committed to the growth of his community, both a good catch by any woman's measure. If the timing had only been different I was not sure Mom would have made the choice she made today, but it was done. For me it was a unique opportunity to compare what could have been versus what was soon to be. The sad part was I had no say in either.

"Good luck to you, Rene," said Doctor Hickman, pumping my hand. "Make sure you show those Indiana boys how to play real hockey," he laughed. "Teach them the good stuff like high sticking, puck flipping and body blocking. All our Minnesota secrets," he joked. "And take good care of your mother if this guy doesn't."

I'm not sure Carl was tuned in to Dr. Hickman's sense of humor because he would look at his watch and then at the car. Everyone waved goodbye as we drove down the driveway, past the nurses' home and turned onto Como Avenue. We passed the guys playing baseball on the vacant lot, the place where I learned the thrill of skating backward and suffered the worst beating of my life. Eddie and Leo ran to the sidewalk to shout good-bye, and it hit me that I'd never see them again, or Father McGowan, who was on his daily dog walk. I thought I saw him make the sign of the cross as we passed but realized he was just trying to untangle the leash. He was not about to bless or be any part of the ceremony that just happened.

As we drove by Booth Memorial, the place of so many experiences in the past year, I saw Ellie walking down the long sidewalk carrying a cheap suitcase, a winter coat over her arm and a bridal bouquet in her hand. I flashed back to the day we arrived when another girl walked the same path on her way to the bridge and to her death.

My eyes followed her until we turned onto Snelling Avenue and passed the Como Theater where I made my first clumsy attempt to hold the hand of a girl who didn't want it held. Memories of Christmas popped up as we passed Olaf's Grocery, the donor of the Booth tree. We stopped at the Happy Hollow Motel to pick up Carl's luggage. He parked at the curb and barked an order that would set the tone of our future relationship.

"Those cans are too damned noisy," he said. "Rene, get out and cut them off and throw 'em in the trash. Carlie, you stay in the car. It's too dangerous out there."

I jumped out and cut the cans loose with my Captain Midnight pocketknife, all the while searching through teary eyes for Ellie. She appeared from a side street and walked slowly toward the bridge. Heavy traffic flowed past and sometimes blocked my view. Afraid of what she might do, I shouted, "Ellie, Ellie," as loud as I could, but the traffic noise was louder. Slowly she set the suitcase down and, for what seemed like eternity, stared over the bridge rail at the busy train yard far below. In the distance I heard a streetcar make its rumbling approach onto the bridge.

"Ellie, it's Rene," I screamed again. "Please don't do it."

She raised the bouquet slowly, pitched the flowers high in the air and looked over the rail as they fluttered to the tracks below. As I stood rooted there, I ran through an emotional gamut of helplessness, hopelessness and then, surprisingly, determination. I really cared enough for someone else to make my first adult decision—I had to stop her.

Just as I leapt from the curb there was a firm hand clamp my shoulder. It was Carl.

"Who're you yelling at, Rene?" he shouted over the din. "Let's go. We've got hotel reservations and we're late. Get in the car."

I was powerless. No longer a man on a mission to save a life but a fifteen-year-old boy who faced the new reality of a stepfather. All the lessons, experiences, and memories of the past nine months had been pushed aside by this newest influence in my life. I choked back tears, took my place in the back seat and looked out for one last glimpse of Ellie. I scanned the streetcar from window to window and saw nothing but faces of strangers. Suddenly there she was with a blank stare and a sad look on her face. I waved frantically but she was already in another world. With the clang of a bell the streetcar glided away. Ellie was gone from my life forever...if I chose to keep my promise.

As the Buick passed the spot where another girl chose to end it all, I realized that life must be nothing but choices. Ellie chose to begin again. Carl chose a new life partner. Mom chose to change her future. When would it be my turn to choose?

CPSIA information can be obtained
at www.ICGtesting.com
Printed in the USA
LVHW03s1240210818
587583LV00002B/2/P